Adirondack Treasure

ADIRONDACK TREASURE

• Isle Royale •

A NOVEL BY

Matthew J. Glavin
& Michael J. Dolan

Pyramid Publishing Inc.
Utica, New York

ISBN 978-1-886166-37-0

This book was printed in the United States of America.

Cover Design: Lindsey Baker Graphic Design
Photo Credit: Photography by Rita Clarke
Map of Isle Royale: Courtesy of the St. Lawrence County Historical Association

Like 'Adirondack Treasure Books' on Facebook

Pyramid Publishing Inc.
PO Box 8339
Utica, New York 13505
www.pyramidpublishingservices.com

To my two wonderful sons who are the highlight of my life
and who provide constant support and inspiration.

Christopher Robert Glavin

Sean Martin Glavin

MJG

To my beloved partner and husband, Guy LaMothe-Dolan, for whose companionship I am ever thankful, and for his support and patience throughout the process of completing this project.

And to my dear friend and co-author who invited me to write with him, and who guided and mentored me throughout my first foray into the creative arts. Without him, I would never have a first novel.

MJD

ACKNOWLEDGEMENTS

THE AUTHORS are immensely grateful to a great number of people without whose help this book would never have been written. Thank you all.

The story of Isle Royale, and the legend of buried treasure, is steeped in the history of northern New York State. Those who keep that history alive provide an important and valuable service to society. Two organizations in particular were instrumental in helping us work through that history so what we wrote was accurate and interesting for our readers.

The mission of the Fort la Présentation Association, in Ogdensburg, NY, is to sponsor the historically accurate reconstruction of Fort de la Présentation in close proximity to the original site, and to administer an ongoing presence. They make history come alive with their educational programs and their heroic efforts to reconstruct the original fort. Association President, Barbara O'Keefe, was generous in providing a list of experts and historians who were eager to share their time and knowledge. Foremost among them was Tim Cryderman. Tim spent countless hours helping reconstruct the history of the French and Indian War and the battle for Fort Lévis. He helped solve the perplexing question of why there was so much gold at Fort Lévis on Isle Royale in the first place. Thank you, Tim. Joe Cosentino, a Board Member of the Association, who worked on construction of the St. Lawrence Seaway in the 1950's, and personally helped remove half of Isle Royale (Chimney Island), was generous with his time. His stories were wonderful and he gave us great insight to that period in history. The knowledge we gained in the books detailing the history of Fort de la Présentation and Fort Oswegatchie written by historian, Jim Reagan, was important in our understanding of the period.

The St. Lawrence County Historical Association in Canton, NY, is truly a treasure in itself. Executive Director, Trent Trulock, and his staff were a great help in our research. In particular, JeanMarie Martello, Archives Manager, helped us dig through the many ancient maps of the St. Lawrence River, Isle Royale and Fort Lévis.

In the Prologue, we wanted to be as accurate as possible with the original Native American names of geographic locations we discuss. We received wonderful help from Carole Katsi'tsienhá:wi Ross, Mohawk Language/Culture Resource Coordinator at the St. Regis Mohawk Tribe. Carol's Mohawk name means, 'She is carrying flowers.'

Mary Beth Curran, Chief Clerk of the St. Lawrence County Supreme and County Courts provided a terrific tour of the beautiful St. Lawrence County Court building in Canton, NY, and the massive records room described in Chapter Six.

Thanks to City of Ogdensburg, Parks & Recreation Director, Matthew Curatolo, for his help with descriptions of the various marinas and contact information for the Port of Ogdensburg.

Sal Pisani, Associate Administrator of the Operations Headquarters for the St. Lawrence Seaway Development Corporation in Massena, NY, was a tremendous help in our understanding of the operation of the St. Lawrence Seaway. A special thank you goes to the United States Department of Transportation for allowing us access to the St. Lawrence Seaway Development Corporation.

Richard Kingsbury spent more than 30 years as a Merchant Marine aboard a freighter. The hours we spent listening to his stories provided a wonderful description of what it's like living at sea. Hopefully we were able to translate his insight and experiences into a realistic description aboard the fictitious ships in our story.

On a trip to Elizabethtown, NY, we stopped, unannounced, at the home studio of stained glass artisan, Dan Belzer. Dan and his lovely wife, Mary Jean Belzer, generously welcomed us into their home and gave us a quick lesson on the art of stained glass works. Like our character, Will, in Chapter Twelve, Dan keeps his very first stained glass piece in his workshop. And, like Will, it allows him, on a daily basis, to see how far he has progressed as an artist.

Thanks to Sue Barton of Blueberry Acres farm in Au Sable Forks, NY, for helping to clarify the proper growing seasons for fruits in upstate New York.

Philip Frederick Jr.; SO-CS/SR/NS, United States Coast Guard Auxiliary, provided valuable operational and background information on maritime safety and operations of the United Stated Coast Guard. We wish to extend a special thanks to all the men and women of the United States Coast Guard who dedicate their lives to keeping our domestic waters safe.

EMPACT America is a Washington, DC-based bipartisan, non-profit organization for citizens concerned about protecting the American people from a nuclear or natural electromagnetic pulse (EMP) catastrophe. They were a great help providing background information on the effects of an EMP attack on the homeland.

We gratefully acknowledge Gordon Lightfoot and the lyrics of his beautiful song, ***Wreck of the Edmund Fitzgerald***, a few lines of which are used in Chapter Eleven.

Taiko is the modern expression of ancient Japanese drumming traditions. We thank Stuart Paton, founder and artistic director of Burlington

Taiko for his input.

Thank you to Nancy Best for proofreading, Lindsey Baker for her beautiful cover design and Rita Clarke for her photographs of the authors. See Rita's website at http://ritaclarkephotography.smugmug.com/

The great writer, Stephen King, said, "To write is human. To edit is divine." No one personifies that more than our editor, Bibi Wein. Thank you, Bibi, for your encouragement and brutal honesty. Once again, your magic has made the book readable.

Throughout the writing of this book, a number of friends and family provided constant inspiration and encouragement. We also had numerous sources who asked not to be named. We are grateful for your assistance and we thank you, one and all.

We want to especially thank those who took the time to read our manuscript and provide their honest criticism and suggestions throughout the writing process, Mark Fenton, Bob Barstow, Kathy & Joe Kopitsky, Maureen Glavin, Christopher Glavin, James Glavin, Stefani Glavin, Wendy Insinger, Mary Jane Connors, Corky Halberg, Norm Santimaw and Susan and Dan Heneka. Numerous changes were made to the story because of their input. They made the story more believable and exciting.

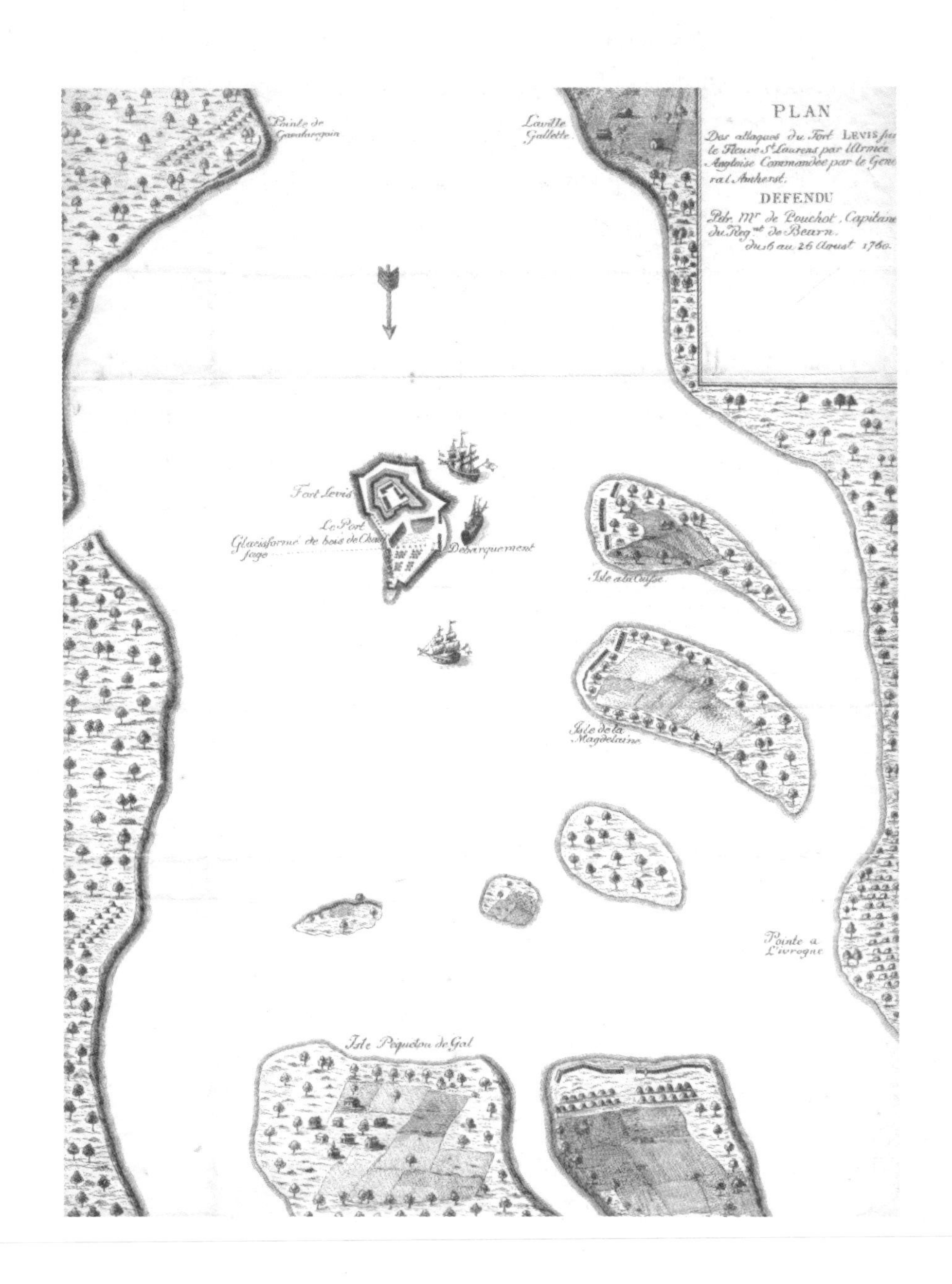
PLAN
Des attaques du Fort LEVIS sur le Fleuve St Laurens par l'Armée Angloise Commandée par le General Amherst.
DEFENDU
Par Mr de Pouchot, Capitaine du Regt de Bearn.
du 16 au 26 Aoust 1760.
Pointe de Gandargoin
Laville Gallette
Fort Levis
Le Port
Glacis formé de bois de Chauffage
Debarquement
Isle a la Cuisse
Isle de la Magdelaine
Pointe a L'ivrogne
Isle Piquetou de Gal

PROLOGUE

IN ANCIENT TIMES, the natives called 'the great river,' *Kaniatarowanén:ne*. It was to play a major role in the exploration of a new land, and would ultimately be the final battleground for what would become a new nation.

The early explorers of *Kaniatarowanén:ne* are legendary in the chronicles of history. Jacques Cartier discovered *Hochelaga*, the native settlement of the ancient forest in 1535. Today, Montreal is one of the great cities of North America. Samuel de Champlain, in 1615, visited on his voyage to Lake Huron, as did the Jesuit priest, Simon Le Moyne, in the summer of 1654 on his way to the country of the Onondagas. After Le Moyne came La Salle and Frontenac, Hennepin and Charlevoix, and many lesser known explorers of the new world.

Since these ancient times, 'the great river,' the St. Lawrence River, has been one of the major highways of the continent.

These were the lands of the Mohawk, one of the distinguished Nations of the *Haudenosaunee*, 'the people of the longhouse,' the Iroquois League. There was a timeworn trail from the Mohawk Valley to *Kaniatarowanén:ne*. In 1749, it was at the end of this trail, on the site of the Mohawk village, *Swagatch*, where the Oswegatchie River meets the St. Lawrence, that a 41-year old French Sulpician priest, Francois Picquet founded the mission of La Présentation. For both the natives and the French, it was a marriage of convenience and self-interest. The Mohawk welcomed Picquet and allowed him to build his mission fort because of their growing concern over the way British settlers were encroaching on their territory in the valley to the south, and on the shores of Lake Ontario to the west. For Picquet, the dual objective was to convert the Mohawk to Christianity and forge an alliance between the native people and the French.

§

During the colonization of North America, Spanish, French, Dutch, Swedes, and English, in turn, each sought a share. The Spaniards fastened upon Florida and Mexico, but their efforts to expand further came to a halt, and in the course of time, Dutch and Swedish holdings along the Atlantic seaboard fell to the English. Only Great Britain and France remained as rivals for the heart and soul of the continent.

At first there was little contact between the two, since their settlements were widely separated by a vast and foreboding wilderness. Engrossed in their struggle to gain a livelihood, the English and French settlers might long have remained at peace. But the parent countries became engaged in hostilities in every part of the world where the two nations had territorial interests. Inevitably, the war spread to involve their New World colonies.

The American phase of the worldwide war would determine control of the vast colonial heartland of North America. Behind this issue loomed an infinitely larger one, however: which national culture was to dominate North America?

The French and Indian War, better known in Europe as the Seven Years' War, and in Quebec, as the War of Conquest, began in 1754 over the specific issue of whether the upper Ohio River valley was part of the British Empire, and therefore open to trade and settlement by Virginians and Pennsylvanians. Or, was it part of the French Empire.

To complicate matters further for the French, corruption and thievery had dominated the culture of leadership in their North American Colonies.

§

Since the mid-17th century, France utilized a dual form of government in its colonies. In Montreal, Pierre Francois Rigaud, Marquis de Vaudreuil, the newly appointed Governor-general of New France, was responsible to His Majesty, King Louis XV, and had control over the military. Francois Bigot was appointed Intendant in charge of trade, finance, justice and all other departments of administration. As a feeble form of checks and balances, the dual government should have resulted in tension between the two men.

Intendant Bigot and his co-conspirators had been embezzling tens of millions of francs from His Majesty for almost a decade when Vaudreuil arrived in 1755. Over the next several years, every conceivable scheme was utilized to swindle the Crown, and tens of millions more were stolen from the King. Certainly, if the new Governor-general was not involved himself, he had become a pawn and provided cover for Intendant Bigot and his band of thieves.

Louis Joseph, Marquis de Montcalm de Saint-Veran, arrived in Quebec in 1756 to take charge of the military. He wrote to his friend, Marechal de Belleisle, French Minister of War, detailing the corruption and plundering he saw, and predicted it would soon destroy the colony. "It seems as if they were all hastening to make their fortunes before the loss of the colony; which many of them perhaps desire as an impenetrable veil over their conduct," he wrote.

The letter from Montcalm resulted in King Louis XV dispatching an investigator to audit the accounts of Vaudreuil and Bigot. The royal auditor ultimately documented the decades of thievery of the royal treasury.

§

While New France was being plundered financially, by 1758, aided by effective blockades off the coast of France, the British won important military victories. In July, the Forteresse de Louisbourg, the guardian of the Gulf of St. Lawrence on Cape Breton Island in Nova Scotia, had fallen to Crown forces. In August, Fort Frontenac capitulated to the British, and the head of the St. Lawrence was sealed. Without reinforcements or supplies, the great French fortresses of Quebec and Montreal were trapped.

After the fall of Quebec in the 1759 Battle of the Plains of Abraham, many thought the war was over. Both Montcalm and his British counterpart, Major General James Wolfe, died of their wounds on the battlefield. But, British Commander-in-Chief, General Jeffrey Amherst, was not finished. He prepared to launch a final three-pronged attack to take Montréal. Columns were to advance along the St. Lawrence from Quebec to the northeast, down the Richelieu River from Lake Champlain to the south, and from Oswego on Lake Ontario to the west. The latter force, which Amherst led personally, numbered some 12,000 men and 100 siege guns.

By August of 1760, the French were building Fort Lévis on Isle Royale in the St. Lawrence River, three miles from Fort La Présentation. Captain Pierre Pouchot was assigned its defense.

Chevalier de Lévis' original design for the fort called for stone walls, 200 guns and some 2,500 troops. What Pouchot had was a small fort with wooden stockades, five cannons and 200 soldiers.

Soon after his arrival on Isle Royale, in an effort to consolidate his forces, Pouchot ordered abandonment of the nearby mission, Fort de La Présentation. Supplies, men, and 200 pounds of gold embezzled from the Crown, were transferred to Isle Royale.

§

Amherst's force set out from Lake Ontario on August 10th. On August 17th, French lookouts sighted the ships, the Onondaga and the Mohawk, from their outpost at Ile aux Chevreuils, several miles upstream from Fort Lévis. The French withdrew in a row galley to Isle Royale to warn Pouchot.

On August 19th, Amherst commenced the attack on Fort Lévis. The siege continued until August 24th, when Pouchot ran out of ammunition.

Before asking for terms, Pouchot ordered the gold be buried so it would not fall into the hands of the enemy. On the afternoon of August 24th Captain Pierre Pouchot surrendered with honors to General Jeffrey Amherst's army.

This was the final battle between the French and the British on what was to become American soil.

§

The fighting cost the British some 26 killed and 47 wounded to the French losses of 275 of the original 400 defenders killed or wounded. Pouchot was amongst the wounded. The British could hardly believe such a small garrison had offered such spirited resistance.

After the battle, Amherst's force remained at Fort Lévis for another four days before continuing on to meet the forces from Quebec and Lake Champlain and completely surrounded Montréal. On September 6th, Montréal was surrendered by New France's governor, the Marquis de Vaudreuil.

The British rebuilt Fort Lévis and named it Fort William Augustus. Upon their return to France, the Marquis de Vaudreuil, Intendant Francois Bigot and their co-conspirators were sent to the Bastille to await trial for their thievery.

The embezzled gold, buried by Pouchot, was never found.

§

The natives called it *Orakonenton*. Today, Isle Royale is Chimney Island. Three miles upriver is the site of the former Fort de La Presentation, known today as the city of Ogdensburg, NY.

The St. Lawrence River not only served as the main route for exploration of the North American interior, it has been a major trade artery since long before the United States or Canada achieved nationhood.

The construction of progressively larger canals along the St. Lawrence River began as early as 1783. By 1900, a complete network of shallow draft canals, locks and channels allowed uninterrupted navigation from Lake Superior through the St. Lawrence River to Montreal.

Between 1913 and 1932, the Welland Canal, connecting Lake Ontario and Lake Erie, was rebuilt. The US was reluctant to enter into a larger scheme, that is, to rebuild the Montréal-Lake Ontario channels. A threat by the Canadian government in 1951 to build a seaway entirely within Canadian territory resulted in a final agreement with the United States for a cooperative project.

Approval of the St. Lawrence Seaway occurred in May 1954. Construction began in August. At the time it was one of the largest civil engineering feats ever undertaken. During the five-year construction project, over 22,000 people took part in some aspect of its building.

ONE

Sunday, May 4th
11:45 GMT – 6:45 am EDT
The Yellow Sea, off the Coast of China

ABU SUNGKAR, Captain of the freighter, Nova, stood and watched.

Flames reached more than 100 feet in the air. Debris was still falling. Screams of men with horrific injuries and burns could be heard in the distance as the two other ships slowly steamed away. "They'll not suffer long," he said confidently. "The sea will swallow them quickly." Even from this distance, heat from the flames could be felt on the faces of the small crew aboard the 575-foot break bulk freighter.

Three missiles had been fired from the North Korean trawler. The first, intended to disable the 45 foot fishing boat's communication systems, was aimed directly at the wheel house. The other two hit the hull to sink her as quickly as possible. The chilling cries for help faded as distance separated the sinking fishing boat from the North Korean trawler and the break bulk freighter.

Sungkar's primary concern was that the column of black smoke would attract attention. He knew the intense fire would be snuffed by the flooding water soon enough, and he hoped the winds would quickly dissipate the smoke that marked the end of the errant vessel. Without hesitation, he had ordered the sinking of the fishing boat with a simple hand signal to the Captain of the North Korean trawler, Paektu. The two ships were positioned far out of the shipping lanes to avoid detection.

He looked at Azhari standing next to him and commented, "the first casualties of our jihad, our holy war."

Azhari said nothing. His smile spoke for him. He understood that the curious fishermen had come far too close to Nova and the rendezvous point. Prying eyes could not be tolerated. The fishermen's attempt to transmit a distress call, however, was their final, lethal decision. Stealth was paramount and the innocent attempts to summon assistance, however laudable, spelled their doom.

Captain Sungkar had hoped the mission would not start this way. But, the fishing boat had to be destroyed and the transfer must take place. For three days, Nova and its North Korean companion had been shadowing each other, waiting for better weather, but the seas remained angry making a transfer too risky.

In only two weeks the summer monsoon season would start in the Yellow Sea. These waters were rich fishing grounds for Chinese and Korean trawlers. Except for the unlucky intruder, the severe weather had kept all but the hardiest fishermen in port.

Paektu, the largest of the fleet of the state-owned, Hamgyong Corporation, was allegedly close by Nova in response to a distress call to provide their mechanics' assistance with phony repairs.

Designed to look like a fishing trawler, Paektu was equipped with sophisticated electronics and weapons. She had been following Nova since they both had left from separate ports near Namp'o, North Korea. Her crew were not fishermen; rather, they were loyal members of the North Korean military. Their mission: to transfer four containers to Nova unnoticed and return to port. They had been well prepared to dispatch any unwanted visitors.

When the weather finally improved in the early evening, Captain Sungkar decided they would wait until daylight to make the transfer. By then they would be far from any leftover debris from their unfortunate encounter. The crew said they could perform a nighttime operation without difficulty, but Captain Sungkar's reply was short: "No lights." His expression telegraphed confidence and agreement his small crew could operate easily at night, but he knew how far light travels on smooth seas, and how easily lights could be seen from satellites and aircraft; a twinkling beacon against a vast, black field.

Their cover story was much more plausible in daylight. Nova had sailed with only one operational bilge pump, the other having been deliberately fitted with burned out bearings. While the operational pump could easily meet the demand, loosened fittings would add to the water leakage and the appearance of trouble. A corroded power cable on Nova's Automatic Information System (AIS) added to the notion that the ship was to be decommissioned upon reaching port.

Nova's officers, however, were getting worried their schedule could begin to slip. Eleven thousand miles lay ahead before their stop in Reykjavik, Iceland, where Nova would be reborn with a new name and new corporate ownership before her momentous trip to America, through the St. Lawrence Seaway, and on to Detroit.

Nova had just completed a three-year refurbishment in Namp'o, where she received new engines, a complete overhaul of her electronics and a custom reconfiguration of her foredeck. Three 15-foot hatch openings had been replaced by one 55-foot opening, large enough to accommodate the special cargo she was about to receive. A newly installed elevator would raise and lower her cargo from deep in the forward hold below the foredeck. Hydraulically operated watertight double doors replaced the three old hatches. The new cargo would be fastened to the elevator deck.

While Captain Sungkar was concerned the new hatch would weaken the ship's structural integrity, he knew that 90 days from now this would no longer be an issue. A new paint job and other cosmetic improvements were the only things that hadn't been done in Namp'o.

By morning, the seas had calmed to three foot swells. Despite the electronics on both ships, radio communication was forbidden. The transponders for the legally mandated AIS system were turned off. AIS sends pertinent information to other ships in the vicinity, including name, call sign, destination, speed, position and course. Additionally, AIS transmits information about manifests and crew to port authorities.

As the sun rose over the horizon, Captain Sungkar authorized communication by signal light. Even though tensions were high, there was no hesitation in the crew's movements. They were ready.

The maneuver had been practiced many times over the past six months. But, this was real. Absolutely no mistakes would be tolerated. Lookouts were posted. The RADAR operator aboard Paektu was not to leave his post. If there were any sign of more unexpected company from sea or air, the transfer would be immediately set into reverse, cementing the illusion of an old, rusty, worn-out ship in distress, taking measures to preserve its cargo from the rising water in her bilge.

Despite the cool temperature and sea spray, Nova's captain shed his jacket. He had broken out in a sweat as the large boom swung over the deck of the ship tied to her port side. After years of planning and preparation, and almost a decade of sacrifice, it was finally happening. To Captain Sungkar, it felt like a dream, but he had to remain alert and focused. This was a dangerous operation and the smallest mistake could be catastrophic. While he and his officers were well aware of the gravity of their operation, they suspected the crew of Paektu didn't know what they were dealing with. They were correct.

The first and the last of the four containers were the most sensitive. The first 53-foot container was transferred onto the elevator deck and brought below. Once in the cargo hold, it was moved off the elevator platform and secured to the deck just aft of the elevator. The next two 20-foot containers were hoisted without incident and placed on Nova's foredeck, forward of the new hatch. The final container was ready for transfer.

The Captain's heart was pounding as the second 53-foot container was lifted. "Slowly," he barked in English. "This is delicate cargo." The North Koreans didn't understand a word he was saying, but his hand signals got the message across. His crew could sense the tension and concern in the Captain. The boom slowly swung around. The rolling seas caused the container to swing too far, making the deck crew uncomfortable. Four stability lines had been attached to each corner of the bottom of the container so they could control the swings. With the rolling of the two ships, several crew members had let go of their lines.

"STOP!" the Captain yelled. With a closed fist he gave the stop signal to the boom operator. "Grab those lines." The crew struggled to control the container. "Slowly now," was the order.

As the boom gently swung around, the container came into position 15 feet above the new hatch. The Captain's hand signals instructed the boom operator to begin lowering. The four lines kept the container positioned directly over the hatch. With only a foot of clearance on each end, officers were in place to make the final adjustments that brought the container to rest on a series of pins welded to the new elevator deck. Once secured, the two smaller containers were positioned on top of the 53-foot container and fastened in place. The contents of these 20-footers would help prevent radiation detectors from identifying the contents of the larger container. The elevator lowered the three containers into the hold, well below the waterline. The hatch doors automatically closed.

The two ships separated and sailed in opposite directions.

TWO

Saturday, July 20th

13:15 GMT – 8:15am EDT

Cranberry Lake, New York, USA

THE COFFEE MAKER had signaled the coffee was ready when the knocking started. It was 8:15 am on a July Saturday. Joseph Benton had just gotten out of the shower and was still in his robe. "Who the hell is at my door at this ungodly hour?" he mumbled. The knocking continued, even louder. Bailey, Joseph's cat, had already headed for the safety of the bedroom. "Hold your horses, I'm coming." There were four more loud knocks before Joseph opened the door.

"If you took a break from the banging you would have heard me say I'm coming." Joseph's initial scowl faded slightly as he took notice of the beautiful woman standing on his doorstep. Softening his tone, he asked his visitor, "Who are you, and what do you want?" He'd had more than his share of uninvited visitors recently.

The woman locked eyes with Joseph for a moment. She had seen pictures of Joseph Benton in newspapers and magazines and knew he was a good-looking man. But, in person, with his hair still wet from the shower . . .

"My name is Savannah Christian."

"I'm not interested, thank you." Although he was interested indeed, Joseph slowly started to close the door.

"Wait Mr. Benton. I left you a message that I'd be here this morning."

"I didn't get any message. If you want an appointment, send me a letter."

"I sent three already."

The woman was holding two books, a thick manila folder and a box of fresh pastries. The look in her eyes revealed her determination.

"What's this about?"

"It's about the treasure my father found and hid. If you'd read my letters . . ."

"I've been a little overwhelmed lately."

"You didn't read any of my letters, did you?"

"No, I didn't."

The stranger lifted her head a bit and sniffed, "Is that coffee?"

"Yes it is, and I haven't had any yet so I'm not ready for visitors. Why don't you come back another day at a more reasonable hour?"

Joseph started to close the door again and a foot prevented his effort.

"Mr. Benton, I've sent you three letters, left several messages and I drove eighty miles this morning, just to see you. The least you can do is give me a few minutes of your time. I even brought homemade strawberry scones. The strawberries are from my garden. I made these fresh this morning."

"My God, what time did you get up?"

"Four."

"Four a.m.? The birds don't get up that early. Look Miss, could we please do this another time?"

"Mr. Benton, I'm here now." Savannah stood her ground just staring. It was evident she was not going away.

"What did you say your name was?"

"Savannah . . . Savannah Christian." Her green eyes were penetrating.

Joseph was defeated, "All right. We can have a cup of coffee and you can tell me your story. I have a friend coming at nine so we don't have much time."

Joseph stepped back and allowed Savannah to walk past him toward the living room. Dressed in tight jeans, pink t-shirt, denim vest and sneakers, Savannah had her strawberry blond hair tied back in a ponytail. Her athletic build and radiant face had captured his attention.

"You can put your things here," pointing to a large library table.

"You have a beautiful home Mr. Benton."

"Joseph, to you, Ms. Christian."

"I'm Savannah."

"Okay Savannah, why don't you pour us coffee while I get some clothes on." Joseph pointed in the direction of the kitchen, "The mugs are in the cabinet on the left. I take milk. If you want sugar it's up there somewhere."

"I'm sure you'll find it," he mumbled to himself as he walked to his bedroom.

By the time Joseph slid on a pair of jeans and a t-shirt, the table had been set with coffee mugs, plates, napkins and forks. He could smell the scones warming in the oven.

Savannah was standing at the large window admiring the view of the lake. She'd taken note of the piles of magazines around the room and smiled to herself when she saw what apparently was the 'Joseph' pile. On top was the most recent issue of People Magazine with a cover photo of a good-looking Joseph Benton. Much different than the man she'd seen this morning. The photos didn't begin to capture how handsome this man really was.

In the corner were three large cardboard boxes full of what appeared to be unopened mail . . . including hers, no doubt.

"Did you find everything?" Glancing at the set table he mumbled to himself, "of course you did."

"Let me get the scones out of the oven." Savannah headed for the kitchen.

"Why didn't you just put them in the microwave?"

"The microwave would have ruined them."

Joseph rolled his eyes. "Oh, of course, I should have known," he murmured.

"What? I didn't hear you?" Savannah yelled from the kitchen.

Joseph realized how sarcastic he sounded and made a mental note to try to improve his attitude. "Nothing," he yelled back to her.

Returning from the kitchen with the six strawberry scones, Savannah let the plate pass slowly under Joseph's nose as she set them on the table.

"Those smell delightful. Look Savannah, I want to apologize if I was rude to you earlier. It's just that it's early and I . . ."

"I understand." She nodded toward the boxes in the corner. "I guess mine weren't the only letters you didn't read. Apparently you don't listen to your messages either."

Joseph was a little embarrassed. He had spent 30 years searching for the treasure of his famous ancestor, Joseph Bonaparte, the former King of Spain and Napoleon's older brother. His recent discovery had propelled him, despite his resistance, into the media limelight.

"But, I haven't thrown anything away. I'll go through it all one of these days."

Savannah was eager to tell her story. "As I explained in my letters, *that you didn't read*."

"Stop right there Savannah. Can we call a truce? I've already apologized for being rude, and I know I've been a bit sarcastic. I'm sorry. Will you please stop with the comments about me not reading your letters?"

"Okay, sure. Like I was saying, my father found a treasure on an island in the St. Lawrence River."

"What kind of treasure?"

"It was a box of gold bullion. Father worked on the construction of the Seaway."

Joseph interrupted again. "When was this?"

"About 1957. After I was born, father wrote me a letter saying he had found the treasure. He put the letter in his journal so I wouldn't find it until after he died. Like I said, father was a construction superintendent during construction of the St. Lawrence Seaway. He was digging up an island when he found it. It was about 200 pounds of gold. I figured it out. That's about $5 million today. Anyway, the letter says he reburied it somewhere. But I have no idea where. The letter says to follow the instructions in the journal."

Their conversation was interrupted by another voice, "Good morning Joe Boy. Whose car is in your driveway?" The sound was coming from the direction of the front door.

"In here," Joseph yelled, "Grab yourself a cup of coffee on your way in."

Looking over the kitchen counter into the dining area, Jerry Doolin was surprised to see a very attractive woman. "Good morning. I'm so sorry. Am I interrupting something?"

"Savannah, meet Baldy. Baldy, meet Savannah Christian. I'm glad you're early, get your butt in here, she has an interesting story."

"I'm sorry, Ms. Christian, but before I forget . . ." Jerry was pouring his coffee and looked up at Joseph, ". . . Will and I had dinner at the Windfall last night. He asked me to tell you he's made something special for you. It's in his workshop and he wants you to stop by in the next few days."

"Okay. Now, get in here."

Approaching the table Jerry put his hand out, "I'm Jerry Doolin. Look, I can come back later if . . . ."

"Nice to meet you Jerry, please don't take offense at this, but what I'm telling Joseph is confidential, so maybe if you could come back . . ."

Joseph jumped in, "Anything you tell me, you can tell him. I trust him with my life. In fact, I did. Well . . . kind of. Jerry was with me every step of the way when I found the Bonaparte treasure. I wouldn't have found it without him. Anyway, for more than 20 years he's been my best friend in the world."

Jerry smiled, "As usual, Joey here is lying. He searched the first 30 years all by his lonesome. I may have helped a little at the very end."

Joseph looked at Jerry, "The name is Joseph, you bald-headed brat."

"I love you too buddy. I see you're in a good mood this morning."

Joseph just rolled his eyes.

"If you two children are done, can we please get down to business?"

"Now, now . . . remember the truce Miss Christian," Joseph reminded her with a wink. He was beginning to enjoy this.

Jerry turned to Joseph with a questioning look.

Joseph just smiled. "Let me bring you up to speed on Savannah's story Baldy."

"Before we get started, Jerry, would you like a strawberry scone, I made them fresh this morning?"

"I was waiting for someone to offer."

Savannah started to get up, "Let me get you a napkin and a plate."

"Please, don't bother. I'll just use my fingers."

Joseph interrupted, "My bald-headed friend here is an expert at eating pastries. He spent 23 years as a cop."

"Don't listen to my pathological buddy. I was a state trooper, not a cop. I never ate donuts. And, I'm retired."

Savannah stared at them, frowning at their antics. They both got her message.

"I'll start from the beginning. Ten years ago I was going through several boxes of my father's personal papers. He died in 1994. In the boxes were his journals. He wrote every day for almost 50 years. In the last journal book there was a hand-written letter dated 1967 and addressed to 'My Dearest Savannah'. He wrote it just after I was born. The letter described how he found 200 pounds of gold while working construction on the St. Lawrence Seaway. One of his primary jobs in 1955 was to remove half of Chimney Island in order to widen the shipping channel. Best I can tell, they just dug it up and dumped it on the other half."

Jerry interrupted, "Where exactly is this Chimney Island?"

"It's three miles downstream from Ogdensburg. You can see it to the right as you go over the bridge to Canada. Anyway, the letter says he reburied the gold somewhere, but it doesn't say where. It just says to find the gold, follow the instructions in the journal."

Joseph asked, "And, what does the journal say?"

"Nothing. I can't find anything in the journals about the gold. I've read them over and over."

"Maybe it was a joke," Joseph said.

"Or it's hidden somehow. Like a riddle or cipher," Jerry added.

Joseph sneered, "Nobody does that kind of thing you idiot. This isn't the movies."

"Joseph Bonaparte did, you brain-dead moron."

Savannah was getting frustrated, "Guys, can you please focus? Are you both ADD or what?"

"Okay, how did 200 pounds of gold end up on some obscure island?" Jerry demanded.

She picked up the two books she had brought in. "It's all in here. There was a French fort, Fort Lévis, on Chimney Island during the French and Indian War. The Island was called Isle Royale then. In 1760, Fort Lévis was being attacked by the British. The French were running out of ammunition. They knew they would have to surrender. They didn't want the British to get their hands on the gold, so the French commander ordered his men to bury it."

"The British never found it?" Jerry wondered.

"Apparently not, they immediately built another fort on the island."

Joseph rescued the train of thought, "Other than the letter, do you have any evidence your father actually found the gold?"

"Not really," Savannah said. "What I know is this: in 1956 he purchased the farm with 140 acres of land in Saranac. He paid cash. I still live there. My father was a hard-working man. Nobody knows where he got that kind of money. When I was a child, I once heard relatives talking about it. They thought he stole it. I remember being very angry and I asked father about it right away. He promised me he didn't steal it and said someday I would know the truth. We never had much money growing up, but we never wanted for anything either. We always seemed to have what we needed."

Both Joseph and Jerry sat there thinking.

Savannah interrupted the silence, "Well, what do you guys think?"

"It's an intriguing story," Jerry said. "But, it's all just circumstantial. You may be on a wild-goose-chase here."

Joseph immediately came to the defense of the pretty lady sitting next to him. "Shut up Baldy, will you ever stop being a cop? Her father obviously found the gold. He paid cash for the farm and left a letter for his daughter telling her how to find the rest. There is something in those journals that says where it is. We just have to find it."

Ignoring his friend, Jerry looked at Savannah, "You really didn't answer my question. Why would 200 pounds of gold have been there? Just because there was a French fort, isn't really an answer. That's a lot of gold for the time. Why was it there in the first place?"

Savannah got up from the table, "I think we're going to be here a while, anybody want more coffee?" Both men said yes.

While she poured, Savannah continued, "As I understand it, the gold had been accumulated by some French colonial politicians and bureaucrats who were embezzling money by the wagon load from the French crown. There was a mission where Ogdensburg is now called Fort de La Présentation. During the war, it was evacuated and the people, along with the gold, were moved to Fort Lévis on Isle Royale."

Joseph interrupted, "And your dad said he found it while excavating the island and he gave you instructions on how to find it in his journal? Did you bring the journals with you?"

"Of course," Savannah replied.

"Dumb question," Joseph said under his breath.

"The originals are all in the car, but I made a copy of the 1955 journal. It's there in the folder. The letter is there, too."

As Jerry was opening the folder, Joseph remarked, "Knowing my cop friend here, he probably has 40 or 50 questions he wants to ask, maybe more. It'll be an interrogation, but I've found it easiest to just play along and answer."

Savannah looked at Jerry, "Ask away, I'll tell you everything I know."

"As my friend here knows, I was a trooper, not a cop. And, I've only got one question. Tell me a little more about your dad."

"I'm not sure what you want to know. He was an honorable man. Lived his entire life in the North Country. He never finished high school. During the war, he was with the Army Corps of Engineers. After the war, he worked a variety of construction jobs until they started construction of the Seaway in 1954. He got a job as a construction supervisor and worked on the Seaway until it was finished in 1959."

"So, he was still working on the Seaway when he bought the farm?" Jerry asked.

"Yes. 1956, like I said."

"And, if you don't mind me asking, when were you born?" Joseph wanted to know.

"1967. My mother died soon after. I never knew her. Father raised me by himself. He only worked odd jobs after I was born. He didn't like leaving me with relatives. I think he knew they didn't care for him much, and he never wanted to feel obligated to them. He raised me."

"He was in his forties when you were born, and you say he didn't work much after that?"

"Not much. He took care of me."

"How did he pay the bills?"

"I don't know. I was a kid and never really thought about it. I guess I always thought he lived off his savings."

"Don't take this wrong, but did he ever get into trouble, was he ever arrested or anything?"

"Of course not! Why would you ask that?"

"Old habits I guess."

Jerry sat thinking. Joseph could tell something was on Jerry's mind and made a mental note to ask him about it later.

Without realizing it, Savannah was biting her nails. "Well? What do you guys think? Are you going to help me or not?"

Joseph realized he'd become intrigued with this self-assured woman. Not quite sure if he was more interested in Savannah, or her story, he responded without thinking. "You bet we're going to help."

"Great," Savannah said, "Where do we go from here?"

"That's a good question." Jerry looked at Joseph. "Where *do* we go from here Mr. Treasure Hunter?"

THREE

Saturday, July 20th

12:00 GMT – 7:00 am EDT

Reykjavik, Iceland

"TODAY *NOVA* DIES," Captain Sungkar proudly announced. "We are now Ares, son of Zeus. The new name will be painted on the bow and stern this afternoon. Within a week, papers will arrive reflecting her new name, ownership, and flag of registry: Isle of Man."

Even in July there was a chill in the austere Captain's quarters of the Ares, now berthed in Reykjavik. The smell of diesel, coffee, sea salt and fresh paint permeated the air. The daily meeting had become a ritual. The Captain expected brief, precise updates from the two other men in the cabin. Other officers were standing watch.

Ares had been in Iceland for 45 days, 30 of those in dry-dock receiving a new paint job. With her new name added, the transformation would be complete.

The entire deck and engineering crew had been released. Even food for the past forty-five days, was brought in by a local restaurateur who came from town every day to feed the five officers on board. A skeleton crew, including a new cook had been hired for the trip to America. They would arrive in five days.

"Rosie, is our sister on schedule?" asked Captain Sungkar, rubbing his hand over his chin. He still hadn't gotten used to the feel of a clean-shaven face. It was the first time in the 40 years of his adult life that he'd shaved every day. For the past three months each of the men in the room had shaved every day, one of the requirements of this mission.

"She's leaving Lisbon later this morning," the short heavyset man responded. They may run into some weather as they approach Ireland, but it shouldn't slow them more than a few hours, sir. Still, they should be here in five days."

Their 'sister' was the freighter Athena, sailing under the flag of Panama. Another break-bulk cargo ship, Athena had been on a carefully orchestrated itinerary for the past five months. After leaving Dar es Salaam in Tanzania, she headed north and made a stop in Mogadishu, Somalia, before sailing through the Gulf of Aden, into the Red Sea, through the Suez, and on to the ports of Benghazi, Libya and Bizerte, Tunisia in northern Africa. After passing through the Strait of Gibraltar, she'd headed south to Freetown, Sierra Leone, then north again for a stop in Agadir, Morocco, before her trip to Portugal. This was her first voyage in the open Atlantic. Her entire life had been spent as a coaster in the Mediterranean and the east coast of Africa. The change in itinerary was the result of new corporate owners. Her Captain, Nurjaman Jibril, was a veteran sailor and was pleased to have the opportunity to visit new ports, though he'd been surprised when the owners had also demanded a change of crew in Lisbon.

Like most ships, the Athena was sailing under a 'flag of convenience', used by shipping companies to avoid heavy taxes and stringent inspections. While the vessels' owners hide behind walls of secrecy created by layers of ownership structures, the crews are typically cheap foreign labor, with few or no rights.

The Athena and the Ares were owned by different shell corporations.

Yet, unknown to the amiable Captain Jibril and his new crew, Athena would be inextricably linked to the Ares for this mission.

Captain Sungkar knew. He had personally chosen the names Athena and Ares, children of the Greek god, Zeus. “Sister and brother, working together for the glory of God,” he would remind his officers.

In just over a week, both ships would be heading to North America. Athena would be going to Boston after a stop in Halifax, Nova Scotia. Ares would head into the Gulf of St. Lawrence, through the St. Lawrence Seaway and on to the home of its new corporate owners. A grand celebration was planned in Detroit for the arrival of newest member of the fleet.

“Timing is critical,” Captain Sungkar reminded his men. “Once Athena arrives, it will take 30 hours to offload her cargo and another full day to take on the textiles and cod oil for shipment to Boston. We must leave Iceland exactly 24 hours after our sister.”

“And what if the papers don’t arrive in time?” The question came from the short heavyset man.

“Don’t worry Rosie; we have nine days before we leave. The papers will be here. Everything is on schedule. The world will never be the same. Satan will be no more.” Captain Abe was pleased everything was going so well. “Tens of millions of dollars have been invested in this mission. Money and years of planning are now bearing fruit,” he said reassuringly.

The three men had been speaking English with slight, unidentifiable accents. Speaking English would ease communication during their passage through the St. Lawrence Seaway.

The officers were trying their best to adopt North American ways. Each had taken an Anglo nickname, and these were the only names used in conversation. The new crew would be given only these nicknames. Amrozi, the First Officer, was called Rosie. Captain Sungkar was called

Captain Abe, in homage to the father of his religion. He was a distinguished looking man with every one of his salt and pepper hairs in place, and always impeccably dressed to impress anyone who might board his ship.

The third man in the room was Azhari. He took the nickname Adam. The youngest of the three, Adam was a dreamer. He had never married. It was a deliberate decision to wait until he had achieved his goals.

While very different in age and personality, the three had a shared passion.

It had been a long voyage since leaving North Korea, but the officers were now well rested.

Reinventing the ship was an expensive endeavor, but necessary to evade the prying eyes of American intelligence. With separate ownership from the Athena, not even the Americans would make the brother – sister connection. And, Athena had taken her name almost five years earlier.

"What about the AIS?" Captain Abe asked.

Adam responded, "I checked the regulations and we can't reprogram the AIS with the new name until the papers arrive. It's okay to have the name painted today, but we need to wait before we change the computer. Don't worry. It will only take a few hours to reprogram." At 26, the tall, muscular officer stood almost a head taller than Rosie. His close-cropped hair and dark eyes sparkled over the beardless chin he had the hardest time accepting.

A sailor for only a few years prior to meeting Captain Abe and being recruited for this operation, he was the least experienced of the officers. He was also the most fervent, despite having been the last to join the group. His computer skills and technical expertise, particularly with some of the specialized equipment they had aboard, were essential to the mission and he was overjoyed to be of help.

Having been raised in the north of Tunisia, in Beni Meslem Village, Adam has sought work in the nearby Port of Bizerte. He started as a port worker and quickly felt a desire to be a sailor. He hadn't been sailing for long when he began keeping company with a group of other sailors and longshoremen who had been heavily influenced by fringe religious elements in Tunisia and Egypt. This had prompted his interest in electronics, particularly weapons systems. He knew what he was doing. For him, it was about the *jihad*, the struggle.

"When we're 40 hours out of Reykjavik we'll begin the final test," the Captain said. "The crew will be assigned to quarters for six hours. Will that be enough time?"

Rosie was in charge of the test and assured the Captain it should be completed in half that time. "But Captain, what will we tell the crew? Won't they get suspicious? They'll also wonder why we're carrying so much ballast."

"Adam will talk to them. He'll tell them operations and weather in the Great Lakes are very different. American regulations require we run a series of tests with minimal crew and under a variety of different conditions. He'll tell them the tests must be completed before we enter the Seaway and the inspections in Montreal. They won't know any different."

The crew was only signed on to deliver the ship to her new owners. Once in Detroit, they would be given flights back to their home countries and a new American crew would take over.

Adam spoke up, "Captain, do you think the new crew will be uncomfortable with the painting on the container?" The painting had not been part of the original plan. Added in Iceland to one of the 53 foot containers now stored deep in the hold of the ship, it had been a last minute brainstorm of Captain Sungkar.

"They should never see it until it's too late." He paused and thought for a moment. "If they do see it, be honest. Tell them the container is a present for the Americans and the painting is part of the present. It's the sacred animal of the Greek god Ares."

"Yes Sir. As they say in America, honesty is the best policy."

FOUR

Saturday, July 20th
16:15 GMT – 11:15 am EDT
Cranberry Lake, New York, USA

SAVANNAH, JOSEPH AND JERRY had been paging through Jack Christian's 1955 journal for more than two hours and had found nothing. Each had taken a third of the stack. After the first round, they exchanged stacks and started over. Pastries and coffee had been traded for pretzels and diet cola.

Joseph stopped and smiled at the entry he was reading,

> ***August 13, 1955*** *– Sara was buried today, leaving behind the* ***grand old lady dog****. The marker can be found on the former Isle Royale. Visit the marker and it will provide you great comfort.*

"Look at this entry. Who was Sara and what ever happened to her dog?"

Jerry fussed at Joseph about staying focused and looking for clues about where to find the gold. "Maybe you are ADD."

Savannah interrupted with a puzzled look on her face, "Wait. I have no idea who Sara was, and Father hated dogs. When I was seven years old, I begged for one. He told me 'dogs were filthy animals.' He said he never had one and would never get one."

Jerry commented, "Sara must have been a relative. Otherwise, why would he put it in his journal?"

"I asked a number of relatives about a 'Sara' in the family and nobody knew of anyone by that name." Savannah thought for a moment. "Maybe she was related to one of the other construction workers, or maybe she worked as a cook for the construction workers."

Joseph was confused, "That doesn't make any sense. He knew you would probably be the only one to read this. If she wasn't someone you'd know, why would he put anything about her in his journal? Why would he say that visiting her grave would bring you comfort? And, if he hated dogs, why mention that at all, much less call her a grand old lady dog?"

Jerry was listening to the exchange when it hit him. "Let me see that." He grabbed the journal page from Joseph and studied it. "Look, it just says 'visit the marker,' and it—'the marker'—will provide great comfort, *not* Sara, whoever she was . . . if she even existed. And why would she be buried on an island in the St. Lawrence River? The island is probably owned by the State of New York. You can't bury a body on state land."

Joseph and Savannah were now standing and looking over Jerry's shoulder.

"The island is owned by the New York State Power Authority," Savannah told him.

Joseph looked at her a bit surprised.

"What? I looked it up."

"That makes this even more unusual," Jerry said. "We need to find out who this Sara was."

"Isn't Sara usually spelled with an 'h' at the end?" Joseph asked.

"Not always," Savannah commented.

Jerry was sitting with his back to the window overlooking the lake as he continued to read the other entries on the page to see if Sara was mentioned again. Joseph and Savannah sat back down. Joseph was sitting directly across from Jerry.

As Jerry was holding the page in both hands, the light coming over his shoulder from the window was illuminating the paper.

From across the table, Joseph saw something. “Let me see that Baldy.” Jerry handed the page to Joseph who then held it up to the window so the light was now hitting the paper directly from behind.

“Look at this you guys.” Pointing to a spot about a third of the way down the page, “Do those four words seem darker than the others?”

“It’s probably just an anomaly from the copy machine,” Jerry suggested.

“Maybe, but maybe not. We can check it out easily enough.” Joseph looked at Savannah, “Didn’t you say you have the originals in the car?”

“I’ll get them.” Savannah headed to her car.

While she was gone, Jerry looked at Joseph and with a smile, “You sly dog. Did you meet her at the Lodge? Bringing a woman home for the night, especially one who has a story about a treasure.”

“I didn’t bring her home. She just showed up at my door this morning.”

”You’re kidding, right?”

“No, I’m not kidding. This treasure sounds like the real thing, Jerry. By the way, what was that about when you asked her if her father had ever been arrested? I know it wasn’t just because of old habits.”

Jerry heard the front door opening and whispered, “I’ll tell you later.”

Savannah returned with a worn cloth covered book. The cover page on the inside simply said – Journal of John T. Christian, 1955. She flipped through the pages and found the entry for August 13, 1955. “Look, I never noticed that before.” Pointing to the words ‘grand old lady dog’ she said, “It does look like they are just a little darker. Actually, it looks like they were written with a different pen.”

Joseph took the book and walked over to the window and held it up so the light could hit the page from behind. Savannah and Jerry followed.

"That is definitely different. You're right. I think he used a different pen."

Jerry had noticed it earlier but hadn't said anything because he wanted to be sure. Now pleased with himself he said, "Look again. What does the first letter of each of those darker words spell?'

Savannah read the sentence slowly, ". . . Leaving behind the G – O – L – D. The marker can be found on the former Isle Royale. That's it . . . That's it . . . You found it! Thank you. Oh, thank you so much!"

Savannah was so excited she turned and gave Joseph a big hug. He hugged her back, holding on just an instant longer than he should.

"All right," she said as she gently pushed away from Joseph. "Where do we go from here?"

Joseph was quick with a response, "We go find the marker. That's what we do."

The three sat back down. "Hey, Joe Boy, Savannah knows where the marker is, and she knows where the island is. She doesn't need our help anymore."

"Yes I do," she quickly said.

"Yes she does," Joseph repeated.

"Okay then, you should have a game plan. You can't just go off without a plan."

"What? You rent a boat and you go out to the island and find the marker. There's your plan."

Jerry just shook his head, "Now I know why it took you 30 years to find Joseph Bonaparte's treasure."

"Well then, what do you suggest Mr. Organization?"

"That island is private property. Are you going to be arrested for trespassing? The New York Power Authority is a state entity. Remember the laws about finding buried treasure on state land? If you find anything of value on state land, it belongs to the state. Also, how big is the island? How long will you be spending there? Are you going to need any tools? Where are you going to get the boat to get out there? And, most important, who's making the lunch that we're taking with us? I'm not going to help if you're making it Joey."

"The name is Joseph, and for your information, I make a mean peanut butter and jelly."

"Like I said, I'm not going if you're making lunch," Jerry looked at Savannah with a question in his eyes.

"Okay, how about a fried chicken and potato salad picnic?" Savannah said.

"When do we leave?"

Joseph jumped in, "You know Baldy, Savannah and I can do this without you."

"No, we can't," Savannah shot back quickly.

Jerry leaned back in his chair. With his hands clasped behind his head and a big smile, he repeated, "No you can't."

"But . . ."

Savannah interrupted Joseph before he got another word out, and with her big green eyes she looked at him and said firmly, "NO WE CAN'T!" After just a few hours together, Savannah was learning how to play the verbal game with Jerry and Joseph.

"Okay, Baldy, it's obvious Savannah and I can't do this alone, will you help us?"

"Of course I will buddy, let's plan on later in the week. Does Friday work for everybody?"

"Friday's finc with mc." Savannah was gctting cxcitcd.

"Me too," Joseph chimed in.

"We probably ought to make a reservation for a boat today." While Jerry went to the desk to make reservations for a boat, Joseph asked Savannah what kind of work she did.

"I'm a translator. I mostly work from home translating corporate reports, manuals, even books from time to time. It works well for me because I set my own hours."

"What language?"

"Bahasa Indonesia, it's the national language of Indonesia."

"Wow, that's unusual. How did you pick that?"

"It kind of picked me. I was in the military, stationed at the American Embassy in Jakarta, and picked up the language. When I got out of the Marines, I went to Syracuse University and got a master's degree in languages. I fell in love with Indonesia while I was there, and went back after graduation to get to know the culture a little better. Like any other business, translation is a matter of supply and demand. Since they're a limited number of Americans who can translate Bahasa Indonesia, I make a good living without working too hard. It leaves me plenty of time for my bees and my garden."

"Okay," Jerry said from the desk. "We have a boat for Friday. I reserved it for the whole day so we can enjoy lunch and we won't feel rushed." Jerry picked up a yellow legal pad and pen that were sitting on the desk and headed back to the table where Joseph and Savannah were talking.

"Look guys, I think better when I write things down. Let's get a few things on paper so I can be thinking about stuff before Friday." Jerry started to write a timeline of events surrounding Jack Christian and his discovery of the gold. Without trying to sound like a former cop, he started to ask questions about Savannah's father and his time working on the Seaway. To Savannah it sounded like a conversation. Jerry knew it was an interrogation.

"You must have been very close to your dad," he started.

"We were close."

"You said he died in1996. How old was he?"

"He was 69."

"That must have been a difficult time for you?"

"It was. It's been 17 years and I still miss him. We did a lot of things together. I still keep the bees and maintain the garden he built behind the house. It's my way of staying in touch with his spirit. He always told me he built the garden for me. Now, I keep it up in his memory."

Savannah turned to Joseph, "The garden is beautiful, I hope you can see it someday."

A bit surprised, Joseph smiled, "I'd like that."

Doing the math in his head, Jerry commented, "Your dad must have been pretty young when he worked on the Seaway."

"Twenty-eight, I think, when he started."

"That means he was born in 1927."

"That's right."

"Let me guess, you still plant something in the garden every year on his birthday?"

"That's amazing. Every May 17th I plant a rose bush. How did you know?"

"Just a lucky guess. Isn't that a little early to be planting roses here?"

"Most years I have to protect them on cold nights. But, I've never lost one of father's birthday roses to a freeze. I'm very proud of that."

"I noticed in the Journal his name was John, yet he went by Jack?"

"Yea, but that's fairly common. Why do you ask?"

"Just curious, I guess I'm trying to get to know him a little better. It may help us down the road."

Jerry had all the information he needed. It would take him a few days to check it out. Neither Joseph nor Savannah would ever know.

FIVE

Monday, July 22nd
14:00 GMT – 9:00 am EDT
Langley, Virginia, USA

"RELAX. You know what you're doing. Just be careful not to make any recommendations until after you've heard all of the information. Don't rush into any decisions." The voice on the other end of the phone sounded tired. Although Lieutenant Preston Evans, USN was about to begin his day, his father, Harold, sitting in his living room in Uruma, Japan had finished his. The retired Navy Master Chief tried to soothe his son's anxiety at having been chosen to lead an intelligence task force. This was his first. Listening to his dad's voice was always a comfort to Preston.

"Any final advice?"

"If you're talking more than you're listening, you're probably doing something wrong. Remember, God gave you two ears and one mouth. Use them in those proportions." His father had a way of condensing everything to simple concepts.

"Thanks Dad. Is Mom around?"

"She's at a meeting. Preparing for *Toro nagashi*." The lantern festival his Japanese mother helped organize every year was just a few weeks away. Preston, who'd grown up in Japan, had enjoyed helping his mother prepare for this ancient ceremony.

"Give her my love, Dad. I'll call later in the week."

"Be good, son. We're both very proud of you."

Lt. Evans allowed himself a smile as he approached Central Intelligence Agency headquarters in Langley, Virginia.

After being cleared by security, he was handed a classified courier package with the latest updates from his office at the Department of the Navy in Suitland, Maryland.

Taking the main stairway to the lower level, he steeled himself for the harsh confines of the CIA. Prior to starting with ONI, the Office of Naval Intelligence, Evans' notions of task force operations were driven primarily by the entertainment media, and his illusions were dashed on the rocks of reality very quickly. Expecting what he'd seen in television and film depictions of task-force meetings, he discovered that there was no wall-sized status board, no dramatic lighting, no midnight flights to the area of operation. Instead, meetings were held in whatever meeting room was available, under cold fluorescent lights, with the same government-contract furniture one finds everywhere, including chairs that provide distraction-free comfort for only the first ten minutes. Information was exchanged and decisions were made, often very slowly; then everyone was off to collect more information to share.

Evans was the youngest member of the Joint Task Force that had been assembled to watch Athena after she left Benghazi. 'The Kid' had participated in several task force groups before, and being asked to lead one was a step toward his promotion to Lt. Commander. He had risen quickly in his navy career because of his education, but it was his quick mind and street smarts that had caught the attention of Navy Intelligence, where he had been for the last seven years.

Evans joined the Navy shortly after 9-11 having just received his Master's Degree in Classical Studies. A baby-faced 5'7", with light brown skin, he was simply referred to as 'kid' by his superiors. He often thought he didn't get the respect he deserved because of his appearance. But he'd made a name for himself on a highly sensitive operation when he connected the dots from a number of separate intelligence sources that resulted in the identification of a significant terrorist operation. His insight averted a strike that could have killed hundreds of people. That event earned him his promotion. It wasn't an official Navy promotion. It was a promotion that showed he was respected by his colleagues. He was no longer just "kid." Now he was referred to as '*The* Kid.'

No one called him Preston, not even his mother. It's a difficult name for a Japanese native to pronounce, so she nicknamed him Mikoto, meaning 'The Noble One.' His African-American father found it easier to just call him Mickey. For his navy buddies, 'The Kid' was acceptable.

Sitting in the Task Force conference room waiting for the other participants, Evans opened the envelope he had been handed and began to read the summary: "ONI first spotted Athena as she passed through the Suez. Her cargo of bananas touched off the gamma radiation sensors as she made the passage through the canal."

He knew bananas in sufficient quantities produce positive readings with radiation sensors because of their potassium content. Potassium-40 is a natural radioactive isotope, and even a single pallet of bananas can set off the sensors. Port managers expect the positive reading when they see bananas on the manifest; an event that must be listed on a radiation anomaly report, but, because of the cargo, nobody pays attention.

After the September 11th attacks, US intelligence agencies installed radiation sensors throughout the world in ports and passages like the Suez and Panama canals. Additionally, ONI has created enormous databases to track any anomalies that could indicate terrorists on approaching ships.

These databases include names and license numbers of tens of thousands of seamen from around the world, many of whom carry fake documents and use pseudonyms because of criminal pasts. ONI has also enlisted informants among port managers, shipping agents, dock supervisors and seafarers' unions. With this massive network, the agency has unique, almost instantaneous, reach-back capability to check just about any ship and seaman in the world.

Standard operating procedure since 9-11 has been to conduct a 'quick-check' on any ship that sets off radiation sensors anywhere in the world, even when bananas, granite or other cargo are obviously the cause of the 'hit.'

The summary went on: "Other than the radiation signature, no anomalies were discovered. Athena appeared to be clean."

From past experience, Evans knew the gamma scintillators used for monitoring these ports were extremely sensitive, able to detect minute levels of gamma radiation over background at significant distances. Many foreign ports do not possess the more selective NBR, or natural background rejection technology, or the ability to identify the specific isotope producing the radiation. The US intelligence community, however, does possess that technology.

Evans kept reading: "After Athena unloaded most of her cargo of bananas in the Port of Benghazi, the Port Manager, a recent intelligence asset recruited after NATO forces helped liberate Libya from Col. Muammar al-Qaddafi, reported that the radiation signature on Athena continued in equal strength."

Evans had already been briefed on what he was reading so he was now just scanning the summary for anything new. The information had been passed on to a nameless, faceless, intelligence officer in Tripoli, who, from the confines of a 1974 Volkswagen Bus, aimed a Radioactive Isotope

Identification Device (RIID), at Athena as she was berthed in Benghazi.

The Identifinder® is a small device, about the size of a hand-held vacuum cleaner that assists in locating the direction from which the strongest signature originates. Once aimed, the touch of a button allows the instrument to capture a spectrum. The VW was not parked at an optimal distance, so what should have been a brief capture of the radiation spectrum turned into a 20-minute process. Fortunately, Athena was stationary and no obstacles stood between the Identifinder® and the second porthole on the port side.

While the CIA officer was capturing the spectrum, he watched the blue LED display for neutron detection. Fortunately, it was not above background. After twenty minutes, the officer looked at the display to see if it was able to identify the spectrum. He stifled a whistle when he read the result: cesium-137, industrial, confidence level three.

From previous reports, Evans knew that since the wars in Afghanistan and Iraq, significant quantities of this isotope had gone missing. Much of it was used in the construction and maintenance of oil wells, pipelines, power plants, water systems, and industrial tools such as radiography cameras. Pavers and builders used it in devices to gauge the density of soil. If there were any records of the locations of all of the contractors who owned these items, and in what quantities, they were never located after the demise of these countries' governments.

The CIA officer in Benghazi used a small laser range finder to determine his precise distance from the source, took a digital picture of Athena, and returned to Tripoli. The information was sent by secure satellite uplink to Washington, where the spectrum was to be passed on to ONI and physicists at Los Alamos and Oak Ridge National Laboratories. Scientists were able to estimate, with astounding accuracy, the mass and probable location of the source within Athena.

Athena was now tagged as a ship with a real radiation signature and, after several additional stops, she was heading to Boston. While the radiation signature had made the situation a priority and bumped it from ONI to Joint Task Force status, the events in Lisbon created even greater concern. CIA, ONI, NSA, and now even the Director of Central Intelligence and the National Security Advisor were involved.

Lt. Evans knew his performance was being watched closely. This was an opportunity for him and he intended to make the most of it. He had requested and assembled much of the intelligence since the Athena had left Benghazi. Her itinerary after Libya included Tunisia, Sierra Leone, Morocco and Portugal. ONI had major assets in each of these ports but Tunisia. The remaining bananas were sufficient to allow local port authorities to write off the radiation alarms. The US would not share their information. Meanwhile, locally-stationed CIA officers were placed in each port, photographing the ship, its crew members, and inspecting off-loaded cargo. Listening and GPS devices were hidden in cargo being loaded on the Athena in case the ship turned off its AIS system.

In Agadir, Morocco, the local pilot who boarded Athena to guide her to her berth on the East Quay had been recruited to secretly place a listening device on the bridge. NSA was now listening to every word said there. Satellites were dedicated to tracking Athena's every move. On cloudy days when the satellites couldn't take pictures, unmanned drones were utilized.

In each port, agents were following crew members to the bars they frequented. Prostitutes, many of whom were on a first name basis with agents and were even considered intelligence assets, were interrogated after liaisons with crew members.

There was no good news in the package of information Evans has just received. Other members of the task force received similar packages from their agencies. Evans had called a meeting to see if they could determine where the evidence was leading. As the other members of the task force arrived, he introduced himself and exchanged pleasantries. There were frequently new faces and names to remember, and Evans' ability to remember a name and face almost instantly was an asset. He finished the introductions and thanked the CIA for providing the facilities for their operations. Then he began his briefing on the materials he had just received. As the group reviewed the new intelligence, a full sense of the gravity of the situation became clear to everyone in the room.

"Except for the officers, the entire Athena crew was released in Lisbon, and thirty new sailors were hired. We need to know why," he told the group. "Backgrounds on the old crew identified nothing out of the ordinary. In fact, all indications from ONI pointed to a capable crew with a great deal of experience."

"What did our Lisbon assets have to say?" someone asked.

Lt. Evans was matter-of-fact in his response, never showing his frustration. "CIA officers talked to several of the released crew as well as managers at the Lisbon Seamen's Hall. Nobody had an explanation. They had never seen anything like this before. The AIS provided license numbers for each of the new crew members and it appears these new guys had less experience than the old, not to mention the fact that several of the new crew had very questionable backgrounds with significant breaks in their time at sea."

The Coast Guard representative jumped in. "Anything on the officers?"

"A detailed background on Captain Jibril is in your packets. Jibril is a dedicated family man, lifelong seaman, clean record. For the past five years he's been Captain of the Athena. As many of you know, one red flag

ONI looks for is long shore time that can be used in terrorist training. Captain Jibril's background is unbroken. His whereabouts can be traced to every ship he sailed since the day he received his mariners' license 37 years ago. There's not a hint that he could be a terrorist, nor has he ever been known to associate with terrorists. He appears to be a seaman through and through."

Trying to keep the meeting moving, Evans continued with his review of the activities in Lisbon. "CIA officers reported the usual drinking by the crew in local bars, but the Athena's officers never associated with anyone. This may be because of the Muslim month of fasting."

Evans looked at one of the two CIA analysts in the room. "Allen, can you help us here?"

Allen Cole was a specialist in Islamic culture. "Ramadan is more than the denial of food and drink. While they are fasting, devout Muslims also abstain from smoking and sexual contact. Our guys in Lisbon report the officers always stayed together and seemed to simply enjoy their time in port. The crew was a different matter. There was activity with local prostitutes, but that is common with seamen, even Islamic seamen during Ramadan." Cole smiled.

"Thanks Allen. Okay everybody, that's all I have except for this; the combination of radiation signature and the unusual events in Lisbon moved the Athena to a top priority. This was mentioned in the President's daily security briefing this morning. Athena is now 12 hours from Reykjavik, her last stop before heading to North America. Canadian Intelligence has been notified of her status and her planned stop in Halifax, Nova Scotia."

The mention of the President's briefing made people sit up a little straighter. Evans wasn't trying to scare anyone, but he wanted them all to know people are watching, and that regardless of the view of anyone at the table, others think this is significant. Evans turned to the other Navy officer in the room, from the US Atlantic Fleet. "Can you bring us up to date, Commander Krieman?"

"The Pentagon is on full alert. Three warships and one submarine have been positioned to shadow Athena once she leaves Iceland. Two separate SEAL teams have already been transported to the warships. Canada had also assigned a warship to the operation. If we receive any indication of a hostile act either in progress or imminent, Athena can be attacked and rendered harmless within minutes. These assets are tasked to this mission for the duration."

"Thanks, Commander. Next is CIA. Joe, anything new?"

Looking at Joe, whose last name was not pronounceable by many, seemingly including Joe himself, you would think he'd just shambled in after a night of heavy drinking, a night that had turned into a morning of heavy drinking. He sat, slouched in his chair with a knee hanging over one of the armrests, an example, nonetheless, of why one is well advised not to judge a book by its cover. With the hand that was not engaged in holding up his head and massive mop of unkempt hair, he began speaking in a smooth baritone that no one would deny was made for radio. The content of his briefing was invaluable, and everyone who did not know him was surprised to glimpse the workings of the brain inside its sloppy wrapping. He concluded with a couple of points: "Our image analysts assure us there were no anomalies in any of the 200-something satellite and drone photographs taken of the Athena since she left Libya. Transcripts of conversations on the bridge offer nothing. Just the excitement of the officers anticipating their first trip to America."

It seemed for a second that he'd finished. Then he shifted slightly in his chair, holding up a hand to indicate he would continue. "There's just one more thing regarding the analysis of the spectrum captured in Libya. Our physicists at Los Alamos have confirmed cesium-137. Depending on where in the ship it's located, and behind how much shielding, it constitutes anywhere from two to three kilograms of material."

Eyebrows were raised and the room briefly went silent. Even the representative from the Domestic Nuclear Detection Office (DNDO) stopped her annoying habit of tapping her fingernails on her coffee mug. "Almost three to six and one-half pounds of radioactive *anything* is a lot. Especially cesium. We consider it a problem when the source from a single radiography camera is loose, and that's about the size of the metal band and eraser on a pencil. That much source material would have to be significantly shielded not to trigger alarms in Boston Harbor," she added before resuming her rhythm-free percussion solo on her mug.

"It couldn't be very heavily shielded, or it wouldn't have been very easy to pull a spectrum in Libya," Evans observed.

"The boat's steel hull is pretty good shielding, and so is the water," replied the DNDO percussionist.

"It's a *ship*. And the spectrum was easily captured from above the water line," Evans insisted.

A young lieutenant from the Coast Guard interjected, "Had she already off-loaded her cargo? Had they loaded fresh cargo yet?"

Evans knew instantly where these questions were going. The ship would ride significantly higher in the water when she was carrying less cargo. The source may have been kept below the water line while laden, but not when most of her cargo was ashore. He leaned to his assistant, a petty officer, and asked her to review the cargo off-loaded and its weight.

CIA Joe pulled out a photo taken by the intelligence officer in Libya and passed it to Evans, who took a look and motioned the Coast Guard officer over to look with him.

"You're much better with merchant ships than I am, Shawn. What do you think?"

After a few seconds' inspection, Lt. Shawn Snow offered his opinion. "She's a break-bulk freighter. Older, but still seaworthy, especially for coastal shipping. She looks like she's riding high, but with the pier in the way I can't see the water line. I'll pass it around my office and see what the others think. Her cranes look to be ready to hook up cargo, but the pier is clean, so I'd say she's off-loaded and the freight's been taken away and she's waiting to be loaded."

"Thanks, Shawn, let us know what you determine, will you?"

"Sure, Mickey," Shawn replied with a smile.

"Mickey?" The question came from a representative from Homeland Security's Office of Infrastructure Protection seated at the opposite end of the table.

"Just a nickname. Short for Mikoto." When he saw that the explanation offered only more confusion he continued, "My mom nicknamed me Mikoto, and my dad shortened it to 'Mickey.' She's Japanese and he's American." He left it there. This meeting was not about him and he wanted to keep everyone focused. He continued immediately with the next phase of the agenda, requesting opinions. This was a time he dreaded because he inevitably had to function as a referee between competing priorities. Sometimes it was a struggle to do so in a way that wouldn't bruise any egos or cause anyone to be reluctant to participate.

DHS expressed their concern that so large a radiation source even be allowed to enter Boston Harbor. The Navy Commander agreed and recommended an assault and boarding of Athena as soon as she left Iceland.

The DNDO percussionist interrupted. “The quantity of material in the radiation source *is* significant, but not dangerous in and of itself. Remember, this is not fissile material so it can’t be used to fuel a thermonuclear device.” She paused and thought for a moment, then continued. “On the other hand, it could be used in a radiation dispersal device or ‘dirty bomb.’ Or, it could be used as a part of a RED, or Radiation Exposure Device. For example, it could be placed near the doors of the New York Stock Exchange, exposing everyone who enters and leaves, repeatedly, over long periods of time. Or, it could be placed in an office or closet to injure anyone who spends time nearby.”

“My point exactly,” the DHS representative said. No one else in the room responded, apparently considering the ramifications of what they just heard.

Mickey Evans broke the silence. “That could be a reason for the crew exchange in Lisbon; swap them out before they become symptomatic from radiation exposure.”

“Maybe,” the DNDO percussionist added. “Maybe this commercial ship is just doing what it does: transportation—moving material for sale to a still-unknown buyer.”

CIA Joe jumped in the conversation. “The history of the crew doesn’t suggest nefarious intent. If we capture the material before any transaction is made, we’ll likely never know who the intended buyer is.”

Evans realized that something throughout this conversation had been nagging at him. If these people were trying to hide this material, they’re doing a rotten job of it. Why didn’t they place it where it would be sure to stay below the water line, like in the ship’s bilge? Water curtails gamma transmission very efficiently, and the transmission would only be further blocked by the steel hull of the freighter. Or, they could just as easily keep it in a heavily shielded container. He elected to keep his thoughts to himself for the moment. He was only speculating and he didn't want to add to the speculation that already existed. Also, the meeting was going long, very long. They could go on endlessly, with progress generally in inverse proportion to time spent.

He decided to end the meeting. "It appears the most important aspect of this case is to determine who the conspirators are, how large a conspiracy it is, what the intended targets are, and who's funding it. The source will remain under constant surveillance; it won't get away. If it were seized now, the unknown perpetrators could easily find more radioactive material somewhere and smuggle it with better stealth.

"Nevertheless, the concerns of the DHS are undeniable. Watched or not, it remains a threat. Athena will never be allowed to come near the U.S coast without a complete inspection. That won't happen until after she leaves Nova Scotia. We'll get the State Department involved and make sure Canadian intelligence officials and the Canadian Armed Forces have full access to the surveillance data and signals intercepts while Athena is in their territorial waters.

"The crew of Athena will almost certainly have to make some form of communication with a buyer if that's their goal. If a transfer of material is attempted in Nova Scotia, Canadian forces, with our assistance, will raid the ship and seize the material. If not, the ship will be boarded before entering Boston Harbor."

Evans looked at Lt. Snow: "Shawn, Coast Guard will have to work with the Pentagon to start planning a couple of boarding scenarios." He turned to his assistant. "I'd like someone from the Department of Energy to be in on our next meeting. No matter what happens, they'll have a big source to secure." Then he looked at Joe. "Keep pulling what you can on the ship and her crew. They'll have to tip their hands at some point."

Mickey Evans reminded the team that Athena still had a stop in Iceland, and that would be their last real opportunity to gather new intelligence.

"We're on it," added CIA Joe. Intelligence officers permanently stationed in Iceland had been placed on alert, and more had already been dispatched to Reykjavik where Athena was scheduled to be in port for only 48 hours.

"Okay, thank you everybody. We'll meet again, same time tomorrow morning."

SIX

Monday, July 22nd
15:00 GMT – 10:00 am EDT
Canton, New York, USA

LEX PARSIMONIAE, or the law of parsimony is better known as Ockham's razor. It is the principle that is often summarized as "simpler explanations are, other things being equal, generally better than more complex ones." Since the 14th century, scientists have used Ockham's razor in the development of theoretical models. Jerry Doolin used it throughout his career to guide criminal investigations. Twenty-three years as a New York State Trooper had shown him the wisdom in this principle thousands of times. After all, criminals can come up with rather creative and often convoluted stories to explain their innocence.

Ockham's razor had served Jerry well over the years. Some of his colleagues nicknamed him 'Cassandra,' after the character in Greek mythology, cursed with the gift of prophecy, but never to be believed. "I was never prophetic. It's just that, more often than not, the simple explanation ends up being the truth," Jerry mumbled to himself as he drove to Canton.

He could not get Savannah's story out of his head. In 1956, her father, a 29 year old construction worker, bought a 140 acre farm with cash from a treasure left over from the French and Indian war. The discovery of hidden treasure was not the 'simple explanation' for the source of that cash.

Jerry always did his best thinking while driving, and today the Jack

Christian money issue was bothering him. Was there really a treasure or was there a simpler explanation? He'd left early in order to check on a couple of things in Canton on his way to Potsdam for his afternoon music lesson.

The two-day trip had been planned for weeks. Since retiring, he'd reluctantly accepted a consulting position with Homeland Security. Only eight months into his contract and these monthly meetings in Massena for Operation Stone Garden were already becoming old.

Coordinated by the Department of Homeland Security, the meeting took place the last Tuesday of every month at the Customs House in Massena. Operation Stone Garden was an effort to coordinate the activities of a number of U.S. and Canadian agencies to protect the border. There would be representatives from the Royal Canadian Mounted Police, Ontario and Quebec Provincial Police, St. Lawrence Seaway Authority, New York State Police, U.S. Coast Guard, Border Patrol, and Customs and Border Protection.

Typically, each organization would give a short overview of specific operations planned for the coming month. Often, two or more of the organizations would be working together on an investigation, usually smuggling-related, that required the help of one or more of the other groups. The agency representative would then discuss current intelligence and possible threats to the northern border and infrastructure. Finally, one organization would give a presentation about their activities.

This month the U.S. Coast Guard would give a presentation on a new stealth boat they were testing. The boat has the same technology the new fighter jets and bombers utilize to avoid radar detection. Equipped with electronic engines along with their diesel engines, they could approach suspicious boats at night without being heard or seen on radar. His reverie caused him to realize he didn't have the latest Infrastructure Threat

Assessments (ITA) for this meeting. He needed to call to the DHS, Office of Infrastructure Protection (OIP).

§

Lillian LaForte had just sat down at her desk. As was her habit on Mondays, she heated a large pan of red beans and rice and left it on the cafeteria counter along with a pile of plates and utensils. A Sunday tradition in her native New Orleans, Lillian had moved it up a day for the benefit of her coworkers at the DHS OIP. She brought enough to feed the entire building, mostly because she enjoyed sharing with her friends at work and never tired of the weekly tradition. Also, she'd never learned to cook on a scale small enough for one. As she was settling in and checking her email, she received a call from one of the consultants in the northeast.

While they had never met, she'd grown to like him from what he'd written and what he said on the many conference calls to which she was a party. If asked why she liked him, she'd be hard pressed to give a clear answer. Perhaps it was his voice or his kind demeanor, but mostly it was because he never took himself too seriously. Seeing the phone number and name on her display, she grabbed the phone and answered, "Jerry, baby! Where y'at?"

Jerry found her New Orleans accent utterly charming. "Lillian! I'm still stuck in the frozen north! And you're not here to keep me warm!"

The ongoing joke made Jerry grin, and widened the perpetual smile on Lillian's face. She always seemed to be just getting over a good laugh. A widow for almost a decade, with grown children who were scattered to the four winds, Lillian had taken the job with DHS initially for something to do, and because her late husband's many years working in the Port of New

Orleans had given her a feel for what was normal and what wasn't. Her skill at recognizing anomalous circumstances was noted by her superiors and she'd quickly been moved into a senior position.

"How come y'all call me on the phone? Can't come see me in the flesh?"

"Wish I could, darlin', but my dogsled is in the shop. And the dogs all take their vacations in the summer."

"Y'all got your excuses. But you didn't call just to pour on the charm. What's up? You're not gonna bail out on us, are you?"

"Why, Lillian! Whatever would make you think of such a thing?"

"Come on, I know you're wishing you never took that contract."

"True, but I did, and I'm gonna see it through to the end . . . the long-awaited, much-celebrated, I-can't-believe-I-didn't-jump-off-a-bridge, end."

"Oh, Jerry, you are a devil with the sweet talk. What'cha need, baby?"

"The latest ITA for this region."

"Jerry-come-lately. That meeting is tomorrow. You're just looking at it now?"

"Tonight I'm gonna get Chinese take-out and a quiet hotel room to do nothing but focus on the product of your office's dedicated hard work."

Lillian could do nothing but throw her head back and laugh. When she finally composed herself she told Jerry he'd find the file in his DHS email inbox. "Chinese take-out? You need some shrimp gumbo to read threat briefs."

"If only! No decent gumbo in these parts. I'll have to suffer until you can cook for me."

"Who's that fellow you had me send the *file* powder to? The windy house?"

"Windfall. John makes some mean gumbo, but he's hours away from here."

"I never get used to how big everything is up there. You got what you need, baby. And I got some red beans and rice getting cold."

"Thanks, sweetie."

"Be good, Jerry."

Jerry wondered why had he allowed himself to be roped into this? His contract with DHS was for one year and he had already decided not to renew it. The best thing about the meeting was the guitar lesson he'd scheduled at the Crane School of Music in Potsdam the Monday afternoon before his DHS meeting. His routine was to drive to Massena after his lesson, get a hotel room, have a quiet dinner and review his notes for the meeting the next day.

§

As he pulled into the parking lot of the courthouse in Canton, Jerry wondered what Joseph and Savannah would think if they knew what he was doing. He was sure they wouldn't understand. The only information he needed for the background check, he had quietly obtained the other day, without either of them knowing what he was doing.

Criminal records are public records, and The New York State Office of Court Administration (OCA) provides the public a computerized statewide criminal history record search (CHRS) for $65.00. The computerized search could have been done from home, but only as far back 1981. The only way to search criminal records from the 1950's was to do it the old fashioned way . . . by hand.

Before heading into the courthouse, Jerry took the guitar from the back seat of his car and locked it in the trunk. It was a Hirade H25, one of the best classical guitars ever made. He did not want to risk it being stolen.

The St. Lawrence County Courthouse was built in the Romanesque style of Potsdam sandstone, Gouverneur granite and Norwood black limestone. An impressive building for a small town. Jerry walked around the outside of the building to the front entrance. He had been in this building numerous times testifying in the trials of people he'd arrested over the years. The glazed tile walls and stone floor in the lobby brought back fond memories of his long career.

Just inside the lobby, and to the left, was the County Clerk's office. Jerry walked past the counter where several clerks were assisting people. Just past the desk was the massive records room. For a moment he stopped and looked. Someone not familiar with the records room would be intimidated. There were thousands of books in shelves lining the walls and on work tables scattered throughout a large open area. Several people were working at the tables. These books contain the history of a people, he thought. Every deed, every mortgage and every last will and testament ever filed in St. Lawrence County since the late 1800s were in this room.

Jerry wasn't here for mortgages, deeds or wills. Jerry was here to see if John T. "Jack" Christian had ever been arrested. The criminal records cabinet was directly in front of him. It had been years since he had looked in these books. The large books with cloth and leather covers were stored horizontally. And every book has its own slot. He pulled Book Three and set it on top of the cabinet. Looking inside, he mumbled to himself, "good guess."

Book Three had a listing of every criminal case in the county from 1949 through 1963. In the front of the book was an alphabetical listing of each entry. There were more than 230 people arrested with the last name beginning with the letter 'C' during that period. Nobody by the name

Christian was listed. While he thought it unlikely, he checked Book Two and Book Four just to make sure. Nothing. For a moment he wondered if John T. Christian was even his real name. He checked his watch. There was one more stop he wanted to make in Canton.

The St. Lawrence County Historical Association has extensive archives on the second floor of their museum on Main Street. Rather than going through hundreds of microfiche films of old newspapers at the Canton library, he thought the archives manager at the museum would be able to tell him if there were any major unsolved crimes in the mid-1950s in the county. After all, to buy a 140 acre farm with cash, and have enough money left over to provide a comfortable living for decades, it would have to be a fairly major crime. There was also another issue about the treasure story that had been bothering Jerry. Why would there have been 200 pounds of gold on an obscure island in the St. Lawrence River in 1760?

JeanMarie, the archives manager, wasn't aware of any major unsolved crimes during the 1950s, but she did give Jerry a little history lesson. "Isle Royale is not an obscure island," she informed him. "It was the site of the last battle of the French and Indian War to take place on what was to become American soil. The battle involved over 12,000 people." Jerry was stunned. He thought he knew his history but he'd never heard of Isle Royale or Fort Lévis.

"How could such a major battle take place without anybody even knowing it happened?" he asked.

JeanMarie thought for a moment, wondering how she should answer the question. The entire subject was a bit of a pet peeve with her. "The St. Lawrence River valley is kind of a 'black hole' of history," she began. "Every school kid in America knows the story of 'Custer's Last Stand' at Little Big Horn. Custer had about 600 troops and there were about 3,500

Sioux and Northern Cheyenne. There were over three times as many troops involved in the battle at Fort Lévis on Isle Royale, in a war that arguably determined the heart and soul of a nation. And even locals aren't aware that it ever took place. I could give you dozens of other examples but I'll leave it at that." Jerry thought he sensed a bitterness in her voice.

"I've heard the stories," she continued, "but I don't know why they would have had 200 pounds of gold at Fort Lévis. It's a question I've never thought of before. That's a lot of gold for that time. Maybe someone at the Fort La Présentation Association can tell you.

They are the real 'keepers' of the history of Fort La Présentation and Fort Lévis."

Jerry had heard of the Fort La Présentation Association and their heroic efforts to rebuild the fort in Ogdensburg.

"The two forts were inextricably linked," she told him. "If the gold was out there, I'd say it had to have been transferred from Fort La Présentation." The archives manager gave him contact numbers at the Fort La Présentation Association.

As he was leaving, Jerry thought of one more question. He turned around, "JeanMarie?"

"Yes, Mr. Doolin."

"I understand that during construction of the Seaway, in order to widen the shipping channel, a portion of the island was dug up and dumped on the remaining portion. Do you know the size of the original island?"

With a bit of a smirk, JeanMarie responded. "Actually, that's incorrect. They did dig up half the island as you said. But, it was not dumped on the other half. It was placed on barges and taken to the mainland. If you drive along Route 37 in Lisbon, those mounds you see between the highway and the river are the former Chimney Island. If you have a minute I can give you a map." JeanMarie photocopied of a map of the original Isle Royale, with a layout of Fort Lévis. Jerry thanked her and left.

Walking to his car Jerry thought about what he had just heard, '*the former Chimney Island . . .*' He then recalled the words from Jack Christian's Journal '*. . . the former Isle Royale.*'

The drive to Potsdam took only 15 minutes and he needed to focus on his lesson. He had finally made a decision about Dr. Kenyon's request and planned on discussing it with him. It wasn't the first time the professor had asked Jerry to give a recital. For two years he had been trying to convince Jerry to do a solo performance at Crane. He'd even promised the Helen M. Hosmer Concert Hall, which boasts some of the best acoustics in the northeast. Most recitals take place in one of the smaller performance halls on campus, but Dr. Kenyon wanted Jerry in the large hall. There was no question in Kenyon's mind that Jerry would fill the space. More important, there was no question this student was ready.

Jerry wasn't so sure.

He had been studying classical guitar with Dr. Kenyon for six years. Only a few people in Jerry's life knew about this passion. He started playing guitar when he was 12. Like most kids that age, he wanted to be a rock star. At some point, Jerry could no longer recall when, he started to play classical music. He'd bought his first classical guitar at the age of 23. The Takamine Hirade H25 had been his retirement gift to himself.

The H25 is a limited edition Hirade, handmade and assembled after a stash of Brazilian rosewood, the rarest and most sought after wood in the guitar world, was discovered in a back room of the Takamine factory. It was Dr. Kenyon who gave Jerry the tip that a former student wanted to sell the instrument. While $5,000 was a lot of money for a guitar, Jerry justified the investment knowing this guitar would increase in value over the years. The H25 has a clarity, dynamic range and transparent tone worthy of a concert hall. That's what Jerry had in mind when he bought it. But, for some reason, not even he could explain, he hadn't been able to commit to a solo concert. While he had gone back and forth on the decision a dozen times, it was his partner, Will, along with Joseph, who finally convinced him to make the commitment.

Other than Joseph and Will, nobody in Cranberry Lake even knew Jerry played classical guitar, much less at a concert level. A week ago, when the three of them had met for dinner at the Windfall, a local restaurant known for its exquisite food, both Joseph and Will were adamant that Jerry go ahead with the performance.

"You jerk, everything you have done for the past 23 years you have done for other people. You've been a trooper, a volunteer fireman, a paramedic. Don't you think it's time you did something for yourself," Joseph said.

"Jerry, this is your dream," Will added.

Joseph thought for a moment before continuing, "You helped me follow my dream and I'm going to do whatever it takes to make sure you follow yours, even if that means dragging you kicking and screaming to that stage."

Will just sat back and smiled.

Dr. Kenyon was thrilled with Jerry's decision and said he had already reserved a date in May of next year for the concert. Jerry was both shocked and relieved. He had more than nine months to prepare, but when he asked Dr. Kenyon why he had already booked him in next years' schedule, Kenyon simply said, "it's easier to take something off the schedule than to add it at the last minute. You were scheduled for a concert in May of this year and I had to cancel. I never told you about it. I didn't realize you would be so stubborn."

"I'm not stubborn, just cautious," Jerry responded.

It was not a great lesson. Jerry made an excuse about not being focused because he was anxious about his decision to go ahead with the concert. Deep down he knew why he wasn't focused. He was preoccupied. He had already decided to extend his trip an extra day. After the DHS meeting tomorrow, he'd drive to Malone and get a room. First thing Wednesday morning he'd check out Jack Christian in the Franklin County courthouse. If he found nothing, he'd go to the Clinton County courthouse in Plattsburgh in the afternoon.

There must be a simpler explanation, he kept thinking. While he was worried about what he would find, he was more worried how Joseph and Savannah would react to whatever he found. He knew they wouldn't understand why he'd gone looking in the first place.

After dinner, Jerry sat in his hotel room and went through a number of scenarios. Several hundred thousand dollars in 1955? It must have been a fairly big job. Maybe a bank heist or payroll heist. That was the simplest explanation. Or maybe some of the larger construction equipment was stolen, transported out of state, and sold. As superintendent, Jack would have access to the flatbed trucks that moved the equipment between construction sites along the river. If it had been done on a holiday weekend, no one would have missed it for days.

One disturbing thing Savannah had said kept coming back to him. *She'd heard relatives speculate that her dad had stolen the money.* It shouldn't be hard to find out if that was true.

SEVEN

Monday, July 22nd
10:30 GMT – 5:30 am EDT
Reykjavik, Iceland

"No! I said spotless. Absolutely spotless! Get rid of those two men and get me clean men."

Adam and Rosie looked at each other with concern. They had never seen Captain Abe so angry. Because Ares would be traveling without cargo, only 17 new seamen had been hired for the trip from Iceland to Detroit. Captain Abe had demanded 'spotless' backgrounds for the new crew. A complete background check had been ordered on everyone. Two men were found to be using falsified documents.

"This is the most important part of the operation and we are not going to risk ten years of planning because of a couple of scum seamen. Do not even allow them aboard this ship. Destroy any record that we even considered them. Pay off the people at the seamen's hall to do the same."

The look on the captain's face telegraphed the gravity of these instructions. He would not be questioned by his subordinates. The process of finding seamen with completely clean backgrounds was more difficult than Adam and Rosie had expected. Many mariners have backgrounds that make frequent travel attractive, and others have a tendency to get into trouble while in port. Captain Abe would take no chances with any men whose history might suggest membership in a watch-listed organization or even an outstanding arrest warrant. They would have to move easily through Customs and the remainder of the DHS apparatus once they entered the St. Lawrence Seaway. He wanted no one who would even raise an eyebrow with an agent of the US or Canadian government. Tensions would be running high when they entered the Seaway and there could be nothing to provoke anything more than a cursory look.

Abe took a quick glance at the clock. The local time was 13:35, time for *dhuhr*, the post-midday prayer. It produced a slight twinge of pain and regret, particularly now during the month of Ramadan. He and his officers had ceased their *salah* six times daily since their voyage began. They had decided, much to their discomfort, that it would be unwise to practice such observances while engaged on this mission. "We must lead a secular life while in the service of the greater goal," was his command to his shipmates. The most they could risk was a moment of quiet reflection while on deck or in the privacy of their rooms. No religious paraphernalia was to be brought on board. There were to be no political discussions among them while the crew was aboard.

While hiring the new crew in Iceland for their trip to America, Adam and Rosie tried their best to find younger, less experienced personnel who had limited time to build a bad record and who would be unfamiliar with the normal workings of a ship of this type. "The misguided youth of today are much less religious and pay almost no attention to politics, a curse of the 21st century," Abe had advised them. "They don't understand what they're doing. With the help of our sister, Athena, soon everyone will. When this is over, we all will make the *Hajj* together."

Abe knew that none of his colleagues had ever visited the Kaaba on the Muslim pilgrimage, but if all worked as planned, they would be received as heroes, "with the adulation of the crowds heaped upon us for dealing such a crushing blow to the Great Satan. All will stand in awe of our accomplishment, the fruits of which will last for years, possibly decades." Abe smiled to himself, "Whose will be the backward society then?"

§

Rosie felt uncomfortable with Abe's anger and volunteered to go to the Seamen's Hall with an envelope of cash to bribe the requisite personnel to destroy whatever records existed that the pair of wayward seamen had been considered for a position on Ares. He asked for two more, preferably fresh-faced youngsters, just out of training. The transaction at the Seamen's Hall was quick and simple; such requests were not unheard of. Rosie was told it would take several hours to find the personnel he sought.

To pass the time, he decided to take a stroll around the city of Reykjavik. He headed south on Naustin between the Harbor House Museum and the Customs House. Turning east, he wound his way through the streets until he reached Laugavegur, the main shopping area bustling with locals and tourists. He enjoyed stopping and looking in the windows of the various boutiques which displayed a variety of eclectic Icelandic and international wares.

Rosie spoke to no one, simply exchanging friendly nods with shoppers and other passers-by. He began to relax, the tension of the earlier conversation with his Captain evaporating like the morning fog. As he walked and looked in shop windows, he caught his reflection, and was surprised to see a relaxed smile looking back at him. For the first time in a long time, he was enjoying himself. His smile broadened and his walk was more relaxed. He lingered when his interest was piqued. He liked this place. After several hours he headed back toward the Seaman's Hall.

Taking a detour toward the Tjörnin, he stopped to pick up a sandwich. Translated literally, Tjörnin means 'the pond' and is surrounded by a manicured park busy with families feeding the ducks and enjoying the summer day. Finding a secluded tree, he sat on the grass to watch the people, enjoy his lunch . . . and think. Foremost in his mind was how angry the Captain had been earlier. His thoughts drifted to the fishermen who had tried to help them in the Yellow Sea. Their screams as Ares sailed away still haunted him. He then thought of the mission and the consequences of what they were about to do. He needed to rid those thoughts from his mind.

A young boy ran by chasing his small dog holding a circular piece of green plastic in its jaws. Rosie smiled and thought of his nieces and nephews about the same age. In the distance he could hear music and singing.

What an unusual country he thought. What impressed him most was not what he saw, but rather what he didn't see. There was no mayhem in the streets, no one committing unspeakable acts, nothing suggesting that these people were terribly different from those at home. Their religious practices were clearly not the same. In fact, he had to look to find any indication of religious leanings at all. A few churches, Lutheran mostly. It all seemed much less important to them. Still, no one was begging on the streets, few if any appeared to be homeless or hungry, and parents obviously loved their children. He felt safe on the streets and others clearly did as well. The smiles with which he was met by locals seemed so warm and genuine that he found himself smiling back. Even the local police seemed friendly and relaxed. No one seemed uptight or afraid. Rosie wondered how different these people were from the Americans.

Stories of the horrors of the Great Satan were commonplace. But the stories hadn't always been the same. Rosie was born in Beirut, Lebanon, at a time when it was considered 'the Paris of the Middle East.' Beirut was replete with western influence when he was young, and it seemed to be a great city and a good place to live. His father's brother had taught at the American University in Beirut. He was a good, happy man, who took wonderful care of his family. It was after westerners fled the country and the trouble started that it became difficult. "How bad could these people be," he thought.

As a young man, Rosie had no interest in a seafaring life. It wasn't that he harbored any animosity toward such a career; he never gave it any thought. He didn't even know how to swim. But in 1977, as the civil war was worsening, his dear mother saw what was happening and had taken it upon herself to look after the future of her children. Rosie's older siblings who were in college were transferred to schools in other countries. He was only 12 at the time, and was taken by his mother to Beirut Harbor to work as a boson's apprentice for a family friend who owned a fishing boat. She knew her son would learn a trade and would have the ability to travel away from the troubles of Lebanon. She was right. Fifteen years later the country had become a shadow of what it once was, with over 120,000 dead and more than 75,000 internally displaced. Rosie had become one of more than a million people who left Lebanon and did not return, except to help move his parents, who lived out their days in Jordan. His family scattered about, he visited rarely, mostly because of his time at sea, and partly because of the memories of the happy childhood taken away so suddenly.

He wondered if Beirut would look like this today if not for the war. It was easy to blame the pro-western factions, or those who identified more with the Soviet Union, but in his mind, all of these non-Middle Eastern cultures were to blame. Islam alone brought peace, or so he'd thought. Now, he wondered. The peaceful beauty of his surroundings shook him from his reverie. His full belly, adding to his contentedness, caused him to drift quietly to sleep. He slept well.

He woke to the sound of laughing children and looked to see a ball rolling toward him. Smiling broadly, he tossed it back to the fair-skinned, blond-headed boy who smiled and waved back at him. It was time to return to the Seaman's Hall to see if they had two clean sailors for him. He didn't want the afternoon to end.

EIGHT

Friday, July 26th
12:45 GMT – 7:45 am EDT
Ogdensburg, New York, USA

JERRY WAS AT THE WHEEL. The drive from Cranberry Lake to Ogdensburg was an hour and a half. The plan was to meet Savannah, who was coming from her home in Saranac. At 8:00 am, the three would have breakfast before picking up the rental boat and heading out to Chimney Island. They had been on the road for nearly an hour and Joseph was upset because he had suspicions. He was reluctant to bring the subject up with Jerry, who hadn't said a word about his 'research.' As the miles passed, Joseph's anger was building. He was confused as to what it was all about and was sure Jerry would eventually tell him.

Jerry could tell something was wrong. "What's up buddy? It seems you're out of sorts this morning. Anything wrong?"

Joseph decided he needed to clear the air. "Yeah, there is something wrong. I stopped by your house Tuesday evening," there was a long pause. "I thought you usually got home around 7 pm from that Massena meeting. Will was there, and he told me you were staying over an extra day doing research. He said you were going to Malone and Plattsburgh, and that it had something to do with Savannah? I thought we were in this together. What the hell were you researching, Jerry? If this had something to do with Savannah, why didn't you tell me?"

Jerry had been expecting this conversation. When he had returned home, Will had mentioned that Joseph had stopped by the house.

"I wasn't sure how to tell you this, buddy. I didn't know how you'd react."

"Tell me what?"

"You know how I always assume the simplest, most obvious explanation is the truth?"

"Yeah."

"Well, what do you think is the simplest explanation for Savannah's father buying a 140 acre property with cash when he was only 29 years old?"

"You tell me, you're the cop."

Joseph's tone told Jerry how upset he really was. "No Joseph, I want *you* to tell *me*. Do you really think a buried treasure is the simplest explanation? Think about it."

"You asshole, you think he stole it, don't you? That's why you asked Savannah if her father had ever been arrested. You were checking to see if she was telling you the truth."

Jerry shot back, "Don't even try telling me you hadn't thought about it."

Joseph was silent. There was a long pause.

"So you had thought about it. Who's the asshole now? Come on Joseph, don't you want to know the truth?"

Joseph didn't say a word.

After a long period of silence, Jerry figured it out. With a big smile on his face he was almost yelling, "So, that's what this is all about. Now I've got it." Jerry then put on his best imitation of Jack Nicholson from the movie, *A Few Good Men*. "*You don't care about the truth.*" He laughed, "you don't care if there is a treasure or not. You just wanted to spend more time with Savannah. You sly dog."

They were getting close to Ogdensburg and Joseph didn't say a word. Jerry glanced at Joseph in the passenger seat and saw that a sheepish grin had replaced the scowl he'd seen earlier.

"So why am I even here?" There was more silence. "Well?"

"Because *she* wanted you here."

Jerry started to laugh again. "It all makes so much sense. This has nothing to do with me checking Jack Christian's background. Joey is jealous the pretty girl wanted me to come along on the search. No worries buddy, she's not my type." They both laughed.

"That's what's so frustrating. I know you're not interested, but I think she's interested in you. Jerry, do you mind if I tell her?"

Jerry just smiled, "Well, she's only human. Sometimes you really are an idiot, buddy. Are you blind? Did you see the way she was looking at you last week? No, let me answer that for you. You didn't, because you wouldn't even look her in the eye. If you recall, it was *you* she invited to Saranac to see her garden. *Not me!* You can tell her whatever you want. You know I don't care."

Joseph wanted to confirm the obvious, "I'm guessing you didn't find anything about Jack Christian, otherwise you wouldn't be here now."

"I didn't. My hunch was wrong. Apparently Jack Christian is clean as a whistle. That's why I didn't tell you. There was really nothing to tell. Do you think we should tell Savannah what I did?"

Joseph thought for a moment. "Since you didn't find anything, I guess not. What's the point?"

"Exactly!"

As they were pulling into the diner parking lot Jerry looked at Joseph, "So are we okay, Joey?"

"Sure Baldy, and the name is Joseph." As they were walking into the diner Joseph said, "By the way, it's . . . '*you can't handle the truth*'."

"What?" Jerry was confused.

"Idiot, you got the line wrong. It wasn't, '*you don't care about the truth*,' it was '*you can't handle the truth*'."

Savannah was waiting inside and heard the end of the conversation. "You guys playing trivia?"

Jerry looked right at her, and again with his Nicholson voice, "*You can't handle the truth*."

"Jack Nicholson in *A Few Good Men*," Savannah shot back.

"Good answer," Jerry said. "You just won a wonderful breakfast and a day on the St. Lawrence River with two young good looking guys."

Over breakfast, they discussed strategy for searching the island. From Google Earth, Savannah had determined the island was about 275 feet wide and 780 feet long, about five acres.

Jerry did a quick calculation. "If we walk three abreast about 15 feet apart, then six passes of the length of the island should let us cover it pretty well. Timing will all depend on the foliage and the terrain. We're lucky to have such a beautiful day. I suggest we try to get four passes in before lunch." Looking at Savannah, Jerry asked, "What did ya bring for lunch?"

"Exactly what I said I was going to bring. Fried chicken and potato salad."

"Excellent."

"What kind of marker do you think we're looking for?" Joseph asked.

"I can't imagine my father would have made it from anything other than stone," Savannah commented.

"I agree," Jerry added.

"I truly want to thank you guys for helping me. This is exciting. I can't wait to see what the marker says."

"I wouldn't get too excited," Jerry responded in a more serious voice. "Who knows what we'll find. Maybe nothing. After all, it's been over 50 years since he put it there. If we find it, it may be weathered and we may not be able to read it. It could even have been stolen. I'm sure there have been 100s if not 1,000s of people on that island since then."

"Don't worry Savannah, my bald friend here is just a fountain of pessimism. That's what 23 years of being a cop does to you."

Jerry ignored Joseph, looked at Savannah and started to say something, but Savannah got the words out first. "I know. You were a trooper, not a cop."

With a big smile Jerry responded, "You're catching on. And, my faux philosopher friend here obviously doesn't know the difference between pessimism and realism." Smiling, Jerry then looked at Joseph, "*Amor fati* buddy."

Surprised at the comment, Joseph shot back, "Shut up."

Savannah had a confused look on her face and looked to Joseph, "What's he talking about?"

"It's nothing but the bald-headed moron being a moron. I'll tell you later. Let's get this treasure hunt started, shall we?" Joseph gave Jerry a dirty look. Jerry returned the look with a smile.

Walking out of the restaurant, Savannah asked Joseph if he knew where the marina was.

"It's not far. About a mile."

"Then why don't you ride with me and we'll meet Jerry there. We need to stop somewhere to get drinks and ice."

Jerry smiled to himself, "I'll go ahead and take care of the boat. See you two at the marina." While Savannah wasn't looking, Jerry gave

Joseph a wink.

When they were alone, Savannah asked Joseph again what Jerry had been talking about.

"*Amor fati*, it means the love of fate. My ex-wife had her doctorate in philosophy and she used to say that all the time. It's from the German philosopher, Friedrich Nietzsche, and she had adopted it as her philosophy. I always hated it. I have my own philosophy. I call it Bentonism."

"I'll bite, what's Bentonism?" Savannah asked.

"You really want to know?"

"Sure"

"It's based on the Socratic imperative 'know thyself' and I add, 'make thine own destiny,' that's Bentonism in a nutshell."

There was a moment of silence before Savannah spoke, "Well then Joseph, *we* should make our own destiny."

There was a tone in Savannah's voice that suggested there was more behind the words. A chill went down Joseph's spine. It had been a long time since he had these kinds of feelings. He looked at her and smiled, "We should make our own destiny, shouldn't we?"

When they arrived at the marina, Jerry had the 18-foot runabout ready to go. Joseph carried the cooler, Savannah had a picnic basket and blanket. Jerry had already loaded a canvas bag containing a shovel and crowbar.

Savannah drove the boat and kept close to the US shore. They didn't want any problems wandering into Canadian waters. They passed the town marina and the Port of Ogdensburg. Two miles down-river, they rounded Chimney Point and passed under the Ogdensburg-Prescott International Bridge. Chimney Island came into sight.

Jerry suggested they circle the island once or twice. "We can get a lay of the land while we look for a place to pull in."

At the northeastern point of the island they found a sandy section of shoreline where they pulled to shore. It appeared other boats had used this same natural landing spot. Once the boat was secured, Jerry trudged up a small knoll and stood looking at the island. He appeared to be daydreaming. Savannah and Joseph watched him for a moment. Savannah finally asked, "What are ya looking at?"

"I was thinking about the battle that took place here. I did some research on the island. Did you know how strategically important this little island was for the French? Look at its location in the river. The fort on this little island protected Montreal and Quebec City from attacks coming down the river from Lake Ontario. At least it was supposed to. More than 12,000 people were involved in the battle for this little island." Jerry told them everything he'd learned from the archivist at the St. Lawrence County Historical Association.

Savannah decided to add her own bit of knowledge, "Did you know this river is one of the most important inland waterways in the world? More than 3,600 ships pass through the Seaway and past this little island each year. Between the Atlantic Ocean and Lake Superior, a ship is raised almost 600 feet by the locks. That's the equivalent of a 60 story building!"

Joseph had enough, "You two are making me feel stupid. Where do you guys get all this stuff?"

Jerry laughed, "They're called books, moron. Don't you ever read anything other than econometric modeling studies?"

"That's what economists read, idiot."

Playing the mother, Savannah stepped in, "All right, stop your quarreling or I'm going to have to separate you boys. Let's get to work."

The three spent the next several hours walking the length of the island and back again. Other than electronic equipment that Jerry speculated was used for navigation, they found nothing of consequence, certainly no sign of the marker they were looking for. Lunch was a welcome break and the three enjoyed watching the ships and pleasure boats moving up and down the river.

After lunch, Joseph suggested that Jerry relax and enjoy the beautiful day. "There's not much left to search. Savannah and I can finish up ourselves."

As Savannah and Joseph were walking away, Jerry yelled after them, "Don't get lost."

It had been a long time since Joseph had been with a woman in whom he was truly interested. Ironically, the last time he'd had a woman in his life was when he was looking for the Bonaparte treasure. But, it was a relationship of convenience, not feelings. He remembered how guilty he felt when he described the relationship . . . 'desperate times require desperate measures.' *That relationship did not end well*, he thought to himself.

Joseph knew this was different. Feeling a bit awkward, and not knowing quite what to say, he pointed to a ship in the river and asked, "What do you think these ships are carrying?"

As it turned out, when it came to the St Lawrence Seaway, Savannah was an encyclopedia. "The larger ones headed east are probably carrying grain headed for Europe or the Mediterranean. Those headed west are probably carrying iron ore from northern Quebec or Labrador. They're headed to the steel mills in the mid-west. The smaller ones could be carrying just about anything. Here's a bit of trivia, those larger ships are 78 feet wide and the locks they pass through are only 80 feet wide. Not much room for error."

Joseph asked "How do you know all this?"

"Because father worked on the construction of the Seaway, I've always had an interest. I've read a pile of books on the Seaway and the construction. Six entire towns were destroyed as a result of the construction. All in Canada. They're known as the Lost Villages."

"I had no idea. You're a truly fountain of knowledge." There was an uncomfortable pause, "You know, Savannah, I'd like to get to know you better."

"I'd like that too, Joseph." There was another longer pause. "I have an idea."

Joseph was intrigued by the new perkiness in Savannah's voice. "What's that?" he asked, mimicking the perkiness.

"Why don't you come back with me to Saranac this afternoon? We can go out to dinner, and in the morning I'll make you a nice Adirondack breakfast. I'll show you my garden and maybe we'll take the horses for a ride and I'll show you the back 140. Then, I'll drive you back to Cranberry Lake. I'm sure Jerry won't mind. He's a big boy. He can find his way back to Cranberry Lake by himself."

"You're not only smart, you're full of good ideas. I'd like that." Joseph was beginning to feel relaxed.

They made a final pass of the length of the island, finding no evidence of the marker they sought. Savannah and Joseph were dejected. Jerry wasn't really surprised. He would have been more surprised if they had actually found something. The three cleaned up the picnic area and headed to the boat. Jerry thought he saw tears in Savannah's eyes. He truly felt sorry for her. Joseph sat in the back of the boat with his arm around her. Jerry wasn't quite sure if Joseph was consoling her, or if there was something else. "Maybe a little of both," he thought. As the runabout left Chimney Island no one said a word.

Passing under the bridge, Savannah finally spoke. "You guys have been great. I'm sorry it didn't work out. Without the marker, I guess I'll never find the gold. I want to thank you two for all your help though."

"I really wish we could have found it for you," Joseph said.

Jerry, at the wheel, was uncharacteristically quiet. In his mind he was going over the conversation he had with the Archives Manager at the Historical Association. "Those mounds you see between the highway and the river are the *former Chimney Island*." Jerry glanced back and to his left and could see the mounds. Then the message Jack Christian had left in his journal came to mind. 'The marker can be found on the *former Isle Royale*. The *former* Isle Royale, Jerry thought.

It didn't make sense. Jack Christian wouldn't have left the marker in the mounds on the mainland. Too many cottages and summer camps were being built along the river at the time. Anybody could have found it. He would have placed it somewhere safe, so only Savannah would find it, he thought.

The words kept running through his mind. "*The former Chimney Island . . . The former Isle Royale.*"

About a mile from the marina, there was a sudden jerk of the boat and the engine stopped. Jerry had put the motor in neutral and for several moments they were just drifting in the river. He didn't say a word. He just sat there. '*The marker can be found on the former Isle Royale. Visit the marker and it will provide you great comfort*'.

"What's wrong?" Joseph asked. Deep in thought, Jerry didn't respond. "Jerry, are you okay?"

Suddenly, Jerry turned around and took three large steps toward the back of the boat. He walked right up to Savannah, leaned over and looked her directly in the eye. She was startled and leaned back toward Joseph.

"Savannah, back in Cranberry last week you said something about half of the island being removed during the construction of the Seaway?"

"Yeah. It was removed to widen the shipping lane."

"I know. But remember what the journal said? '*The marker can be found on the former Isle Royale.*' Maybe your father literally meant the '*former*' Isle Royale. You know, where the island formerly was . . . the part that's now underwater." Jerry threw his arms in the air and yelled, "Fasten your seatbelts folks. This treasure hunt isn't over yet!"

"You're brilliant," Savannah jumped up and gave Jerry a big kiss on the cheek. Both worked to keep their balance as the boat rocked.

Jerry was an experienced diver and suggested they come back and he would search the '*former*' Isle Royale. "You two can be my spotters in the boat."

Savannah quickly corrected Jerry, "You mean *we* will search for the marker."

"Do you dive?" he asked.

"Do I dive? Between my embassy assignment in the military and my return stay after college, I spent eight years in Indonesia. With 20 percent of the world's coral reefs and over 6,000 species of fish, it's the best diving in the world. Of course I dive."

"Perfect. Joey can be our spotter and you and I can look for the marker."

"His name is Joseph, bonehead. And, in case you haven't figured it out, I'm on his side. One more thing . . . you're driving back to Cranberry Lake by yourself today. I'm kidnapping him."

Jerry was pleased to see Savannah take part in the banter but wasn't expecting this news, at least not this soon. "Fine, you can have him," Jerry said. "But, you need to know something. I'm not going to pay ransom to get him back. "By the way, next Saturday is good for me to dive."

"Saturday works for me, too. How about you Joseph?"

"Looks like I'm just a pawn in your little games. That's fine with me."

NINE

Friday, July 26th
14:30 GMT – 9:30 pm EDT
Reykjavik, Iceland

THE SMELL OF NEW PAINT pervaded the Ares. Abe and his two senior officers sat in the captain's galley. Most of the food was prepared at a local restaurant and brought to the ship ready-made, but on occasion when meals required last-minute preparation, the ship's facilities were used.

As the cook became comfortable with the galley, he used it more frequently. This required the help of one of the restaurant's waiters to carry supplies, set tables, and assist with serving. It quickly became clear to the entire wait staff at the restaurant that the trip to the ship represented a long period of time in which only one table was served, and no tip would result. No one volunteered for this task and the owner of the restaurant had to recruit unwilling wait staff to go along. Captain Abe, Rosie and Adam were extremely careful about what was said in their presence.

Almost every day before the cook and his assistant arrived Abe reminded the others that eating these meals during the month of fasting was their own sacrifice for the glory of Allah.

§

Elsewhere in the harbor, Athena was off-loading her cargo. The listening device placed on her bridge by the harbor pilot recruited by the CIA in Morocco was providing information on the conversations nearby. A small panel van trained a laser on the window of the captain's office and quarters. Noises inside would vibrate the window, and the laser would use the vibrating glass as a microphone. Additionally, a large gamma scintillator, known as "the blue sausage," was trained on Athena's cargo hold to make sure the radioactive cargo wasn't moved.

While in port, the captain of Athena treated his crew to locally-available cuisine and fresh produce, rare on long voyages. Local vendors made these deliveries to ships in port, and the delivery people were easily recruited by intelligence personnel.

The young man who delivered the produce to Athena was given a hefty sum of cash to carry a small plastic device aboard. He knew the layout of these break-bulk freighters. Finding the crew busy, he suggested he leave his boxes of fruit and vegetables on the small table in the room adjacent to the galley. It was the captain's table. He took a small piece of plastic out of his pocket, peeled the backing off the adhesive strip, and stuck it on the underside of the table. Once verified by CIA agents it was properly installed and operational, the delivery man would find his pockets laden with more cash. And, he'd be eager to do more.

As expected, Athena's exchange of cargo went smoothly. Local intelligence agents began to wonder if the crew knew anything about the radioactive source on board. The strongest signal hadn't moved despite the rearrangement of cargo. No one seemed to be avoiding the area where the source appeared to be located. There were no precautions taken and no one had specialized protective equipment. Evidence was mounting that the crew were completely unaware of the hazard.

Perhaps only a few of the crew, perhaps only one, knew there was a substantial radiation source aboard. U.S. intelligence operatives were paying attention to every word overheard from Athena, no matter how benign it appeared. And much of it sounded benign.

Athena was loading cargo for Nova Scotia and Boston. The cargo had been thoroughly searched by intelligence officers in the warehouses before it had even been transported to the wharf. It was under constant surveillance by American agents until it was secured in Athena's holds. There was nothing unusual. Textiles, raw wool and fish oils. Samples of the oil were analyzed to ascertain that it was indeed fish oil. The fabrics and wool were tested for anthrax spores. The air downwind of the ship was electronically sniffed for nitrates and explosives.

Everything was normal. Nothing appeared the least bit unusual. Nothing except for the radiation emanating from Athena's hold.

As intelligence streamed back to Washington, DC, the task force was puzzled. It seemed so bizarre. Who were these people working with? What were they going to do with cesium on their ship? How were they communicating . . . and with whom? As Mickey Evans went around the table, his team responded with more questions and no answers. His team was becoming more uncomfortable with the situation and Evans' concern was mounting as well. In a few hours, Athena would be sailing to North America.

§

At Iceland's northerly latitude, sunrise was 4:15 on the day of Athena's departure. Captain Jibril and his senior staff had eaten early in the officers' mess. With Ramadan, it was required that the meal be eaten before sunrise. Ramadan or not, today Athena was departing and the early meal would have occurred regardless.

Like any good captain, Jibril was a safety-conscious man, even more so considering a trans-Atlantic crossing. It had been some time since he had made an open ocean voyage; he was careful to test each piece of equipment and check all systems thoroughly before leaving port. Nothing could go wrong in the middle of the Atlantic. At one time, he would have used a checklist, but over his many years at sea, the process had become second nature, and he usually recited orders from memory.

Today, however, he referred back to his old list just to be sure nothing had been overlooked. His mechanics had been ordered to catch up on any minor repairs that had been put off; little-used equipment was dusted off and tested for reliability. He would have a chance to test his engines before sailing too far from Iceland. Apart from that, he was confident his older, but exceedingly well-maintained vessel was up to the trip. He was proud of his ship and her crew, and wouldn't hesitate to put her up against any other ship of similar purpose.

At precisely 6 am the Chief Officer advised Captain Jibril that the harbor pilot was aboard. As he made his way to the bridge he paused to do one last mental review. After cordial introductions, Jibril sounded the horn and gave the order to cast off the mooring lines. He turned to the harbor pilot, "Sir, the ship is yours."

Athena was piloted out of port and between Engey and Akurey islands, at which point the harbor pilot was to be collected by a chase vessel. However, the harbor master's well-greased palm insured a radio call to Athena advising there would be a delay in retrieving the pilot, thus giving him additional time aboard. The harbor master advised Athena they would intercept southwest of Akurey Island, as she entered the shipping lanes for her southwesterly trip to Halifax.

The news of the delay was met without negative comment from captain or crew. Once outside the harbor limits, control of the ship was returned to Captain Jibril. The harbor pilot was permitted to move about freely and was able to place two more listening devices, one in the crew's mess, and another on a bulkhead in the ship's forecastle. The latter, it was hoped, would pick up conversations between crew members who were in the vicinity of the cesium source.

Several miles from the harbor buoys, the pilot was retrieved without incident and Athena steamed on, her crew unaware that just out of the range of their RADAR, US Navy vessels, both on the surface and submerged, were shadowing her every move, monitoring every conversation, and biding their time for the opportunity to board her. Weather permitting, small helicopter drones would be launched from a Navy cruiser. The drones would photograph and observe the ship's activities. Satellites were trained on her. No one aboard that ship could sneeze without 50 people knowing about it. On she headed toward the shores of North America. Toward the homeland.

§

One of the anonymous intelligence officers on the pier was packing up his listening devices when he was distracted by harsh voices. Two men were arguing right outside his old van. He sat still and heard the words "*those people on that ship*." One was complaining they never tip the waiters and that he'd gone there entirely too many times. The other man, apparently the complainer's superior, was clearly tired of hearing these comments and said that they would be rewarded handsomely before the ship left port.

"They're going to America!" the angry man said. "We'll never see them again! What do they care about us?"

This piqued the interest of the intelligence officer. He didn't know what ship they were talking about, but it sounded too familiar. Athena had been taking food deliveries. He turned on his digital recorder and sat silently as the two men went on.

The calmer man in charge was trying to reassure the angry man. The ship would only be here one more day; leaving too early the day after for the restaurant staff to serve.

"And then what? You heard them talking, they're never coming back. They don't care if they leave us empty-handed."

Looking through a side window and into the rear-view mirror, the intelligence officer was shocked at what he saw: another ship, almost identical to the one he'd been watching, berthed further down the wharf. Sure, he'd seen it and others like it, but another break bulk preparing to sail to America? It was probably coincidence, but he'd be remiss not to collect more information on that ship to see what their story was.

§

From the bridge of Ares, Captain Abe watched Athena glide gently out of Reykjavik harbor. He couldn't stifle a smile as the hulking ship moved silently past him. A couple of glances toward the pier revealed what he was sure were surveillance vehicles driving away. He was unaware they had also taken photographs of Ares. Rather, he was admiring Athena. A beautiful ship, he thought. Moreover, she was doing her job well. Abe was satisfied things were coming together.

His thoughts on his plans for the next 48 hours was cut short by a worker who asked him to step aside so a nearby instrument panel could be unbolted for polishing. He had hired some locals to complete a few final repairs, some interior painting, replacement of worn decking, and a little cleaning.

The cosmetic changes were necessary because the ship was to be turned over to new owners in Detroit, the captain said. He wanted everything 'ship shape.' This English phrase — the only colloquialism they learned that suggested the goal in mind — was used, overused really, by Abe, Adam and Rosie when directing the workers' activities. The newly re-born Ares was beginning to gain a showroom-worthy appearance.

Abe and the crew were proud to be aboard her.

As Athena disappeared from view, Abe picked up a small glass jar of black paint and a small brush and made his way to the cargo hold. For the second time on this mission he was about to break one of his own cardinal rules. Standing beside the largest of the four intermodal containers, he looked at the painted image of the sacred animal of the Greek god Ares; a coiled cobra, hood displayed as though it was about to strike. It was a large image, at least a meter high, and rendered in surprising detail. He smiled as he took his small brush and painted amidst the scales of the serpent's body. One would have to look closely to discern it, but he knew it was there. That would have to be enough.

Captain Abe closed his eyes to silently thank Allah. He could see in the darkness of his mind the words he had just painted in Arabic, 'Insha'llah,' '*if God wills*.'

TEN

Tuesday, July 30th

16:00 GMT – 11:00 am EDT

Cranberry Lake, New York, USA

"Good Morning Mr. front cover of People Magazine. How is Cranberry Lake's most famous resident this morning?"

Joseph Benton's face was turning red. He looked at the postmistress, "Cindy, you're embarrassing me."

"It's a great photograph, Joseph. You know we're really proud of you."

"Who are we?" Joseph asked as he opened his box to get his mail.

"Everybody in town. You've made Cranberry Lake famous. I heard there hasn't been a room available at the Lodge or Stone Manor in over two months. And they're both booked solid through Labor Day."

Joseph glanced at the thick pile of mail and saw yet another yellow card indicating there was more to be picked up at the window. Cindy had the extra mail waiting. This had been a daily ritual since the extraordinary events more than three months ago. Joseph had already switched to a large postal drawer to handle the volume, but every day there was more that didn't fit in the box.

"Can I get your autograph Mr. Benton?"

"Not you too Cindy?"

Cindy laughed, "You have a certified letter. You have to sign for it."

"Oh." Joseph was embarrassed again. "I'm sorry; I'm just getting tired of all the attention. You know, I can't even have dinner out any more without being interrupted a half dozen times for my autograph."

"Poor baby, it must be so, so difficult being such a famous celebrity and all. Sign here." Cindy handed him the card. "It must take forever to get through all your fan mail."

As he was placing the pen on the card he glanced at the return address and a chill went through his body. His felt the blood drain from his face. His hand started to shake.

"Joseph, are you all right? Joseph?" Cindy was becoming alarmed.

There was no response. He just stood there.

"Should I call someone?"

He snapped out of it. "Sorry. I was just surprised at who this letter was from." His hand still shaking, he signed for the letter, gathered up the rest of his mail, and left without saying another word.

In the car, his hands, still trembling, Joseph propped the letter against the steering wheel and stared. He didn't understand why he was reacting this way. Moreover, he didn't quite understand why he was *feeling* this way. He thought it was over and he would never hear from her again. Yet, here it was. A certified letter, no less. And it wasn't from her attorney . . . it was from HER.

Joseph wasn't sure if he was sweating because of the letter or because of the unusually warm day.

Finally he threw the unopened letter on top of the pile of mail on the passenger seat. His head was spinning and his thoughts were jumbled. He had spent 25 years with this woman as the center of his life.

"The center of my life," he mumbled. He thought for a moment. "She never saw that. She thought the Bonaparte treasure was the center of my life. She never saw that it was so much more than a search for my heritage.

It was for us."

Joseph was talking to himself as he turned onto Route 3 and headed to Jerry's house on Columbian Road. The love he'd had, and may still have for this woman, was beginning to turn to anger as he remembered how much her words hurt as she left him. He loved her, he also hated her.

For a brief second, his mind turned to the past few days he had spent with Savannah. It was a tender and beautiful time. They had walked the gardens and rode the horses around the property. In the evening they sat holding hands staring at the stars.

But his thoughts quickly returned to Lucia S. Benton. Joseph could almost see her. Her olive skin and chestnut hair, a result of her Mediterranean descent. Her deep, sultry, unmistakable voice. Joseph smiled to himself. Their marriage together had been the epitome of synergy. Together Joseph and Lucia were more than their individual parts. They were partners in life and in business. They complemented each other.

They had met at the University of Chicago and became instant soulmates. Initially, Joseph knew her by her middle name, Sharon. After the death of her mother with whom she shared a first name, Joseph convinced her to go by her given name, Lucia. It was a decision she never regretted. Joseph and Lucia understood each other and shared everything.

While Lucia had a doctorate degree in philosophy, in undergraduate school, her minor was economics. Joseph had received his masters in economics. While married, they even worked together on investment strategy.

A typical evening at home would find them discussing the differences between the Austrian School of Economics and the Chicago School of Economics. Lucia would always call Ludwig von Mises and Ayn Rand "intolerant" and "extremist." Just for "intellectual fun," Joseph would call Milton Friedman a "Keynesian" and a "statist." This cut to the bone. Both

Joseph and Lucia believed in free market economics, and had taken classes from Milton Friedman. Joseph knew how to press Lucia's "buttons."

It was the intellectual discussion itself that provided the stimulation. It was like a drug for them both. Neither took the discussions personally. It was as much the verbal sparring as their individual positions that provided the stimulation.

Joseph remembered it was the philosophy discussions that were most stimulating. Almost a love potion. After a lively debate on existentialism, they would have an evening of passionate love making.

Maybe, deep down, it wasn't the search for the Bonaparte treasure that led to their divorce. Maybe it was their differences in philosophy. They had a fundamental disagreement on life.

Lucia's doctoral dissertation had been on Friedrich Nietzsche, the 19th century German philosopher and his influence on 20th century existentialism. She would often remind Joseph how Nietzsche had viewed *Amor fati* – the "love of fate," as the "formula for man's greatness." Joseph could never accept the *Amor fati* view. Nietzsche opined, "*Freedom consists in desiring what is, and what has been, and in choosing it, and loving it, as if nothing better could be desired.*"

Deep down, Lucia was really more an adherent to Kierkegaard, who though greatly influenced by Nietzsche, also believed that the negative aspects of existence, such as pain, frustration, sickness and death – were the essential features of human reality.

Joseph often mistook Lucia's 'dark' existentialist philosophy as depression. Lucia was adamant it was something else entirely; an interpretation of human existence that stressed what she called, '*its concrete and problematic character.*'

Joseph didn't have the deep knowledge or understanding of philosophy that Lucia had, but he did believe in the Socratic imperative '*know thyself.*'

Not only was Joseph not a fan of Nietzsche, he had his own philosophy—Bentonism.

As he contemplated Bentonism, Joseph's thoughts turned to Savannah and the remarkable past few days they had spent together in Saranac. The quiet time sitting in the garden. Not talking, just holding hands and being with each other. He wondered, not for the first time, if he was falling in love with her. Then his thoughts again returned to Lucia.

The divorce had been bitter. They still desperately loved each other. But things had changed. Apparently, her way of handling the divorce was simply to accept it . . . *Amor fati.*

Since the divorce, Joseph had battled his own demons: Guilt that his search for the Bonaparte treasure had driven away the only person he really loved.

Guilt that he prostituted himself in a relationship with another woman simply to gather more information for his search and disgusted that he justified the relationship by convincing himself that '*desperate times require desperate measures.*'

Guilt that he hadn't trusted his best friend, Jerry, when things were at their worst. Yet, Jerry was the only person who stood by him. Jerry was almost killed because of Joseph's search for his family treasure.

Finally, he was disappointed in himself that his life had become unmanageable because of his abuse of alcohol as a means to drown his feelings after the divorce. '*How could I have been so weak?*'

More than anything, he felt his behavior, as a result of his obsession over his heritage and the treasure, might have tarnished the Bonaparte legacy.

As he approached Jerry's house, Joseph realized how grateful he was that he had a friend who stood by him and believed in him during the worst of times. "This friendship saved my life," Joseph said softly. He smiled to himself as he remembered how much Jerry liked Lucia and how he would only call her Lu.

In the driveway he sat for a moment looking at Jerry's house. He could see Jerry working on his old pick-up. In the distance he could see Will in the garage working on a stained glass project.

But again, his thoughts returned to Lucia. Dr. Lucia S. Benton was an elegant lady. A philosopher, cerebral, yet full of subtleties. She was, at one point, the perfect complement to Joseph.

Lucia was not a person to make a quick decision. Her decision to bail out on Joseph wasn't made lightly. Presumably, nor was her decision to contact him today. "What does she want?" he quietly asked himself.

Joseph looked down at the envelope sitting on top of the pile of mail in the passenger seat. He needed to talk through his thoughts and feelings with someone. He grabbed the unopened letter.

ELEVEN

Sunday, July 28th

17:00 GMT – 12:00 pm EDT

Reykjavik, Iceland

WHEN ALL THE new crewmembers were aboard Ares, Rosie gave them their stateroom assignments and assembled them for a short briefing. He explained that their job was to safely deliver the ship to new owners in Detroit, Michigan, USA. Each sailor had with him a one-way airplane ticket to a city of his choice.

Captain Abe was introduced and explained there was no cargo with the exception of spare parts. "The extra ballast we are carrying makes up for the displacement of cargo," he said. Therefore, of course, there would be no deck crew and no off-loading upon arrival at their destination. The job was mainly to keep the ship running in good repair, and to guide her safely to her new assignment as a 'laker.' The job would be easy. Many were new to the sea and this would be a good voyage to gain experience. Some systems tests were required while underway, during both daylight and nighttime conditions; the officers would give instructions when the time comes. The Captain's first and only order of the evening was to stow all personal gear and get some rest; it would be an early morning departure.

§

At three a.m., Captain Abe was on the bridge giving orders to the crew and preparing to disembark. The harbor pilot was on time and ready. After double-and triple-checking ballast requirements, hc gave the orders to get underway. The sky was cloudy and there was a light mist falling. As with Athena, a chase boat followed Ares as she maneuvered easily out of port. The pilot transferred at the expected point and returned to Reykjavik.

Ares headed south and west toward Greenland. The final stage of their mission had begun. Captain Abe, Rosie and Adam had been apprehensive about this most sensitive part of their five-year odyssey.

During the first day, tests would begin. Many would be for show, but Adam and Rosie were genuinely anxious to test the new enhanced RADAR unit that had been installed in Iceland. It would alert them if any uninvited guests were approaching.

Now that the ship was underway with a new crew, Abe fell into his decades-old habits as commander of a merchant ship. The day would progress as any other. Officers made sure the crew were made to feel comfortable. It had been part of the original plan that one officer was assigned to eat supper with the men in the crew mess every evening. Ostensibly to appear to be friendly, in fact it was an opportunity to keep a close eye on the crew and monitor their conversations.

There were no plans for the first two days other than routine equipment tests. The crew needed time to become comfortable with the newer equipment and the Korean labels on much of the machinery. But, it didn't take long to learn how to get around the obstacles. For a one-way trip, they'd be fine.

Suppertime of the third evening brought the crew a message from the captain: ***"All crewmembers are to be assigned to their quarters for a three-hour period from 2130 to 0030 hours. This is necessary to facili-***

tate a minimal-manpower cargo-jettison exercise." None of the crew had ever heard of such a thing. Captain Abe was prepared for this and assigned Adam to 'convince' the crew of the test's authenticity. Adam was scheduled to dine with the men and deliver a speech he'd prepared over a year ago, and had rehearsed many times.

In his affable way, he chatted about the colorful history of shipping on the Great Lakes. Then he explained how heavy traffic, combined with fog, cavalier captains, and late fall and early summer gales, made sailing on these lakes some of the most hazardous on earth. Thousands of ships had blown ashore, foundered, exploded, or collided during the past 150 years.

Adam became more animated as he spoke, "You must have heard of the Canadian singer, Gordon Lightfoot?" he asked.

Several of the men acknowledged they had.

"Then you have heard of the last major shipwreck on the Great Lakes, the Edmund Fitzgerald. Every American and Canadian has heard the story." He went on to tell the crew the story of that horrific day and night on the legendary ship. In great detail, and quoting liberally from the Lightfoot song, he captivated his seaman audience in the mess. At one critical point, Adam paused and looked down. Some of the men thought they saw his eyes getting moist.

Adam let a few crewmembers finish translating to their buddies who didn't speak English. The only sound in the mess was the humming of the ship's engines and the occasional creek of the hull.

As he looked up, he spoke the final verses of the ***Wreck of the Edmund Fitzgerald***. Slowly, in a soft voice, he continued with the rhythm of the lyrics . . .

"Does anyone know where the love of God goes when the

waves turn the minutes to hours?"

Adam continued the tale, with the haunting images of a ship in distress, going down in a storm, never to be recovered. All of the young sailors had enough experience to have found themselves on a ship in a storm. The very thought of meeting such a fate made them queasy.

"And all that remains is the faces and the names of the wives and the sons and the daughters."

Adam brought his voice to a near whisper, as though he'd gone down with the ship, and all that remained was a ghostly remnant of his former self. The crew were transfixed.

"Superior, they said, never gives up her dead when the gales of November come early!"

Mimicking Adam's whisper, the translators finished. There was another long silence. To a man each of the crew bowed their heads.

Knowing he had done his job, Adam cleared his throat and went on, "Since that tragic accident, the 'minimal-manpower cargo-jettison exercise' was a maneuver required by the USA and Canada for cargo ships operating on the Great Lakes. They must be able to jettison their cargo in the event of severe weather and a danger of sinking," he told them. He emphasized, "It must be accomplished only by three senior officers, in this case, Captain Sungkar, myself, and Rosie."

"Are there any questions?" Hearing none, Adam finished, "This regulation was the reason this ship was fitted with an elevator. Only for the

Great Lakes are break bulk freighters fitted with the large hatch on the foredeck which opens and allows the heaviest cargo beneath to be elevated automatically to the deck level. The Captain will have to certify, under oath to the inspectors in Montreal, that the maneuver was accomplished with minimal crew."

The dramatic story satisfied the young crew. Even the more experienced men, a few of whom had initially questioned the maneuver, saw the logic. The crew was, however, sorry they couldn't watch the 'test.' Adam finished his dinner and returned to the officers' mess and reported to the Captain, "Job done."

When the time came to test their operation, Captain Abe would be too busy to watch for prying eyes. Nevertheless, he was confident the cover story he and Adam had concocted, and Adam had so expertly delivered, would stand up. If one of the men were to become too suspicious, he could be disposed of before arriving in North America. Accidents do happen.

At 2130 hours the weather was as good as it was going to get for a test of this nature. Abe, Adam and Rosie had gone over each step together and separately, dozens of times, committing their roles to memory. They would have no need for a crew once the ship arrived in Detroit. Alone, they could easily finish the final and ultimate goal of their mission while the ship was berthed. Then they would take advantage of the ensuing chaos to load fuel drums into the old Land Rover stored in one of the 20-foot shipping containers, drive across the Ambassador Bridge from Detroit to Windsor, Ontario, and continue either east or west until they reached one of the coasts. From there they'd gain passage to Asia or Europe.

The officers had kept the crew busy that day. When the time came for the men to remain in their quarters, they were tired and well fed. Apart from two crew members who were working in the engine room, the three officers had the ship to themselves. Winds and seas were calm. Their course was set; the ship had slowed to eight knots and was on auto pilot. There was no traffic within range of their enhanced RADAR. Cloudy skies would prevent prying eyes in the sky from watching.

Everything was ready to test their capability. If anything were seen as an impediment, they would have sufficient time after the test to make whatever changes were necessary.

The first step was to load fuel. A flick of a switch activated the lights in the hold. Deep below deck, Adam worked at transferring fuel from the container mounted off of the elevator platform, to the large container on the platform. Starting early, he was able to finish this delicate and dangerous task alone while Abe and Rosie prepared the deck. When he was finished, Adam made an intercom call and climbed atop the three containers on the elevator platform. With minimal deck lighting, Rosie manned the controls and retracted the water-tight hatches on the foredeck, revealing a yawning opening that disappeared into the cavernous cargo hold, empty with the exception of four intermodal containers, three neatly stacked and secured to the elevator platform. They checked to make sure none of the crew had become curios enough to lurk about.

With the 'all clear' the elevator moved with surprising speed and silence as the ship gently listed. There was more than sufficient ballast aboard for such a minor shift in cargo, and no one was concerned with the speed of the elevator's ascent. The more quickly they could accomplish this, the better. Rosie stopped the platform short, so that the upper two containers were even with the deck. Working quickly he positioned the crane over the first 20-foot container. Adam attached the cables that would lift it to the deck. Abe disconnected the cables after the container was gently placed on deck. The process was repeated with the second 20-foot container. Once both containers were secured on deck, Rosie returned to the elevator controls and brought the platform to its full elevated position.

Taking a split second to admire the painted cobra on the 53-foot powder blue container, Abe was already unlocking the doors, securing them to the sides. A stack of boxes containing spare parts, secured on four pallets, provided a shield for the real prize. Inside one of the container's doors was a collapsible pallet jack, which was quickly unfolded and used to move the palleted cargo free of the container.

Behind the cargo was another single door to the three foot wide, heat-shielded, control room. Inside the main portion of the customized Klub-K container, built in Russia and equipped in North Korea, was a Rodong-1 single stage, mobile liquid propellant medium-range ballistic missile. Developed by North Korea in the mid-1980s, it was an adaptation of the Soviet SS-1, more commonly known by its NATO reporting name, 'Scud.'

The missile loomed silently inside the steel box, patiently waiting to release its lethal cargo when asked. With the press of a button just inside the control room, the rear three-quarters of the container started its ascent until it elevated the nose of the missile. A green light appeared when the inclinometer mounted inside the container indicated the requisite 72 degrees necessary for launch. The distinctive markings on its warhead revealed its source.

Adam retrieved a key from a chain around his neck and inserted it into a small lock mounted on the wall. One quarter turn, and the control panel came to life. Two small, shielded buttons were adjacent to the key switch, labeled, "igniter enable," and "launch." He slid back the shield and pressed the 'igniter enable' button. The square switch lit up yellow and a buzzer sounded. A window labeled "Time Delay" came to life, flashing '00.00.' Setting a number would begin a countdown to an automatic launch sequence. He slid back the second switch cover, revealing a flashing red square beneath his thumb. He held his thumb over the button without touching it. A press of the red button would ignite the liquid fuel and send the missile flying off of the port side of the ship and into the North Atlantic sky. He quickly turned the key to its off position and the control panel went dark. Done!

The entire operation took 27 minutes. Abe, Adam and Rosie looked at each other confidently, silently congratulating each other before putting everything back in place. A half-hour later, the watertight hatches were again closed, the fuel was off-loaded, the ship was secured, and the three conspirators retired to the quiet confines of the captain's office to discuss what they'd learned.

All were pleased with how quickly their plans had been executed. Captain Abe reviewed the plan to have the Land Rover and fuel prepared, along with their luggage, documents and cash, prior to the launch. If they were able to leave quickly enough after the real launch, they might even get across the border before the effects were felt. If they couldn't cross in Detroit, they would travel through the US to a remote point along the border where they could cross unseen. Each had sufficient documentation in different names: passports, family photos, credit cards, receipts and other "pocket litter," to establish a different identity. They weren't terribly worried about being caught. Communication would be dramatically curtailed, if it existed at all.

The expression on Rosie's face was unmistakable. He looked concerned. Since his visit to Iceland, he'd been having intrusive thoughts about the mission, and it was beginning to show in his expressions. Abe queried Rosie about what was bothering him, thinking it must be an operational issue. Rosie replied, "What will this do to the innocents?"

Abe and Adam were stunned for a moment. They looked at him, puzzled. Rosie continued, "There are good people in America. What will this do to them? Are we going to kill farmers, merchants, mechanics, sailors? What have they done? Why don't we point this toward the politicians?" Adam didn't know what to say. He was uneasy hearing such talk. Captain Abe sat silent for a moment before answering.

"Rosie, I know how you feel. I've felt the same way. That's why we decided to use this device. It's not a bomb. Well, it is, but it doesn't land on people. It will detonate at the peak of its arch, a 150 miles up, and send out an electromagnetic pulse. That's all. It'll erase every computer, every credit card, everything that has a microprocessor in it, including automobiles.

"Electricity generation requires computers now, so they'll lose the capability to produce electricity. The electrical grid will go black. The effect will cascade throughout the country, and probably much of Canada. Telephone service will fail. So will all commerce that requires computers, machines or transportation. No one will be able to get money from banks because the computers will be useless. They'll be brought back to their 18th century. It will affect every person in America, but it won't kill anybody. It won't knock down a single house. Nothing like what we've seen with American drones. It will make their lives as difficult as our brethren in Afghanistan. The difference is they're not used to it. And, it'll take them a very long time to repair it. Perhaps years."

Rosie hadn't given much attention to the specific weapon and didn't understand what an electromagnetic pulse device was. Although still not completely understanding the technology, Abe's explanation set him somewhat at ease.

The conversation ended and Adam notified the night shift that they could return to duty.

The officers headed for their quarters. Out of earshot of Rosie, Abe remarked to Adam that they would have to watch him. "We might have to complete this mission without him," Abe whispered.

The Captain settled his head onto his pillow, but couldn't sleep. Rosie's remarks had disturbed him. So was the fact that he lied to his dear friend. Abe knew very well that, while the weapon would not burn someone to death, nor would the radiation be of serious harm to anyone, the effect of the pulse would certainly be deadly. Hospitals, police, fire departments, water utilities, and more would all lose power, and their critical equipment would be irreparably damaged. Most critical infrastructure was equipped with back-up generators, but these are controlled by microprocessors, which would be wiped out. Emergency services rely on vehicles, which, like every other vehicle within the considerable range of the pulse, would be rendered useless. Even with older vehicles manufactured prior to the use of microprocessors, fuel would be limited because it takes power to pump. Without cash, which would dwindle quickly, there'd be no way to buy fuel even if it were available. Many would die quickly as pacemakers, infusion pumps, ventilators, dialysis units, and fire alarms failed.

Those vast "amber waves of grain" could never be harvested without operational machinery. Even if an army of people were willing to help, communicating with them, much less getting them to the right place, would be a monumental if not an impossible task. Aside from shouting for help or sending someone to summon nearby people, there would be no communication. Obtaining replacement parts for anything would take months, if an order could be placed at all.

There would be massive food shortages. Starvation. Panic. Violence. It would indeed be lethal. Abe had read the declassified American documents estimating up to a 90 percent death rate one year after a major Electromagnetic Pulse event.

They were two days away from the shores of America. Abe said a silent prayer to Allah, and fell asleep.

Adam could not sleep. He returned briefly to his cabin only to unpack his secret stash of religious paraphernalia and say his evening prayers, along with a prayer of thanksgiving for a successful day. He had not for a moment felt guilty about disobeying the order that no religious items be brought aboard ship. He made a cursory attempt to sleep, but soon surrendered to his youthful exuberance. He dressed and ventured out on deck.

He was proud of himself. He had convincingly persuaded the crew to provide the much-needed privacy for their test. Two days before departing Iceland he had completed the necessary wiring, power supply connections, and plumbing fittings to facilitate the fueling and launch of their weapon. Everything had worked as intended. Everything would work as intended when they arrived in Detroit. This would be the first major accomplishment in his young life, his *jihad.*

He tried to suppress the immodest feelings that were flooding him; the history-making success, the adulation of the crowds, the gifts and rewards that would be lavished upon him and his compatriots. He would become a cleric after returning home to Tunisia, a powerful and influential cleric. Tens of millions would harken to his advice and counsel. A *fatwa* above his signature would be taken almost as seriously as scripture. He would be both a religious and political leader.

Strange, he thought, how events conspire to produce the unexpected. When he went to seek work at the Port of Bizerte, it was because there were no job prospects in his little village, and he wanted a chance to travel, to see other lands, to learn. Soon after beginning work as a sailor, he met people who taught him what needed to be done in the service of Allah. He threw himself into it, ravenously reading everything he could get his hands on, listening to the sermons of firebrand clerics around the world. The more radical, the more extreme the rhetoric, the more he was drawn to them.

His family wanted him to marry and had, several times, tried to arrange appropriate meetings with young women, but he would have none of it. He did not want the distraction. Upon his triumphant return from America, however, he would have his choice of wives; many of them. Hundreds of beautiful women would be longing for the chance to be the wife of the successful, rich and handsome hero he was to become.

Riding high on the wings of his youthful imagination, he was suddenly brought back to reality by a crewman who asked if he needed anything. Adam smiled his warm, charming smile and said no, he was just off to bed. He wished his young crew member a good night and walked back to his cabin.

TWELVE

Tuesday, July 30th
16:10 GMT – 11:10 am EDT
Cranberry Lake, New York, USA

JERRY HADN'T EVEN HEARD the slam of the car door when he saw Chester, his 110-pound Great Pyrenees, run up the driveway. He looked up from the engine of his 1978 Ford F150 pick-up to see Joseph walking down the drive and Chet following, wagging his tail. Jerry had a love-hate relationship with his truck, which sometimes seemed to burn more oil than gas. "Hey buddy, how was your weekend with Savannah?"

Another voice came from the workshop in the garage. "Hey, Joseph."

"Hi, Will," Joseph yelled back. He then lowered his voice. "Jerry, we need to talk." Joseph handed the unopened letter to his friend. Chester seemed to sense something was wrong. His tail had stopped its wild back and forth, and he just watched.

Jerry noticed Chester's concern. After wiping oil from his hands, he took the envelope and looked at it. "What's this?"

"Look who it's from."

Seeing the return address, he was surprised. He looked up and saw sheer panic on Joseph's face. His friend was sweating and his skin had a grayish white tone. Jerry realized Chester had picked up on Joseph's state right away.

"Why is she writing you now? Have you guys been talking?"

"Of course not. I haven't talked to her since that day in court. I haven't wanted to talk to her."

"Let's go inside, get some water." Jerry needed a moment to think about how he should respond to this unexpected development. By the time he joined Joseph at the round oak kitchen table, placing a tall glass of ice water in front of his friend, he was sure.

"Don't open it."

"What do you mean, don't open it?"

"I mean, don't open it." Jerry was matter of fact. "Ignore it. Act like you never received it."

"I can't just ignore it, Jerry. Lucia was my life for 25 years. What do ya think she wants?"

"It doesn't matter. She walked out on you. She gave up on you. Do you really care what she wants?" Jerry's voice was steady and firm.

"Maybe I do."

"Joseph, we've been friends for a long time. I saw what her leaving did to you."

Joseph didn't respond. Images of Lucia were flashing through his mind. Her hair. Her soft olive skin. Her smile. Together they would sit on the deck looking at the lake. He remembered their philosophy discussions while lying in bed. The lovemaking. A brief smile disappeared as he remembered the bitter words as she left. The depression. The drinking. The nights sitting on the deck alone. The loneliness. A tear rolled down his cheek.

Jerry had watched as it all happened. The joy of the marriage, the bitterness and sorrow of the divorce. He put his hand on Joseph's arm. "Ignore the letter buddy. You don't need this in your life now."

They both sat silent for several minutes. Then Jerry spoke the words he'd heard Joseph say a million times. "Know thyself." He paused. "Make your own destiny."

When Joseph didn't respond, Jerry decided to sound a bit more upbeat. "It's time to move on buddy. Practice what you preach. Make your own destiny. Look what's happening in your life now. You're happy, sober, living life again. You're working on a new treasure hunt with a very pretty lady, I might add." Joseph remained silent. "Hey, you never answered my question. How was your weekend?"

Joseph ignored him. "I need to find out why she wrote me. He reached for the letter that had been sitting on the table. Jerry was quicker, and grabbed it first.

"Let me hold it for a while. Maybe you'll change your mind. She probably saw your picture on the cover of People and wants more money. Maybe she thinks she deserves part of the Bonaparte treasure."

Joseph looked his friend in the eye. "I need to know what's in that letter."

Jerry's voice started to get louder. "Why do you need to know? That letter may just open wounds that don't need to be opened. Look at you. The wounds are still raw. Don't forget what she said to you when she left. What that *did* to you."

Joseph shot back, "I know exactly what she said. That doesn't make her a monster. That was her way of expressing her hurt."

Jerry lowered his voice and softened his tone. "Joseph, you know that's not what I'm saying. I've known Lu almost as long as you. I love her to death. This isn't about her. I'm . . ."

"You're what, Jerry? Suspicious? You can't even allow for the possibility that she's written for a good reason, that she's sincere, that she…" His voice trailed off. Jerry let him finish his thought silently.

"And you're not suspicious?" He picked up the letter and shook it at Joseph. "Then why didn't you rip it open the minute you got it? Look buddy, I'm not questioning her motives, okay. It's just that I've been by your side for the past three years, and I've seen the dark places you've stumbled through. You've come so far . . . I just want you to think about it. Let me hold on to it for a few days? We'll talk again. The words aren't going to change. If you decide you need to read it, it'll be the same letter."

"You're not going to burn it, are you?"

Will poked his head through the door from the garage. Jerry glanced his way and Will knew he shouldn't come any further. "No, buddy. I just want you to think hard about the possible ramifications of opening up any dialogue with this person, at this time. I'm not inside your head, but you seem to have something good going with Savannah. Before you . . ."

"Leave her out of this! She has nothing to do with it."

"Sorry. You're right. She doesn't. But any possible relationship could be scuttled before it even gets started if you're still haunted by your marriage to Lu."

"Haunted? Lucia isn't a ghost."

"The marriage is."

Joseph sat still, stunned for a moment. "You're an asshole."

"I know."

"But you are occasionally right. I don't know what to do."

"Then don't do anything . . . for now. Take your time and be sure what you do is what you want to do, for you and your future. Let's change the subject. Will's been making something for you. I think he wants to show you, but I don't know if he's finished yet."

The two got up and headed for the workshop and studio in the garage. The letter sat on the kitchen table.

Jerry's partner, Will, had been working with stained glass for more than 15 years.

His small and medium-sized objects d'art, created in the style of Louis Tiffany, had won him a national reputation. Occasionally he would take on commissioned works, but he preferred to create his own pieces.

The space had not been used as a garage for years. It was more of a showroom and workshop. Finished lampshades and framed stained glass windows hung from the rafters. One wall was lined with custom-built shelves that created more than a 100 vertical slits, each with glass panels in every conceivable color. The workbench was positioned in front of a newly installed window that captured the afternoon sun. Hanging from the rafters over the workbench was a simple stained glass rainbow, mounted in a wrought iron frame. This was the very first stained glass piece Will had ever made. He kept it as a daily reminder of his progress as an artist.

On either side of the workbench were several dozen small drawers and cabinets that stored items of the trade. To the left a small rack held spools of copper foil of various widths.

Throughout, track lights highlighted the finished pieces. Will looked up with a big smile when he heard the door open from the kitchen. "Hey guys."

Joseph tried to put a smile on his face. "Hey Will. You really have turned this place into a studio. It looks great."

"It's just a garage," came the sullen response.

"No Will, I mean it really looks great. It's not a garage anymore."

"Yes Joseph, It's—just—*Jerry's*—garage." Each word was individually emphasized. There was a half-smile on Will's face. "On the other hand," he continued, "if our bald-headed friend here ever decides to ask me to marry him . . . maybe I'd call it my studio. Until then, it's just

Jerry's old garage. I'm only here on a temporary basis."

Jerry rolled his eyes, "whatever."

Will's half joking, half serious comments about marriage had been increasing lately.

"You know, Will," Joseph said, "throughout history bald men have always had trouble making commitments. Be careful what you wish for." He was always quick to try and play both sides whenever Will brought up the subject of marriage. Remembering a comment Jerry had made about Savannah, Joseph turned to Jerry, "Be careful my friend, it looks like you hooked a wild one here. One of these days you're going to have to reel him in or you'll lose him."

Will gave Joseph a thank you wink. "Joseph, come look what I made you."

As he walked toward the workbench, it took him a minute to understand what he was looking at. He stopped and stared in amazement.

"You made that for me?"

"You're the only Bonaparte I know."

The piece was like nothing he had ever seen. The frame was carved Spanish Oak. Inside the frame was an 18 inch by 28 inch stained glass window with an image of the Coat of Arms of his ancestor, Joseph Bonaparte. "It's almost done. I just need to add some copper sulfate to give the leading the right patina. It'll be ready in a day or two."

"Will, this is remarkable. Why?"

"Because you are such a good friend to my honey."

Joseph gave Will a hug and whispered in his ear so Jerry couldn't hear, "Thank you, Will. I'll keep working on him to pop the question."

"Okay guys, I gotta go. I've got stuff to do." Joseph looked at Jerry. "Hold on to that letter for me, will you?"

“You bet,” Jerry responded with a wink. “See ya Saturday?”

“Of course. Savannah is coming up on Friday.” He turned to Will. “Wanna come? The boat sleeps eight. With Jerry’s split personality, Savannah and me, that’s only four. There’s plenty of room.”

“I’d love to, but I have a show this weekend. Maybe next time.”

“Smiling as he walked away with a new bounce in his step, Joseph turned, “You’re still an ass Jerry Doolin.”

“You bet he is,” Will agreed.

THIRTEEN

Wednesday, July 31st
18:10 GMT – 1:10 pm EDT
Langley, Virginia, USA

ATHENA WAS SHADOWED throughout her voyage to Halifax, Nova Scotia. Every conversation on the bridge, in the captain's office, and in the galley was monitored. All digital communication was intercepted and analyzed and appeared to be completely benign. Cryptologists detected nothing to indicate coded language in the conversations or emails.

Various theories were floated in task force meetings, the most prominent being that the crew might be unwitting mules. The cesium could have been secreted aboard ship without the original crews' knowledge. The exchange of crew in Lisbon might be coincidental, or might indicate that someone in a higher position was pulling the strings.

Berthed in Halifax, Athena remained under constant surveillance. Nothing noteworthy was observed. No one, aside from the usual port personnel approached, and no one on board did anything beyond their jobs. The crew exchanged cargo, refueled, and filed paperwork. Intelligence officers who tailed crewmembers while on shore found them to be friendly and well-behaved with port authorities and locals. They prepared for sea and were awaiting clearance to depart. Next stop: Boston.

The Task Force decided to wait and watch. But, one thing was certain. Before entering Boston Harbor, Athena would be boarded and inspected.

The US Coast Guard would take the lead, citing as pretext a "routine safety inspection for hazardous material."

"We'll have to get on board and have the time to look around," the Coast Guard commander remarked to the Task Force, "We can't just jump on board and count life jackets. If the stuff is there, it'll take some time to locate it then get a good assessment of it."

"Why don't we use a couple of DOE radiation specialists on the boarding party?" Mickey Evans suggested. "We can dress them in Coastie uniforms." He was always reticent to suggest anything that had a cloak-and-dagger connotation, but he recognized that this situation required skilled personnel to locate and access what they were looking for. While they were receiving the strongest signal through a port hole near the bow, this didn't mean that the source was actually near that location, only that the radiation moved more easily through the glass. Everyone knew it could take some time to locate, particularly in a ship laden with cargo.

The suggestion garnered nods of assent from the rest of the Task Force. Buoyed by their agreement, Lt. Evans continued, "We can send them with a couple of Ordnance Disposal (OD) teams." This comment was met with puzzled looks. "Suppose the ship itself is the Radiation Dispersal Device (RDD)? It could be command-detonated while berthed without the crew knowing anything about it." Eyebrows were raised. This possibility hadn't yet been discussed. The Coast Guard agreed to send in three two-man ordnance disposal teams along with the radiation specialists and dogs. There would be sufficient resources to locate any device and enough help to minimize time on-station . . . essential, given the known radiation hazard.

Debate soon followed on what to do once the source was located. The intelligence community and FBI wanted to disable any potential explosive device and allow the ship to operate as normal, under heavy surveillance.

They were looking to catch the bad guys and find out who they were working with. The Homeland Security viewpoint was to mitigate the hazard, secure the cesium, and remove all risk to the public before the ship got too close. Safety was their primary concern.

Mickey decided it was time to end the debate. The possibilities of what they might encounter aboard the Athena seemed endless. Contingency plans were developed in the event the device was too dangerous to leave alone, the radiation source was too insecure, or if there was clear evidence that the crew were the perpetrators. They couldn't plan much further without more information from the ship itself.

§

Athena received departure clearance from Halifax. She was ready to steam south. More eyes than imaginable were on the freighter's every move, every communication, and every change in course. The little conference room at CIA headquarters was going to be in use for a while. It would remain staffed with direct audio communication to each agency's commands, until the threat was over. If a marker light went out on Athena, everyone in the room would know about it before the crew did. The raid would be conducted 50 miles from Boston Harbor. Until then, all they could do was watch, wait, tweak the contingency plans, and keep the antacids within reach.

The Coast Guard, Department of Energy, and the Department of the Navy liaisons all quickly left the room to get their necessary personnel assembled and transported to the Coast Guard cutter that was preparing to engage Athena on the initial intercept. The Department of Homeland Security representative dispatched the news through their chain of command to the

Domestic Nuclear Detection Office that a source might be on course to enter Boston Harbor. The communication made clear the source would be examined, and under heavy surveillance.

With so many disparate agencies involved in the US security apparatus, communication between agencies was one of the most difficult aspects of any such operation. The creation of the Department of Homeland Security, as well as other intelligence-sharing reforms resulting from the 9/11 Commission, did little to diffuse the tension between agencies. What no one wanted was for one agency to sound an alarm that would blow an investigation conducted by another agency.

Mickey Evans sat quietly at the table. The possible scenarios the Task Force had discussed ran through his head like a swarm of bees, each colliding with another and producing a cacophony of thoughts that were difficult to tease apart. His youthful appearance gave way to a visage of stern, determined concentration. His meditation was interrupted by the arrival of his relief. He had occupied that room since the prior evening and needed to get some rest before returning. The young Lieutenant J.G. would contact Mickey if anything significant developed. Plus, he had a rehearsal later that afternoon that he couldn't miss.

§

Shortly after being transferred to Washington, Evans tried to find an activity that would help him maintain a connection to his Japanese heritage. With the exception of trips to the States to visit his father's side of the family, he'd grown up in his parents' house outside of Uruma, not far from the US Naval base at Okinawa where his father worked. After high school, Mickey moved to America to attend Columbia University and remained there until he received his Master of Arts in Classical Studies.

As a child of his time, western influence pervaded his life, but his mother was conscientious in her efforts to balance it with her ancestral culture. She was observant in the Shinto tradition. Mickey's belief in the supernatural waned with the passing years. Nonetheless, he very much enjoyed the rituals and festivals.

As a youth he found himself fascinated by Taiko drummers and spent quite a few of his school years actively participating in a group. Later in high school he was distracted when an aikido craze swept through his social circle and he went off in another direction. An accomplished martial artist, once he joined the Navy Mickey looked for something to provide some contrast to the technical, analytic nature of his vocation.

His past interest in Taiko was rekindled when he saw an ad in the Washington Post inviting interested persons to visit an open house. The Potomac Taiko Drum Society had been in existence for decades before Mickey visited on that day, and their interest in him began immediately after the short performance they offered for the attendees of the open house.

After the demonstration, everyone had left except Mickey. The membership looked at him skeptically, initially judging him by his appearance. Clearly he was not completely Japanese, they thought he would be another of the many young people who come with an initial interest in the music and quickly go, uninterested in the deep cultural traditions of Taiko.

Their misgivings gave way to warm smiles when they introduced themselves in English and received a response in impeccable Japanese. Introducing himself as Mikoto, in the manner that would be expected of a Japanese native, he informed them, "My friends call me Mickey." He was peppered with questions. His answers inspired many of the members to reminisce on their lives in Japan. They wondered how life was for him and his mixed-race family, living in the old country.

Mickey said it was difficult at first, especially with his maternal grandparents. The family stayed in Japan after his dad retired from the Navy, visiting America only a couple of times a year. His father eagerly adopted the culture of his wife, but his maternal grandmother was distant to her American son-in-law. After the death of her husband, her son-in-law joyfully welcomed her into his home. She warmed up quickly and boasted to her friends about his dedication to family and his loving care of her.

The musicians weren't at all surprised to learn Mickey had some experience with Taiko and were delighted to see he was eager to renew his interest. At rehearsals they always referred to him as Mikoto, but while enjoying an after rehearsal beer they called him Mickey.

The basics came back to him with relative ease, and his dedication to learning was rewarded with increased skill. He practiced with the group every chance he got, and when circumstances precluded attending a rehearsal, he'd practice at home or wherever he could. Once, he even resorted to striking a pillow with rolled up newspapers in a hotel room. The more he worked at it, the more he liked it. And the more the rest of the group liked him. He was talented, interested in learning, and accepted correction and criticism in the spirit in which it was offered. It also didn't hurt that his well-developed body looked good when they performed bare-chested, or on the occasions when they performed in nothing but fundoshi.

It wasn't long before he was asked to perform with them at a reception at the Japanese Embassy. He was deeply honored, and threw himself into the performance with unsurpassed zeal. His efforts were rewarded with outstanding reviews for him and his fellow performers. They were asked to perform at the annual Cherry Blossom Festival in Washington, DC. Photographs of their performances adorned the walls of their rehearsal space, drummers' backs arched, rearing back with huge drum sticks held high overhead, ready to crash down on the heads of the massive drums.

Their rehearsal space was part of a warehouse converted for that purpose. It was one of the few places they could find where no one would complain about the hours of thunderous drumming.

Mickey loved Taiko more with each passing year. He loved the outlet, such a departure from the fluorescent-lit, analytical, data-mining nature of his job. Taiko was creative, physically demanding, ancient, emotive, expressive, erotic. He could not miss this rehearsal. He had a performance coming up at a reception for Japanese businessmen and diplomats.

FOURTEEN

Wednesday, July 31st
19:45 GMT – 2:45 pm EDT
Saranac Lake, New York, USA

THE LETTER HAD BEEN bothering Joseph for the past 24 hours. A hundred times he asked himself, "Why did I leave it there?" He knew if he went back, Jerry would say the same thing, and not let him read it. But, he couldn't get Lucia out of his mind. "Was something wrong? Was she sick? Did she need money?" The divorce settlement had been generous.

While worry about Lucia's health and financial status bothered him, Joseph was more confused about his feelings. He still cared for her. Did he still love her? Did she still love him?

Sitting on his deck, Joseph thought of another piece of advice Jerry had often given him, "Make a decision, even if it's wrong." There was only one thing to do.

The drive to Saranac Lake seemed to last longer than the hour it normally took. By the time he turned on to Park Avenue, he had convinced himself something was seriously wrong. The house number had been ingrained in his mind from the many documents he'd received during the divorce proceedings almost four years earlier. He had never forgotten it.

Two-twenty-four Park Avenue was a small pleasant looking white cottage with a hint of a gingerbread trim. Joseph slowed as he drove by, looking for a car in the driveway. Parked by a side door was the 2009 black

Lexus SUV he'd bought her for her birthday. He continued for another block and turned around. This time he looked for movement inside the house. There was nothing. Again, he didn't turn in the drive. Rather, he continued to Catherine Street and turned left, back toward the village.

The Blue Moon was a bistro Joseph and Lucia had frequented. Ordering an iced tea, he took a table half-hidden in a corner. Briefly, he reminisced. There was the time Lucia had a paper published in a second rate philosophy journal. It wasn't much. But, it was a start. They had a small dinner and celebrated with too much wine. They laughed for hours, not caring what people thought. They had to get a room for the night because neither of them could drive back to Cranberry Lake. Joseph smiled.

But, his fond memories were short lived. "*Am I doing the right thing?*" He asked himself the same question a dozen different ways. The answer was always the same. "*I don't know*."

He went over all the reasons not to open the letter Jerry had brought up the day before. '*Now I'm here, ready to knock on her door*,' he thought. '*This is crazy*.' Joseph thought about the rough time he went through after the divorce. It did hurt. It was hard. He was still going to AA meetings. "That's not her fault," he said out loud. "Maybe the bitterness has faded." He took a sip from his drink. "Has it? Or am I just trying to convince myself it's faded?" was the new question. The answer was the same as earlier.

Briefly, Savannah came into his thoughts. Joseph looked out the window on to Main Street. "She only lives 30 miles up the road," he whispered.

He finished his drink and went to his car. Without starting his engine, he placed both hands on the steering wheel and bowed his head. "Savannah or Lucia?" He was surprised at how quickly he made his decision.

Turning from Catherine Street back onto Park Avenue, he could feel sweat forming on his forehead. He made the right turn into the driveway and parked a respectable distance behind the Lexus. As he walked to the porch he took a deep breath, pausing a second before knocking three times.

It was an agonizing 15 seconds of waiting. Joseph felt his heart jump when he heard the door knob turning.

"Joseph." The raspy, unmistakable voice always melted his heart.

"Lucia."

There was an uncomfortable pause. He noticed how beautiful she was without make-up.

"Come in, come in. You must have gotten my letter."

"Not really. Well, kinda . . . but not really."

"You're not making any sense. Either you got it, or you didn't." The words were spoken in a light hearted manner.

"Yes. I got it. But I didn't read it."

"Then what are you doing here? Why didn't you read it? It was Jerry, wasn't it? "

"It's a long story. I came to see if you're all right. I thought something might be wrong."

"Of course, I'm all right. You should have read the letter."

"I've been accused of that a lot lately. Not reading my mail, I mean."

"What are you talking about?"

"Forget it," Joseph was looking at the floor. "I thought maybe we could talk. You know, catch up a little."

"That would be nice. I'd like that. It's a beautiful day. Let's sit on the porch. Can I get you something to drink?"

"Sure." Joseph made his way to the porch while Lucia went to the kitchen. Joseph was shaking his head and asking himself, "What am I doing here?"

Within moments Lucia arrived carrying a tray with two tall glasses, a glass pitcher of lemonade and a small plate with lemon wedges and a tiny fork. Sprigs of mint were already in the glasses. Another plate had four English biscuits. Out of habit, Joseph got up to take the tray and set it on the glass top of the wicker table while Lucia sat down.

Feeling a little uncomfortable and not knowing quite what to say, Joseph tried to start the conservation while Lucia poured their drinks. "This is a lovely home."

"Thank you. It's cozy."

"Are you happy here in Saranac Lake?"

"Reasonably."

Joseph shifted in his wicker chair. He decided to get to the point. "So, what was in the letter?

There was a slight laugh. "If you wanted to know so badly, why didn't you just open it instead of driving all the way here?"

"I couldn't."

"Jerry! I knew it. Well, I'll say one thing; he's a loyal friend, always trying to protect you. I heard what happened to him a few months ago. Is he okay?"

"He's fine. The bullet just went through some muscle. He retired soon after. If he knew I was here I'm sure he'd want me to say hi. You know how much he likes you."

"Say, has he ever gotten around to asking Will to marry him?

"Not yet. But I think he's getting close."

There was another laugh from Lucia. "He's no better than you when it comes to making decisions."

"What do ya mean?"

"I thought I recognized your car. I saw you drive by earlier and not turn in. Twice!"

"I wasn't sure I should." Her olive skin and chestnut hair were sparkling in the late afternoon sun. He thought of the scores of afternoons they'd spent sitting on the dock at Cranberry Lake. Lucia always made lemonade with extra lemons and mint sprigs. The sun always highlighted her lovely features.

"By the way, congratulations on finding your treasure. It's got to feel good to get that out of your system."

Joseph thought for a second about telling her about his new treasure hunt, but decided against it. A flash of Savannah's sweet face went through his mind. "I'm glad it's over. I'm not thrilled about all the fuss though."

"I've been reading about you. Impressive. It must have been satisfying to return King Joseph's crown to France?"

"Yeah. Jerry went with me. It was an emotional trip. Jerry's a good friend."

"Yes he is."

Joseph reached into his pocket and pulled out a solid gold coin. "Look at this."

"You've had that for years. It's King Joseph's coronation coin. Why are you showing me that?"

Joseph was deep in thought and didn't hear what Lucia had said. "It was minted when Joseph was crowned King of Spain. It's the only one passed down through my family."

Lucia took the coin and looked at it closer. "Okay. I've heard that story a million times. What's the big deal? You've carried this with you ever since I've known you. For 25 years you said it's your most valuable possession."

Joseph had a change of heart and decided not to say what he had planned. He changed the topic.

"How have you been since the . . . Since I saw you last?"

"I've been fine." Lucia put the coin on the tray. "I had a pacemaker put in. Some problems with the heart. That little thing keeps me going, and keeps the heart from stopping."

"Why didn't you call me?"

"After the divorce hearing, I didn't think you'd be interested."

"Lucia, of course I'm interested. I still care about you. By the way, you still haven't told me what was in the letter."

"It was an apology for all the horrible things I said to you. That's all."

Joseph was silent for a moment. "I know what you said was in the heat of the moment. Don't worry about it. A lot of time has passed. I said things too. I'm sorry."

"Joseph, I was hoping we could be friends. Maybe talk every once in a while."

"I would like that, Lucia. I've been thinking about you a lot lately. I miss our talks."

The conversation went on for another two hours, gradually drifting from somber to cheerful. "Hey, I have an idea. How about a treasure hunt?" Joseph had a new playfulness in his tone.

The Bonaparte treasure had been one of the issues in their marriage. Her voice had a new tension in it. "What are you talking about?"

"Let's go on a search for a nice restaurant in Lake Placid and have dinner?"

Relieved, she was on her feet instantly. "That would be nice. Let me change and freshen up."

Joseph took the tray and placed it on the kitchen table. He saw the gold coin Lucia had set there earlier. He started to reach for it. He paused . . .

and left it on the tray.

Dinner was three hours of catching up and reminiscing about old times. Both had relaxed after the awkwardness of the initial conversation. “I don’t want this night to end,” Joseph said. “I am so glad we got together. You are a special woman, Lucia. You always have been.”

“Funny thing, I guess my letter did its job, and you never even read it. I had hoped we could get together and be friends again. *Amor fati*.” Joseph didn’t respond.

Lucia continued. “The night doesn’t have to end here, Joseph.”

FIFTEEN

Thursday, August 1st
10:30 GMT – 5:30 am EDT
The North Atlantic

Mickey Evans had barely shaken off the sleep. At home, he was abruptly awakened when word came via the US Coast Guard that Athena was approaching the 50-mile perimeter that had been established. They were preparing to hail her and order her to stop and be boarded. Three Ordnance Disposal (OD) teams with dogs and two radiation experts from the Department of Energy's National Nuclear Security Administration were brought aboard with equipment to secure the source if necessary. One US Navy SEAL team was placed as back-up in the event they encountered violent resistance. Further back-up was provided by a Navy frigate, a cruiser, two F-14's, and an attack submarine, under orders to maintain a firing solution while the Athena was within 75 miles of Boston Harbor.

Open communication was maintained between the Coast Guard ship, the task force headquarters, each agency's chain of command, and the White House Situation Room. POTUS had been briefed by the National Security Advisor and would be summoned for decisions requiring his authority.

Everyone was on edge. It was one of the rare occasions when Mickey found his job exciting. Most intelligence work is people talking and collecting information. Not exactly James Bond stuff. Today was different.

He secretly wished he could be on board Athena with the rest of the boarding party, participating in the interviews, searching for the cesium. But he also knew that he'd be of little help. He wasn't a specialist in any of those areas, and would probably just be in the way. Still, it would be exciting to see it all in person, and be there when the bad guys were captured. But he'd have to be happy monitoring it from the confines of his task force room in Virginia.

The IT specialists had come in wheeling a large cart with several computers and 50 inch flat-screen monitors. They connected and tested everything with surprising speed. The Task Force Operation Room now had live audio and video links to the Coast Guard Ship, FBI Headquarters, the Director of National Intelligence, and the White House Situation Room.

The orders for the Coast Guard crew, along with the FBI agents, ONI intelligence officers, NNSA specialists, and OD specialists, were to detain the ship, interview her crew, locate and assess the radiation source, locate and disable any explosive devices, and report their findings for further instructions. Armed resistance was not expected, but the possibility could not be ruled out. Everyone was ready.

The ball was now in the hands of the captain of the National Security Coast Guard Cutter *Stratton*, which had been moved weeks earlier from her base in Alameda, California to the First District in Boston. The USS Stratton was the newest of her type, placed in service March 31, 2012. Planning for a total of eight ships of this class to be placed into service, the Coast Guard command wanted to put the Stratton and its weapon technology to use in this case to demonstrate its capabilities as part of the national security apparatus.

The captain of the Stratton gave the 'go' order.

On the bridge of the Athena, Captain Jibril had just taken his first sip of sweet mint tea when a young crewman took off his headphones. "Captain, we're being hailed by the USA Coast Guard. They are ordering us to come to an immediate stop and prepare to be boarded."

"Boarded? What for? Report our position. Are we out of the shipping lane?" The orders kept coming. "RADAR operator, report all contacts. Have we encroached on protected waters or another ship? Are there any obstructions or emergencies in the area?"

Jibril got up from his chair and made his way to the radio, barely letting the crewman communicate to him that their RADAR showed one Coast Guard ship on an intercept course and nothing else. While he hadn't been in command of a ship that sailed to the United States, this was something he hadn't heard about, nor was he prepared for it. Grabbing the microphone from the radio operator, he answered the hail in his best English, "This is Captain Jibril of the freighter Athena, calling the US Coast Guard vessel hailing us. Please state the reason for your order to come to a halt." He reached for the switch to put the response on the bridge speakers.

Aboard the Stratton, Captain David Knowlton monitored his radio operator's reply. It was exactly as ordered in the briefing. "Athena, you are within the territorial waters of the United States, and are ordered to come to a dead stop. Prepare for a Coast Guard safety and security inspection." The radio operator did his job perfectly, delivering the message in a tone of voice not unlike ordering a cup of coffee. He added in a drone, suggesting profound boredom, "This is pursuant to Title 14, USC, Section 89."

Jibril, unfamiliar with US practices looked around at his bridge personnel. He was met with shrugs. After a moment he spoke to his helmsman, "All stop." Raising the microphone to his mouth, he replied, "Very well, we will prepare to receive you. On the port side there is a ladder amidships."

The radio operator aboard the Stratton reported Athena's compliance, stating he could hear the engine telegraph ringing in the background. "Prepare the boats, ready the boarding parties," Knowlton ordered. "Bring us up off of her port beam. I want an escape course constantly calculated. Hands on throttles at all times. If we need to get out of there, we'll need to do it quickly."

The navigator advised, "Contact with target in 12 minutes."

The crew of Athena were unaware of the drone flying overhead, providing images of the ship to the Task Force and others. Nor were they aware of the number of guns, missiles and torpedoes trained on her.

Mickey and his group in Langley were watching the monitors intently. He hadn't realized he was sitting on the edge of his seat until he heard Jibril's confirmation and assent. Leaning back in his chair and almost slipping off, he remarked, "Now they know we're coming. Watch the deck, shout if you see anything that looks like they're preparing to resist." He knew the Stratton had the same video feed he did, and at the first sign of trouble, a Maritime Security Response Team (MSRT), would raid the ship from boats and the helicopter waiting on the Stratton's deck.

The Jayhawk helicopter pilots were ordered to power up with their compliment of MSRT members as the boarding party was launching for Athena. Their orders were to orbit Athena until recalled.

From his desk, Mickey listened. The conversations between Athena officers and crew members were as one would expect for the operation. Jibril gave orders pertinent to the ship's operations, and told a seaman to collect all of the ships records and bring them to his office. The only ship-to-shore communications were to their shipping agent and the Port of Boston, advising of a delay in arrival.

It all seemed so normal. Mickey felt uneasy.

Two of Athena's seamen walked across the deck to the rail along her port side. The drone's video camera zoomed in with remarkable clarity. The monitors showed nothing in their hands, their jackets open enough to suggest nothing hidden beneath. They opened the rail and prepared to assist the boarding party.

Mickey could see from the video feed how startled the crew members of the Athena really were. When the drone zoomed out sufficiently, the source of the surprise was clear. The 418-foot Stratton is larger and significantly more heavily armed than the next-largest cutters in the Coast Guard fleet. An imposing ship, she maneuvered with exceptional grace along Athena's port side. The instant she stopped, the Long Range Interceptor II launched, bearing the first group of the boarding party, consisting of Coast Guard and ONI personnel. All were armed, as was standard practice with any boarding and inspection.

The next personnel to be brought over were the OD and radiation specialists. MSRT members were already aloft in the Jayhawk, and more were in an Over-The-Horizon IV boat, waiting for the signal to commence a raid. They were told to stand by.

Captain Jibril met the Coast Guard officer on the bridge of Athena, politely introducing himself and his first and second officers with a warm smile. As is the custom of his culture, he offered tea and his hospitality to his guests. The USCG officer politely declined his offer, apologizing for the delay and asking for the cooperation of Captain Jibril and his crew. "You shall have anything you need. My crew are at your disposal," was the reply he received from Athena's very professional captain. Jibril pointed the way to his office where all of the ship's records were neatly stacked.

Mickey, Captain Knowlton, and a dozen others were monitoring the conversation on the bridge, and on another channel, the bug planted in the cargo hold nearer the radiation source. They were listening for something that would indicate anyone was trying to hide the source. Or worse, arm an explosive. No one appeared to be in the cargo holds.

A couple of the Coast Guard personnel, along with the OD and radiation specialists, had button cameras on their vests, allowing for audio and video feed of their activities. They watched as the OD specialists got their dogs and gear together and walked to the cargo area. The NNSA radiation specialists were some distance behind them. It didn't take long to rule out other sources of radiation, aside from the strong source near the ship's bow. The radiation specialists wouldn't approach, however, until OD cleared it for explosive devices or booby traps.

The OD team already knew the cargo was clean, but looked over the surfaces and between the loads in the event a device had been placed after the cargo was loaded. They worked quickly and efficiently. There was no indication of an explosive device anywhere on the ship. It all appeared normal. As OD cleared sections of the cargo hold, the radiation specialists followed, trying to narrow down the exact location of the source, or sources. Once everyone was satisfied there was no threat from explosives, all watched the video as the RAD guys moved in.

An initial search of a section of the hull near the forecastle showed nothing obvious. It didn't take long before they were able to report on the radio, "We have one source. I don't know if you can see this on the camera, but it looks like it's hidden behind a steel plate that's been tack-welded between two of the reinforcing . . . whatever you call them . . . ribs, on the hull." He used a flashlight to illuminate the area for the camera. "To get it, we'll need some cutting tools. I'm not sure yet how big a container we'll require."

The frame on the video feed suddenly panned 90 degrees to the right, framing one of the radiation specialists who had dropped the long black scintillator he was holding. He had been leaning against some of the cargo and was staggering backward. The specialist was noticeably pale, and appeared to be struggling to breathe. He leaned forward, hands on his knees and began to gasp, just as the Coast Guardsman escorting them slung his weapon and grabbed the struggling man from behind. The Guardsman's radio crackled, "medical emergency! HST, meet us on deck." An OD specialist swept an arm under the ailing man's knees, lifting him up, and the two men carried him along the catwalk, toward the ladder leading up to the deck. Evans and his task force sat stunned for a moment.

Watching his own feed, Captain Knowlton reacted instantly. "Masks. All personnel don your masks. Ready our chemical response personnel."

The Stratton was fully equipped to respond to any chemical, biological, nuclear or radiological incident with state-of-the-art technology and highly trained crew members. Evans, Knowlton, and many others involved in the boarding and surveillance operation knew such rapid onset of symptoms could not be the result of a biological or radiological source. Chemicals must be the culprit.

In Captain Jibril's office, the intelligence officers going through the ship's paperwork and interviewing Athena's officers suddenly stopped what they were doing and immediately tensed. Captain Jibril couldn't hear the radio messages coming through the earpieces of his guests. He stood by in shock as every American in the room simultaneously grabbed their weapons and changed their demeanor. The intelligence officer in charge said only two words, "Nobody move."

The Health Service Technician or HST, the Coast Guard's equivalent of a medic or corpsman, had been standing just outside Athena's bridge when word came through. Instinctively, he grabbed his backpack and bolted for the hatchway toward the cargo hold. He simultaneously grabbed his respirator and swung the hatchway open.

Jibril felt his body go cold. He didn't know what to say. He didn't understand what had gone wrong, and there was nothing he could do.

By the time the two rescuers got him into open air, the ill man was visibly worse. He was ashen, and had begun to take on a blue tint. The HST took a quick look and asked his patient a question. There was no reply. The man appeared to be losing consciousness.

People throughout the government were riveted to their monitors as the scene played out. Elsewhere, a submarine was preparing to fire torpedoes to destroy the contaminated ship.

The HST looked at the two unmasked rescuers, silently sized-up the situation and plunged his gloved hand into the open backpack, withdrawing an auto-injector. Pulling off the safety cap, he pressed it against the thigh of the now critically ill man. He held it in place for a moment and tossed it aside. Within seconds, he had oxygen on his patient. His legs were elevated on his pack and the HST was trying to raise a vein in the man's arm. Not finding a suitable vein, he dropped the man's arm and picked up a pair of shears, cutting the left leg of his patient's pants to mid-thigh. He grabbed hold of a povidone/iodine swab, and asked his colleagues to arrange evacuation of the patient to the Stratton.

The radio was buzzing with questions for the far-too-busy HST. His only reply was a firm, "not now." His hand plunged into his backpack and located a device that vaguely resembled a syringe. Holding it to his patient's shin bone just below the knee, he deployed the bone injection gun, driving a stainless steel spike into the marrow cavity of the unconscious man's tibia. The core of the spike was removed, leaving behind a hollow needle which he attached to an IV. Diphenhydramine and methylprednisolone flowed into the patient's leg. A quick reassessment indicated the man was improving.

As the MSRT was preparing to fast-rope from the helicopter to Athena's deck, the HST advised his command, and everyone else eavesdropping, that this was not a chemical weapon exposure. It appeared to be an allergic reaction. The crew from the Long Range Interceptor arrived with a stretcher. The patient continued to improve and was able to communicate, albeit weakly. The first question the HST asked was about allergies. The RAD specialist replied, "Fish." The cargo hold had been loaded with fish oil.

Everyone, from Mickey Evans and his task force room full of people, to Captain Knowlton, to the skipper of the attack submarine, to the White House staff in the Situation Room, breathed a collective and simultaneous sigh of relief.

Jibril saw everyone in his office relax as suddenly as they had become tense. The intelligence officer smiled and apologized, stating that one of their colleagues had taken suddenly ill and needed to be evacuated. Jibril and his crew asked about his condition, offered assistance, and appeared genuinely concerned.

The interviews progressed, with all of the crew members answering everything asked of them with forthrightness and apparent honesty. Nothing they said contradicted what the intelligence officers already knew. Everything was corroborated by the evidence collected, including the order to exchange the crew in Lisbon. Jibril was unable to offer an explanation, stating the orders came from his corporate offices.

When questions about undocumented hazardous materials were asked, Jibril chuckled. "There is nothing undocumented on this ship, sir. I am not in the practice of transporting hazardous materials, nor contraband." When the interviews were completed, intelligence officers met to compare answers given by the other crew members. All seemed to be consistent.

Mickey Evans found himself scratching his head. It seemed the crew of Athena was clueless about the cesium hidden in her hold. Knowing it wouldn't be long before the Captain of the Stratton asked for instructions on how to proceed, Mickey asked for input from the representatives in the room. The opinions were as predicted. The Department of Energy wanted to seize the cesium immediately and bring it to a secure facility. So did Homeland Security. Even though they were confident that there were no explosives or other means of using the ship as an RDD, they were uncomfortable with such a hot radiation source in the Port of Boston and not under their control.

Before the FBI representative could say anything, the communications link with FBI headquarters crackled to life. The Assistant Director of the WMD Directorate was emphatic in his objection to seize the source. "We have to find out who's coming for that material," he shouted, "we have no idea who is behind it or how big the cell, if any, may be. I can't stress this strongly enough. I'll put teams all over that pier if necessary. We need to capture these people. If we make it just another failed attempt without getting our hands on the perpetrators, they'll just try again, and we won't even know who they are. I'll take it to the Director, the Attorney General, or the White House if necessary. This has enormous national security risks, not just for this incident, but into the future." The FBI agent in the room was nodding his agreement, a singular nod against a tableau of heads shaking, "no."

Before Mickey could move the conversation toward a consensus, opinions started to come from all sides, degenerating rapidly into something resembling the trading floor of the New York Stock Exchange.

The feed from the White House Situation Room showed several National Security staffers sitting around the large table. In the background, Evans saw the door of the Situation Room open and the National Security Advisor walk in. As the camera zoomed in, her image filled the screen. She was trying to say something, which was inaudible over the cacophony in the room and over the COMM link. Lieutenant Snow, of the Coast Guard, saw Mickey's frustration and emitted an ear-piercing whistle, which instantly quieted everyone. "Thanks, Shawn. I believe the National Security Advisor has some input. Please proceed, ma'am."

The NSA explained that this situation has been a part of the President's daily security brief since the ship left Lisbon. She was perfectly comfortable speaking for POTUS in stating that the criminal investigation must continue. "There are very dangerous people involved in this. Their capture, and the intelligence we can glean from them is of paramount importance to the country's security."

That ended the conversation.

Athena would be permitted to sail to Boston with the source aboard. The 'level one' surveillance would continue. One FBI hostage rescue team would be placed in the port, augmenting two Maritime Safety and Security Teams (MSST's), ready to take the perpetrators into custody at any time. The Domestic Nuclear Detection Office would be alerted to not sound any alarms. They would monitor the location and status of the cesium, along with the Coast Guard and NNSA. The cesium would be collected after those intent on gaining possession were taken into custody, along with the entire crew of Athena. The Athena crew would require more extensive investigation and interrogation.

Intelligence assets in Boston were engaged to derail the delivery of Athena's cargo. She was scheduled to sail out of Boston to Calais, France within 48 hours of arrival. Arrangements were made to ensure her cargo would not arrive on time. The entire crew would be under close surveillance and able to be apprehended in an instant. The ship would not leave port with the cesium aboard.

For Mickey Evans and his team, it was back to the waiting game. Everyone was uncomfortable. The risk of failure was high.

SIXTEEN

Thursday, August 1st

20:00 GMT – 3:00 pm EDT

Cranberry Lake, New York, USA

THE RIDE BACK to Cranberry Lake was rushed. Joseph hadn't planned on spending the night at Lucia's, much less sleeping till noon. He'd made no preparations for the trip to Chimney Island. They had rented a 43 foot Bayliner and planned on spending the night on the boat.

Even though he felt rushed, the drive gave him time to think about the extraordinary past 24 hours. He pondered his future. Would they remain friends? Close friends? Was there even a remote possibility they would remarry? He had more questions than answers.

Turning into his driveway he saw a familiar car. His heart stopped. "Oh shit!" he mumbled. For a second he thought about backing out of the driveway and heading to Jerry's, but the front door opened.

"Hey, handsome. Surprise! I tried to call to let you know I was coming up today. I thought I'd surprise you and we would spend the day together tomorrow and head up to the river Saturday morning." Savannah ran up to him, gave him a hug and tried to give him a passionate kiss. Joseph tentatively hugged her back, but resisted the kiss.

She was a little surprised at his reaction. She also noticed the stubble on his face. "Are you okay? What's wrong? Don't you like my surprise?"

"Of course I do." Joseph said, trying his best to sound excited. "It's just that I'm . . . surprised."

"I got here two hours ago and the door was open, so I let myself in."

"I wasn't expecting you." Joseph was still trying to make excuses for his appearance and unusual greeting.

As they went inside, Savannah spoke of how excited she was to have a second chance of finding the marker. "Do you think it's there, Joseph? Do think we'll find it?"

"I don't know, Savannah." Joseph seemed distant. "Look, Savannah, I need to shower and shave. I've been in these clothes since yesterday. Why don't you make yourself comfortable? Give me a few minutes."

"Is anything wrong? Are you okay, Joseph?" A new sense of concern was in her voice.

"I'm fine. Just let me get cleaned up."

With no other explanation, Joseph headed to the bedroom.

Savannah headed to the deck to resume reading the book she had found on Joseph's shelf earlier. The book sat on her lap as she pondered Joseph's unusual behavior. She could hear the shower running. Her thoughts shifted to the warm naked body she had cuddled to just the week before. She was wondering if she should offer to join him in the shower, when the phone rang.

Trying to be helpful, she went inside and picked up the phone, "Hello."

The woman on the other end of the line was taken aback. "I'm sorry, I think I have the wrong number," was the reply.

"Are you looking for Joseph?"

"Yes I am." There was surprise in woman's voice. "Who is this?"

"I'm a friend of his. He's in the shower. Can I tell him who called?" There was a long silence. "Hello? Are you there?"

"Yes, I'm sorry. Tell him Lucia called. Tell him he left something very valuable at my house last night. I know it's important to him. It's too valuable to mail, so just tell him I'll hold on to it for him."

"Can I tell him what it is?"

"He knows." The line went dead.

Savannah looked at the receiver and simply said, "Okay." She set the receiver on the cradle.

Joseph was unusually long in the shower. He took advantage of the privacy of the shower to try and sort out his feelings for Lucia, and now Savannah.

"Feel better, handsome?" Joseph had just walked onto the deck in fresh khakis, polo shirt and sandals. The afternoon sun was warm. "Actually, I feel a lot better." He rubbed his clean shaven face. "I needed that." Walking up to Savannah, he gave her the kiss he should have given her earlier. "You've been here two hours and haven't gotten yourself something cold and wet?"

"I felt bad enough helping myself to your house. I thought helping myself to your fridge was pushing it too far."

Joseph let out a short laugh. "You did all right last time you were here. Come on, let's get something to drink." The two walked to the kitchen. "Coke or Sprite? Sorry, I don't keep any liquor in the house."

"I'm not a drinker anyway. Sprite is fine. Lots of ice please. By the way, while you were in the shower, you got a call."

Joseph chuckled again.

"What's so funny?"

"You help yourself to my house. You answer my phone. But you won't get yourself a soda pop. So, who was on the phone? Someone looking for a buried treasure?"

"Funny." She gave Joseph a tap on the butt. "It was Lucia." A chill went down Joseph's spine. "You left something important at her house last night. She said she would hold on to it for you."

Joseph wasn't sure what to say. "Lucia is my ex-wife. We had some things to discuss about the divorce. It got late, so I spent the night on the sofa." The tone of his voice had a guilty sound to it. "We talked until three in the morning. I ended up sleeping till noon. I was pissed she didn't wake me sooner."

Smiling, Savannah was waving her hands in the 'stop' motion. "Slow down partner. You don't owe me any explanation."

"Nothing happened." He was still sounding guilty.

Savannah started laughing. She reached over to Joseph, put a hand softly on one cheek, and kissed him on the other. "You're sweet."

"What was that for?"

"For being sweet."

It was a completely different reaction than he expected from Savannah. While he was relieved, he was somewhat confused as to why she wasn't a little jealous. He got thinking, maybe she didn't have the feelings for him he had thought.

"So what are we doing for dinner?" Savannah asked with a big smile. "You're not making me cook, are you?"

"Well, that fried chicken was so good last week, I thought . . .

"You creep."

"I'm just kidding. Why don't we call Jerry & Will and see if they want to go out?"

"Who's Will?"

"Will is Jerry's partner. I guess I didn't tell you. Jerry's . . . ."

Savannah interrupted, "You dope, I figured that much out. Call them. I'd like to meet Will. It would be like a family dinner." She got up and kissed Joseph on the lips. "I'm going out to the car and get my bag."

Joseph called Jerry, almost in a panic. "Jerry. I think I've really done it now. I need your help."

Worried Savannah would walk in, he was speaking in a whisper. "I spent last night at Lucia's. We talked about everything."

"Hold on Joseph, did you say you spent the night at Lucia's?"

"Yes. We had a terrific time."

Jerry was startled by this news. "What were you thinking?"

"Listen to me Jerry, Lucia's not the problem. I got home this afternoon and Savannah was here waiting for me. She's planning on spending the night. She wants to spend the day together tomorrow, then ride to Ogdensburg with us Saturday."

"Yikes," was the only response Jerry could get out.

Joseph heard the front door open and instantly changed the subject . . . and his voice. "So, Savannah and I were wondering if you and Will would like to join us for dinner at the Windfall?"

On the other end of the line, Jerry started laughing, realizing what was going on at his friend's house. "You do know how to step in it, don't ya?"

Savannah walked by and said in a loud voice, "I'm going to your bedroom to change and freshen up."

Jerry heard the comment and was laughing even harder. "I'm sorry buddy, just tell her to make herself at home."

"Come on Jerry, this is serious."

"I'm sorry, buddy. Do you need Will and me to come over and rescue you from the pretty lady?"

"No." was the instant response.

"So what's the problem? You have feelings for two beautiful women, and you can't decide who to choose?"

"Something like that. But, I'm not sure Savannah has the same feelings for me. She actually talked to Lucia on the phone this afternoon. She knows I spent the night at Lucia's, and she didn't seem jealous at all."

"So the plot thickens. Now the two beautiful women are talking to each other." Laughing again he continued, "You beat all, Joey. And you want me to get you out of this predicament."

"I just want your advice."

"Okay. Here's my advice . . . pick one! You can't serve two masters."

"You're no help."

"Seriously, Joseph. Listen to me. First of all, you need to relax. You hardly know Savannah. She's very sweet and clearly she has feelings for you. And, I know you like her. You've talked to Lu once in the past three years. You have no idea what your real feelings are for her. Why don't you just let things play out a while? See where they go. There's no reason to panic. And, definitely no reason to make any rash decisions."

Savannah came out of the bedroom and walked up to Joseph and hugged him from behind. Speaking toward the phone she yelled, "Jerry, can you hear me?"

Joseph answered for him, "He can hear you."

"You and Will are going to join us for dinner, aren't you?"

"Tell the lovely lady we're sorry, but we already have plans. I think you two need to spend some time alone. By the way, Will's show this weekend is in Burlington, Vermont, so he's leaving real early tomorrow. He's taking Chester with him. I've got lots of stuff to do tomorrow to free myself up for the weekend. We ought to get an early start on Saturday. I'll be ready by seven. Since the lovely Savannah is riding with us, we'll have to take the SUV. I'll ask Will if he'll take the pick-up. Want me to pick you guys up at seven . . . or are you planning a Saturday morning romp under the covers?"

"You jerk! We'll be ready. See ya Saturday."

"Okay, have fun tomorrow."

SEVENTEEN

Thursday, August 1st
13:30 GMT – 8:30 am EDT
The Laurentian Channel, off the coast of Newfoundland

"ALL AHEAD ONE-THIRD," Captain Abe ordered. Ares had just completed her ballast exchange in the calmer waters of the Laurentian Channel. It was a requirement of the American and Canadian governments to prevent invasive species from entering the Great Lakes system. The salinity of their ballast water would be tested during their inspection in Montreal, only a day away. Regulations mandated the exchange take place prior to Ares reaching 63° west longitude. Transport Canada had been advised of their inability to make the exchange in the open ocean, due to lack of cargo and the dangers associated with a ballast exchange in heavy seas while the older ship was riding a little high in the water.

Even though the ballast exchange had gone smoothly, Captain Abe was becoming apprehensive. Thoughts of their sister ship, Athena, weighed heavily on his mind. There had been no news in several days. Abe knew he would soon be busy dealing with pilots and maneuvering the St. Lawrence Seaway. "Hopefully, Athena is dealing with her own problems," he thought.

After notifying the St. Lawrence Seaway Development Corporation of their position, he requested the first of five pilots who would guide their ship through the Seaway. The pilot would board in 12 hours as they approached Quebec City, Canada. "Sleep," the Captain said to himself. There wouldn't be much of it once the pilot was aboard and they made their way to Lake Ontario, he thought. Abe turned the ship over to Rosie with instructions to notify him when they were an hour outside of Quebec. He returned to his stateroom and laid his head back on his pillow, turning his head to look at the photograph on the bedside table. His wife, holding his young daughter, was smiling back at him.

The twinges of grief felt no less raw despite the time that passed since their deaths. Her family lived in Kabul, Afghanistan. While Abe was at sea, she and their daughter made a frantic trip to Kabul in an effort to convince her parents to leave with her for their home in Kiamari, Pakistan. They never returned. Nothing was recovered. There was no *janazah* or funeral rite; he had nothing to bury. The crew on the bridge when Captain Sungkar received the news of his family's death would never forget the look on his face, nor how stunned they were at the sight. They would say he was never the same thereafter. His ship was commanded by his first officer for three days. He never left his stateroom. He never answered the intercom. None of his crew ever heard him laugh again.

Abe spent weeks in a futile attempt to untangle the series of events that had led to their deaths. He was not successful. The US military blamed "insurgent attacks" for the explosion, while the locals called them military strikes. The fog of war had reached the threshold of his stateroom, thousands of miles away. That fog would never lift.

Either way, military attack or counter-attack, Abe concluded that nothing would have happened if the Americans had not invaded and occupied Afghanistan. It was shortly thereafter that he began looking for ways to exact revenge on the infidel invaders. His timing was prophetic. Al-Qaeda was always looking for a plan to follow 9/11. Planning, connections and funding were forthcoming. The long process required patience, but events along the way served to buoy their efforts and funding requirements. More recently, Al-Qaeda wanted to avenge the death of Osama Bin Laden, and North Korea wanted to let the world know they were still a force to be reckoned with following the death of Kim Jong Il. The plan, which by then had been underway for years, was seen as a perfect response.

§

Notification came precisely at 7 p.m. Abe had gotten nine hours of sleep and was in the officer's mess eating supper when the call came. "I'll be up shortly," he said. Ares had already slowed to 12 knots when Abe reached the bridge. In a few minutes the radio transmission came. "Ares . . . pilot intercept in approximately 15 minutes. Please reduce speed to five knots and prepare for transfer on port side." "Ares copy. Fifteen minutes. Five knots. Port side transfer." was Rosie's response.

On the bridge, 40 feet above the deck, the Captain put out his hand. "Welcome aboard the Ares, sir. Captain Abu Sungkar at your service. Please call me Abe."

The pilot, dressed in a starched white shirt, navy blue shorts and Birkenstock sandals, put out his hand with a friendly smile, and in his distinctly French accent, responded, "Thank you Captain. Welcome to North America and Canada. I'm Captain Jean Lapierre. I'll be your pilot and your tour guide until we reach Montreal."

"The ship is yours Captain. Please help yourself to anything you would like." Abe said, as he stepped aside and gestured to the spread of food and tea laid out for his guest.

"I've got to say, I haven't seen a break bulk freighter in these waters in quite a while. She's a beautiful ship. Bring her up to 8 knots, please," he ordered.

The sun was setting, and the lights of Quebec City were beginning to work their magic. "That's magnificent," Abe was looking at the building on the top of the cliffs off the starboard side. It was a stone castle awash in artificial light, its turrets silent sentinels over the river. "It looks like we're still in Europe. What is it?"

"That, *mon ami*, is Le Château Frontenac, one of the most historic hotels in all of Canada. It's overlooking Old Quebec City. And, you're absolutely correct; Quebec is the most European city in North America. Take a good look. It's your last chance to see the charm of the continent. Between here and Montreal we'll be going through a very rural part of Canada. Then, once we reach Montreal, everything changes. The sun will be rising as we approach the city, and you'll have a chance to see our industrial underbelly. Do you have all your paperwork ready for your inspections?" the pilot asked.

"The papers are ready. We expect everything to go smoothly." Abe was nervous and wanted to know as much as he could about the inspections. "In order to schedule my crew, how long a stop should we plan for in Montreal?" Abe knew the warhead was well shielded against radiation detectors. The container in which it was held was originally designed to hold four cruise missiles. Now it held only one ballistic missile. The remaining space was used for shielding. His concern was a physical inspection of the 53-foot container. While the ship manifest indicated the boxes contained spare parts, and they did, they were only two boxes deep before the control room wall in the Klub-K container. If there was a chance their plan would fall apart, Montreal would be the first place it could happen.

"We'll arrive by 0630 hours," Captain Lapierre said. "I would expect you'll have a fresh complement of inspectors. You should be on your way by 1030-1100 hours, assuming no hiccups."

"Hiccups?" Abe asked. He didn't understand.

"I'm sorry . . . assuming no problems. There are several ships behind you. They'll want to get you processed out so they don't get backed up. The Seaway can get busy this time of year."

The next 12 hours went by slowly. The crew was performing to perfection, but the anticipation of the upcoming inspections made sleep difficult for Adam and Rosie. Both drifted in and out of consciousness, worried about what would happen if they were asked to empty the Klub-K container or the container with liquid fuel.

Rosie was thinking about his conversation with Adam and Abe, just a few days earlier. He wasn't totally convinced his friends had been completely honest with him. "Could there really be a bomb that would just destroy electronics? How could that be?" His thoughts kept going back to his walk around Reykjavik and the innocents.

Captain Abe had gotten his sleep, and was with the pilot asking questions about navigation on the Great Lakes. Using his inexperience in North America, Abe had skillfully worked into the conversation questions regarding what to expect in Montreal. All the arrangements had been made by the shipping agent they had hired. In addition to the inspections, the agent had arranged for Ares to take on a fresh shipment of food supplies while in Montreal. "You can load your food stuffs once the inspections are complete. They should be waiting for you on the pier by the time you're ready to depart," the pilot told him.

0500 hours. came with a series of bells over the ships communication system. All hands were ordered to be available as they approached

Montreal. Adam and Rosie were grateful the agonizing night had come to an end. Both said a quiet prayer to Allah, asking his blessing that the morning go well. Adam whispered to himself, "Your will, Allah, is about to be realized. Watch over us, and guide us. Make these infidels blind to your great plan. Let today pass without incident."

On the bridge, the pilot ordered the ship to slow to six knots. He notified La Corporation de Gestion de la Voie Maritime du Saint-Laurent, they were one hour out, and would be available for inspection and resupply as soon as they arrived.

The St. Lawrence Seaway had been built as a bi-national partnership between the U.S. and Canada, and continues to operate as such. Administration of the system is shared by two entities, the Saint Lawrence Seaway Development Corporation in the U.S., a federal agency within the US Department of Transportation, and La Corporation de Gestion de la Voie Maritime du Saint-Laurent, or the St. Lawrence Seaway Management Corporation in Canada. All inspections are joint operations. Ships entering the Seaway don't have to repeat the process in each country. Abe was relieved they would only have to go through the inspection process once.

The sun was still low and orange, and at their back, as Montreal came into view. In the distance, light was reflecting off the windows of the downtown buildings like fire. On shore, they passed pier after pier. Some had ships loading or unloading their cargo. Others were empty, waiting for the next ship to arrive. The pilot, commenting on how remarkably well the ship handled, gently guided Ares into pier 66. Parked just six feet from the edge of the pier was a white passenger van. A group of seven people in various uniforms were standing around engaged in an animated conversation. Abe was surprised they appeared to ignore their approaching ship. As Ares' engines thrust into reverse, dock workers were grabbing lines and securing the ship. The Captain was pleased his young crew wasn't showing their inexperience.

Once on dry land, Abe put out his hand, "Thank you for the lesson on the Great Lakes Captain Lapierre." Hiding his nerves, he smiled and added, "And Captain, thank you for the guided tour. It was a delight."

"My pleasure, Sir. Safe voyage to you."

Abe turned and headed toward the group of men talking. He stood for a moment at what he thought was a respectful distance, surprised not one of them acknowledged his presence. An officer with the Canadian Coast Guard was emphatic about something being "a big deal." Another man jumped in, "Why wouldn't they just seize it in Canada . . . or even wait until they're in Boston? It doesn't make any sense . . . unless something big is going on."

"Excuse me," Abe interrupted and pointed to his right. "I'm Captain Sungkar of the Ares, are you the inspectors for my ship?"

"Me pardonner le Capitaine. Je suis si désolé. I am so sorry for being rude. We were just discussing some news. Let me introduce myself. My name is Walter Bousse. I'm with Canadian Coast Guard, Vessel Traffic Service." Bousse was a no-nonsense officer, overweight and balding. "I will be coordinating your inspections today. Please, let me introduce you . . . Mr. Pelltier and Mr. Dufour are with Customs, Ms. Jeannet and Mr. Andrews are with immigration, Mr. Vigneau is with Transport Canada and will be checking your ballast water. And finally, Mr. Elliot Triot and I will be inspecting your ship for seaworthiness." Each of the inspections officers had portable radios attached to their belts with an earphone in one ear.

Abe was surprised that Mr. Triot looked at least 15 years younger than any of the other inspectors.

"May we board her?" Bousse, asked.

"Of course," Abe replied.

Rosie was assigned to work with the immigration officers, reviewing marine green cards, passports and background on each of the officers and crew. He escorted the Immigration Officers to the mess where the crew was assembled along with all their files and necessary paperwork.

Adam was assigned customs. "Well, I got the easy job," he laughed. "We don't have any cargo. Just spare parts and a 1962 Land Rover." The Customs officers already had the manifest downloaded from the AIS.

"Why the Land Rover?" one of the Customs Agents asked.

"The President of the company we're delivering the ship to, I think he's a collector."

"It must be nice," the other agent quipped.

"I wouldn't know," Adam responded, sarcastically. "Gentlemen, follow me." Adam directed the officers down several ladders toward the cargo hold.

Abe had assigned one of the engineering crew to escort Mr. Vigneau through the ship to the ballast tanks. The officer from Transport Canada was carrying a kit to test the salinity of the water in each.

Abe picked up a microphone and addressed the entire ship over the PA system. "All hands, this is the Captain. We have inspectors aboard for the next several hours and they will require our assistance. You are to provide whatever assistance is requested without hesitation. If you have any questions, provide the requested assistance, and then bring your concerns to me. That is all." This had already been briefed to the crew before arriving in Montreal, but Abe was restating it for the benefit of the inspectors. It worked. The cadre of inspectors, upon hearing the announcement looked at each other as if to wish such were the orders on every ship. Noting the accent-free English of the ship's officers they speculated Middle Eastern but guessed the officers had been raised somewhere in the West.

"Where would you like to start?" Captain Abe was concerned about how nervous he was. He had expected to be calm.

Bousse didn't hesitate. "Why doesn't Mr. Triot begin at the bow? You and I can meet with your chief engineer in the engine room. We'll all start in the bilge and work our way up to the bridge." Another crew member was assigned to escort Triot.

In the forward cargo hold, Adam was holding a ladder for a customs inspector who was climbing on top of the 53-foot container. It was uncomfortably warm in the hold and the lighting was poor, and that's just how he wanted it. He hoped they wouldn't notice the elevator and ask that the containers be brought to the deck where the inspectors would be more comfortable.

"Can you open these two 20-footers for me?"

"You bet," was Adam's response. "Nothing here is locked or sealed." Adam climbed the ladder and opened the container holding the Land Rover. The second customs officer looked up from the floor.

"Wow, she's a beauty. Completely restored! Let's look under the hood." The two men stepped around the straps securing the Land Rover to the interior of the container. Under the hood, the inspector took note of the battery leads, disconnected and secured to the chassis of the vehicle as required. "Looks good, let's look at the other container. They would have to climb down, move the ladder, and climb back up to reach the doors to the other container.

Adam could hear the doors to the 53-foot Klub-K container being opened below him. His heart was pounding. "Hey," he called to the inspector below. "Could you hold the ladder for us?" In the distance he could see a flashlight and hear the sound of footsteps echoing through the cargo hold. He wondered who was coming. Every five or six steps he heard metal on metal.

Adam climbed down the ladder and waited for the other inspector to join him on the floor of the hold. The footsteps were getting closer. The doors to the 53-foot container were open but not secured to the sides. The pallets were full of boxes, wrapped in cling wrap and piled to the top of the container. Each box was labeled in Korean. The folding pallet jack was still in its proper position secured to the inside of the right hand door. "Nothing for resale?"

"Nothing." Adam answered. "They want plenty of spare parts so they wouldn't have to wait for anything from Korea."

The senior customs inspector saw another inspector approaching accompanied by a member of the Ares crew. "Adam, meet Mr. Triot, he's checking your ship for seaworthiness."

Young Triot shook hands and nodded, turning to his two colleagues, "Did you hear the Coast Guard is actually boarding her? They're dead in the water, 50 miles from Boston Harbor. They say there are at least two warships following." He paused. "I told you guys it was a big deal." Triot switched to French. In a firm tone he continued, "*Je vous ai dit que ces chiffon-têtes essayeraient encore neuf onze. Ce temps est par l'eau au lieu de l'air.*"

Embarrassed at Triot's assumption that Adam wouldn't understand French, the customs officer interrupted, "These radios don't pick up a thing down here."

"I heard it as I was coming down," Triot said, "but I lost my signal."

Being Tunisian, Adam understood French. Without changing the expression on his face, he said a silent prayer, "*Allah Akbar. Al-hamdu lil-lahi rabbil 'alamin.*" . . . "Allah is the greatest."

"Mr. Triot, we're done here. You need to finish up your inspection so we can get this ship on its way." He turned to Adam. "As far as I'm concerned, you're all set."

Adam held back a sigh of relief and smiled. "I told you I got the easy job."

"The others will probably be another hour or two. Mr. Dufour and I are going to grab a ride back to the office. Thank you for your cooperation." The three weaved their way up several sets of ladders and gangways to the deck and said their final goodbyes. As he was leaving the ship, the senior customs officer turned around. "I see your supplies are here. You're clear to load them while the others are finishing their inspections."

§

"Captain Sungkar, you have a fine ship here. I'm certifying her for operation on the Great Lakes." While Walter Bousse was completing the seaworthiness certificate, Abe looked toward the deck as Adam was finishing the loading of supplies. Rosie was on the bridge overseeing their refueling.

"And the new pilot? When does he arrive?

"He should be here any minute. The van that dropped off the customs agents was going to swing by and pick him up. You'll be off in 30 minutes."

"Thank you Mr. Bousse. I complement your team on their efficiency." The inspections had been completed in less than three hours.

"Our pleasure. It was a delight to see an old ship in such beautiful shape. And of course, the lack of cargo made the process much easier."

Abe smiled and warmly shook Bousse's hand. Then, worried that the inspector might notice how sweaty he had become, he was all business. "Rosie, prepare for departure. We'll leave as soon as our pilot arrives."

Walking down the steps from the bridge, Abe heard the call on the intercom for all hands to prepare for departure. When he reached the ship's deck he saw the familiar white van pulling onto the pier. The four other inspectors were quite animated as they talked among themselves. One comment was louder than the others. "It's not just the Coast Guard. There are warships."

Bousse interrupted sharply. "Mr. Triot, we don't need to be discussing this here."

"Yes Sir. Sorry Sir."

Abe wasn't sure what they were talking about. But he had his suspicions. Still, the hum of the engines was a welcome sound and he invited the new pilot to join him on the bridge.

Captain Frank Lacoste was a veteran pilot. Abe instructed the helmsman to take orders from Captain Lacoste then gave a short blast of the horn, signaling the dock crew to let go all lines. He turned to the pilot, "The ship is yours, Captain."

Ares' bow moved off the concrete wall of the pier. Abe stepped back and let Captain Lacoste do his job. They had successfully made it through the most dangerous part of their journey. He was anxious to talk with Adam and Rosie once the ship was maneuvered through this part of the Seaway, but he couldn't help but feel relieved.

In minutes, Ares was in the river. The sky was clear, the winds light and, to Abe's surprise, the river was busy. Power boats, sail boats, tour boats, even kayaks and personal watercraft shared the river with the break bulk freighter. They passed La Ronde, a Six Flags amusement park on the eastern tip of Île Ste-Hélène, where Expo 67 had been held. Beneath one of the two arches of the Jacques Cartier Bridge, they entered the shipping channel toward the St. Lambert Lock, the first step in their ascent to Lake Ontario.

In a calm reassuring voice Captain Lacoste issued constant orders as the ship maneuvered into the concrete chamber. Ares came to rest in the lock at 10:10 am, and was tied up 12 minutes later. At 10:30 am, water rushed into the chamber and lifted the ship 18 feet in eight minutes. The gate opened and Ares resumed its journey to the South Shore Canal.

It would take several hours to pass through the length of the canal. Abe informed Captain Lacoste he was leaving the bridge to meet with his senior staff.

In the Captain's stateroom, Adam spoke first. "They're boarding Athena,"

Rosie hadn't heard. "What are you talking about? How do you know that?"

"I heard the talk too. They boarded her in the open ocean." Abe whispered. "It's exactly as we planned. American intelligence is focused on our sister. She'll keep them occupied for a while. The Americans can't focus on more than one thing at a time."

"What if they make the brother-sister connection?" Rosie asked. "They'll track us down."

Adam jumped in. "Rosie is right, Abe."

"Even if they make the connection, it will take them a long time. We stay with our plan. Nothing changes." Abe was adamant in his order. "Our plan is working as we intended," he repeated. "Look how well everything went in Montreal. Keep working toward our goal."

By 3:30 pm, the ship had passed through the Côte-Ste-Catherine Lock, lifting her another 30 feet. Ahead, the river widened and by dinner time, they arrived at the first of the two Beauharnois Locks. Each lock lifted Ares 42 feet to the Beauharnois Canal.

At sunset, Abe was alone in his stateroom. From the porthole he could see the lights of a summer fair as fireworks lit the evening sky. He smiled as he thought about a fireworks display of a different kind, just a few weeks away. The people of Detroit will think our gift to America is just another fireworks display. Abe stared a long while. A feeling of terror then filled him. "What if Adam and Rosie are right? What if the Americans make the connection?"

§

By six a.m., Ares had passed through the two locks on the American side of the Seaway. They had changed pilots again and were approaching the final lock in the St. Lawrence River. The fifth pilot, Captain Edward Tucker, flashed an ear-to-ear grin as he complimented Abe on his ship's condition. Abe soon realized this pilot was a chatterbox. Once he was comfortable with the ship's controls and proportions, he started making small talk. Almost every remark was accompanied by a joke. Abe and Rosie enjoyed his company which provided respite from their doubt and worry. All were relaxed to the point their guest began to share information. "I hadn't seen a break bulk in a decade. Then all of a sudden, on the same day, I hear about one getting raided and I'm piloting another." Abe still smiling replied, "Raided? What for?"

"I don't know. Has to be something important. They boarded her way offshore. I heard there were warships with the Coast Guard. The Navy doesn't care about smuggling, so it's definitely more than that. Rumor is, someone got hurt on the raid." Rosie raised an eyebrow. "We've been listening to American and Canadian radio. Haven't heard a word about it." Ed grinned. "Press blackout. But you can't keep a secret in the Pilot's Union. We have a fully-functional rumor mill."

Abe was curious. "Did they seize the ship? They didn't sink her, did they?"

Ed shook his head. "Helm, come to 188, please. Maintain our current speed." He then looked at Abe, "Last I heard they cut her loose and she sailed in to Boston. No one seized the ship. They off-loaded their cargo from what I understand." The conversation continued, but Abe wasn't listening. His mind was spinning. Could the Americans have seen through their deception so quickly? Ed's words about a crack-down on ships and port security snapped him back to attention. A wave of nausea came over him. For the first time in all the years of this operation, he felt pursued.

Abe excused himself from the bridge. He called Adam and Rosie to his stateroom. "We are in America," he began. "We've passed every test we have faced over the past years. But we must not risk waiting until we reach Detroit." The Captain looked at the two men. "My brothers, soon it will be Laylat al-Qadr, the Night of Power. It is the holiest night of the year . . . the night in which the Qur'an was revealed." Abe took a deep breath. A chill went down Rosie's spine. The Captain continued, "It is said that if a person performs voluntary worship on this day, that worship is equal to a thousand months. My brothers, what better way to worship Allah, than to destroy the Great Satan? We shall prepare now."

He looked at Adam, "Rig something to fail that will require us to stop. Do it quickly. The last port before Lake Ontario is just a few miles ahead. We'll dock there and give the crew leave while we make repairs. We can even send them home. Tell them we'll pick up an American crew. The pilot can disembark. We'll have the ship to ourselves. Go. Move quickly."

They cleared the Iroquois lock on the Canadian side of the river. Ares was 110 miles west of Montreal and 224 feet above the city.

As they moved out of the canal, Ares sailed past the tiny Chimney Island, and under the Ogdensburg-Prescott International Bridge.

Suddenly, the fire alarm sounded. Near the stern, smoke came billowing out of every open vent.

EIGHTEEN

Saturday, August 3rd
13:30 GMT – 8:30 am EDT
Ogdensburg, New York, USA

THE 43-FOOT BAYLINER was an older model. When he'd rented her, Jerry had been assured she was in good operating condition. She had recently been overhauled with twin 400 horsepower inboard engines. A lot of power for a 43-foot vessel. More important, she had an oversized dive platform.

"Why don't you guys take the master stateroom and I'll take the forward cabin." Jerry was making room assignments as he familiarized himself with his surroundings. "Joey, do you want to help me get the gear?"

Jerry and Savannah had each brought their own dive gear. They'd arranged to rent plenty of spare air tanks at the marina. Savannah had also brought her laptop and underwater camera, which she hadn't used since she lived in Indonesia. During her years in the Pacific, she'd become an accomplished underwater photographer and was very proud of her work. She'd brought the laptop to show Joseph and Jerry her hundreds of photographs.

They hadn't yet decided if they were going to spend the night moored at the marina or the island. Jerry had promised to cook a special dinner of pan seared sea scallops and shrimp with garlic and wild rice. Savannah planned her famous Adirondack breakfast. But without Jerry's pick-up, there was no room for groceries.

Once their gear was loaded, Joseph and Savannah were off to do the grocery shopping while Jerry took the boat on a test run with the owner of the marina. He was unfamiliar with the craft and wanted to get a feel for the operation of the boat. A one-hour lesson was included in the rental fee.

"Don't forget the garlic," Jerry yelled as Joseph and Savannah headed out.

Joseph gave a dismissive wave.

"And plenty of fruit," Jerry added.

Jerry finished stowing the dive gear on the aft deck. After throwing his bag in the forward cabin he headed to the marina office to find the owner.

"When you called, I thought I recognized your name. And you look familiar. I'm sure we met somewhere." The marina owner, Matt Russell, was an affable man with an enormous belly and crooked nose that clearly had once been broken and never properly repaired.

"I rented a runabout here last week," Jerry responded.

"That's it! Sorry I didn't remember," Matt said. "Let's take this baby out, shall we? You're gonna love her. She handles beautifully."

On the dock, Matt stood for a second admiring the boat. "If you like her, she's for sale. Less than a hundred grand and she's yours."

"I'll keep that in mind," Jerry responded, rolling his eyes.

Before leaving the marina, they spent 20 minutes going over the necessary mechanical and electrical operations, followed by a quick run through the galley equipment. They spent most of their time on the flybridge with the radar and GPS. Jerry was thrilled the boat was equipped with the marine Garmin. It not only had river charts, it also featured both depth and forward sonar. "Perfect," he said to himself.

"Run the blower for five minutes then start her up. I'll go down and grab the lines and fenders. Easy on the throttles, she's over-powered."

"Aye, Aye skipper."

With the lines free and the marina owner safely onboard, Jerry confidently put the engines in reverse. Matt waited until the boat cleared the slip before bringing in the fenders.

They glided out of the marina into the open river. "You handle her like a pro," Matt commented.

"I've had a little experience. I'm with the volunteer fire department in Cranberry Lake. We have a 30-foot fireboat." Jerry headed east and slowly pushed the throttles forward. They passed the town marina in front of the Ogdensburg Recreational Center. Another mile and they passed the empty pier of the Port of Ogdensburg. Ahead they could see the bridge to Canada.

"Open her up," Matt suggested. He held on to a rail.

Jerry pushed the throttle all the way down. The boat jerked forward with surprising force. "Wow!" Jerry gasped.

"I just wanted you to see what she could do. I wouldn't run her this hard too long … unless you're independently wealthy. She eats a lot of gas at this speed."

Under the bridge they passed an old freighter off their port side. "She's heading to Lake Ontario," Matt advised.

"Let's circle Chimney Island and we'll head back. That all right with you?"

"I'm fine with that. Looks like you're comfortable with the boat. Let me call ahead and make sure your air tanks are on the dock." Matt reached into his pocket for his cell phone.

Just under the Ogdensburg Bridge, Jerry noticed the freighter they had passed earlier seemed to be dead in the water in the shipping channel. As they got closer, he steered the boat to port to get a better look. There was dark smoke coming from her vents. Huge doors, to what must have been a forward cargo hold, started to open. Smoke billowed out of the hold and he could see the crew running in all directions on deck. Over the din of his engines he heard an alarm signaling a fire on board. Suddenly, something started to appear from the cargo hold. Two small white shipping containers on top of a larger blue container were rising through the smoke. Jerry slowed his boat and watched.

Matt had finished his phone call and joined him in watching the unusual event. "Ya don't see that very often. He had better get that heap out of the shipping channel or he'll be in big trouble." He reached over Jerry's shoulder and switched channels on the VHF radio. Jerry and Matt listened.

". . . . is the freighter Ares, reporting mechanical problems. We just passed the Ogdensburg-Prescott Bridge. Bilge fire onboard and under control."

"Copy, Ares . . . Coast Guard will be notified. Do you have power or do you need tugs?"

"It appears one drive shaft is down. We still have power in the other. We should be able to hobble to the nearest port."

Jerry and Matt looked at each other and listened to the instructions being given to the freighter. Jerry was curious about the name of the freighter. "Ares . . . the Greek god of war. That's an unusual name for a freighter." He dismissed the thought.

"Doesn't sound too serious," Matt commented. "It sure could have been a lot worse if they blocked the channel. I've seen 30 ships backed up before. It would have been a nightmare for the Seaway. " he said.

Jerry asked Matt if he would take the helm. "Are there any binoculars onboard?"

"Of course. In the storage space under those seats. Why?" He pointed to a bench seat behind him.

Jerry didn't answer. He'd lifted the seat and was searching through a pile of rolled charts, flares, a flare gun, and a dive flag. Frustrated, he called back, "They're not here."

Matt put the boat in neutral and walked back two steps. "Let me look."

Off their starboard side they were still 100 yards from the freighter. Matt found the binoculars and handed them to Jerry as he heard the remaining engine of the freighter come to life. The ship began to move toward them as it sounded its horn in warning. Taking the helm, Matt maneuvered the boat away from the massive freighter.

"Hold on, go slow." Jerry requested. "I want to look at something." He had noticed a strange logo painted on the largest of the three containers. "I've seen better glasses," he said as he held the binoculars to his eyes and examined the container.

"Binoculars have a nasty habit of disappearing from rental boats. That's why I only buy cheap ones."

"I understand." Jerry focused the glasses on the image of a coiled cobra in a striking pose. He realized it wasn't a logo, just a painting. But it reminded him of the DHS Center for Domestic Preparedness school in Anniston, Alabama, where the C.O.B.R.A. (Chemical, Ordnance, Biological, Radiological) live-agent training facility is located. He had been there several years ago for training and had a polo shirt with the school's logo, almost identical to this cobra image. Again, he thought of the name of the ship. *Just a coincidence*, he tried to convince himself. He wondered what the cobra meant? The sacred animal of the Greek god of war, he remembered. The combination of the name and the painting nagged at him.

"All set?" Matt asked. "You guys probably want to get your weekend started."

"Aye, Aye."

At the marina, Jerry was not at all surprised Savannah and Joseph hadn't yet returned from their shopping. Besides groceries, they needed to stop for plenty of ice. Jerry shook his head thinking of the predicament his friend got himself in with Lu and Savannah. It worried him and he hoped he would have some private time with Joseph so they could talk about it.

Dock hands loaded the spare air tanks and secured them with bungee cords as Jerry relaxed on the aft deck. He pulled out his cell phone.

The automated telephone system at DHS is a maze of menus and submenus. Thanks to his experience in navigating such systems, Jerry had known enough to make notes and save them in his phone. After a few minutes of button-pressing, he was connected to the extension of Lillian LaForte. He expected her voice mail but was delighted to hear Lillian's New Orleans accent singing back to him, live and in person.

"Jerry! Two calls in one week. I'm starting to think y'all are smitten with me. That Will of yours had best be careful!"

"Oh, darlin' you know you're the only woman in my heart."

"The last time I fell for charm like that, I found myself married with four kids. But you're not here to propose. What'cha got a need for?"

"Some information, Lil. There's a cargo ship in the St. Lawrence Seaway, looks like she's had an on-board fire. The name is 'Ares.' I can't tell what flag she is sailing under, but she would have cleared Montreal either yesterday or the day before. Can you get me her background and cargo?"

"Worried about zebra mussels, baby?"

"Not at all. With a little garlic butter, they're delish."

"Bring some down and we'll toss them in with the crawfish boil."

"You're on."

"What's got ya fussing 'bout a boat, baby?"

"While the smoke was pouring out of the vents, she hoisted a few intermodal containers out of her hold onto the foredeck. The largest was all blue with a coiled cobra painted on it."

"Jerry, those boats have gajillions of containers on them."

"Not these ships. This one is old, World War Two style, with the cranes on it. Besides, no reason to pull the container out of the hold unless the fire was pretty bad. And it looked like it came up on an elevator."

"Like on an aircraft carrier? Break bulk freight ships don't have elevators. That's what the cranes are for." Lillian was clearly puzzled.

"That's what I thought. There's something weird with this ship. It may be nothing, but all of that smoke was definitely significant. It looks like they're pulling up at the Port of Ogdensburg."

"Whose-in-burg?"

"Og-dens-burg. It's a small port on the Seaway. It's just northeast of Lake Ontario."

"And they used to get confused with Thibodaux."

"At least it's not in Gananoque or Oswegatchie."

"True that. I'll call you when I have something baby."

Conversations with Jerry, she'd discovered, often provided as much information as she gave back. He'd never called with any request like this before. And knowing him as she did, he wouldn't have asked for this information just out of curiosity. She also knew that every incident on the Seaway was considered a reportable incident. It wouldn't be difficult to get what Jerry needed.

NINETEEN

Saturday, August 3rd

13:45 GMT – 8:45 am EDT

St. Lawrence River, New York, USA

"Looks like we've burned out some bearings on one drive shaft," Adam said over the intercom. "The sparks set a fire in some bilge oil. The hold is full of smoke." Captain Abe's reply was quick, "Can you get it under control?"

"The crew are knocking it down now, but it's becoming very hot down here. I think we should...protect the...cargo."

"I'll send Rosie down to help you retract the hatch. We can lift the platform into the open air." Smoke billowed out into the summer air, briefly obscuring the pilot's vision. The pilot ordered the remaining engines to stop. It only took a minute to see again and for Adam to advise that the starboard drive shaft was out of order. As smoke billowed out of the open hatch, the intermodal containers floated into view, two white small ones mounted atop a larger light blue one.

The pilot whistled as he saw the elevator lift the cargo. An elevator was a surprise on such a vintage ship. Abe remarked on the improvements, citing the purchaser's specifications, adding, "I'll be sorry to give her up. I've grown to love this ship. At least until now." Captain Tucker advised that any shipboard incident is treated as a marine casualty and would have to be reported to the Seaway Authority and the Coast Guard. The fire was out now, but the considerable smoke produced by burning oil was still venting from the massive hold. The Seaway Authority ordered Ares out of the shipping channel, directing the ship to the nearby Port of Ogdensburg. A radio call to the port directed them to berth on the west side of their pier.

Captain Abe made profuse apologies to Captain Tucker for the disruption of his schedule, assuring him they would make immediate arrangements for his return. "Hey, you sailed half-way around the world. Something's going to break. It's no big deal. Just give us a call and let us know when you're ready to get underway again. We'll send someone out," Tucker said with a smile, shaking Abe's hand vigorously. "I hope it will be me. I'd love to come back and pilot her. She's a beauty." The bridge staff made small talk with Captain Tucker until a taxi arrived to pick him up. Once he was gone, Abe called Rosie and Adam to his office.

"We need to give the crew shore leave. They have to be gone so we can begin our mission."

The grimace on Adam's face betrayed discomfort. "The engineers have started to disassemble the damaged drive train. They expect to make the necessary repairs and get us underway. If we offer leave, they probably won't take it. They want to finish the job and get home."

"And where would they go?" Rosie asked. "We're in this little city in America. Most of these men don't speak any English."

Abe sat ruminating for a moment. "Then we'll have to send them home now. We can say that we will require another inspection and it will take too long to keep the crew on, so we'll have to bring on an American crew when we're ready to sail."

"I'll contact the shipping agent," Rosie offered. "I don't know how long it will take to change their travel arrangements, or even where the nearest airport is. This may take longer than we want."

"Call right away." Abe ordered. He turned to Adam and instructed him to get the crew packed and ready to disembark the ship and travel home. "We have to get them off of this ship before we off-load the Land Rover or handle the fuel. I will tell the Port authorities that we're waiting for parts, and repairs will be delayed."

§

The crewmembers disassembling the drive shaft looked at each other in disbelief. Never before had they been ordered to stop working, let alone leave a ship with such a job unfinished. It made no sense to any of them. Some were frustrated, wanting to finish the repairs and make the delivery. Others were elated to learn they would be going home early, with no reduction in pay. They put their tools away, showered, changed and began packing their belongings.

While the crew were occupied, Rosie advised that it would take some time to re-book airfare and arrange for transportation to an airport. They would be delayed in their plans.

"Tomorrow is Laylat al-Qadr. We will deliver our blow then," Rosie reported. "The crew will be on their way home. The port will be quiet. On a Sunday, there may be no one here. That will make it easier to move the ship into the channel and launch."

Adam looked puzzled. "Why move the ship? We can launch it right from here. We'll just need to turn the container around."

"That would be dangerous. We would have to fuel first, then move the container. The fuel tank is not placed to fuel the missile after turning it around. The fueled missile is very unstable, and it will have to be lifted by the crane, rotated 180 degrees and remounted." Rosie was shaking his head which telegraphed his discomfort.

"True," was Abe's response. "Plus, I intend to scuttle the ship in the channel. The Seaway is a huge gravity-fed system. It can be navigated easily without computers or electricity. Ships from all over the Great Lakes and around the world could use it to deliver supplies and assistance after the impact. Sinking the ship in the channel would slow them down substantially."

Adam smiled. "Perfect." Rosie sat still and quiet.

"We can pull the propeller shaft and allow the bilge to flood." He asked Adam to calculate how long it would take for the water level to flood the engines and stall the Ares. Abe went on. "Once the ship is anchored in the channel we won't need the engines. We will launch the missile on a 195-degree course. It will detonate somewhere between New York City and Washington, DC. Both cities will be impacted by the EMP effects. The power failures should cascade through the remainder of the east, south, and into the mid-west. It may even extend through the rest of the country. I can't be sure. In any case, it will still be catastrophic. Thousands of government computers will be destroyed in Washington, DC, at the Pentagon and the CIA. The financial centers in New York will be wiped out. The beast will be beheaded. It will be a clear and decisive victory. We'll use the Zodiac to get to shore and escape in the Land Rover. The ship will be left to sink perpendicular to the channel. Obviously we must move as quickly as possible. There is no telling how long it will be before they track us down."

Abe was unsure about this new plan at first, but the calculations he made for the new target area gave him some comfort. His primary concern was getting caught before they could launch the missile. He wished they weren't required to report the mechanical failure. Better they stayed out of sight. "It is a weekend for the Americans," he thought, "Perhaps they will not be working until Monday. By then it will be too late."

He went ashore to find a representative of the Ogdensburg Bridge and Port Authority to give his cover story. They had a minor failure of a drive shaft bearing. Some sparks ignited a small amount of bilge oil. It was extinguished almost immediately. No damage. They will have to wait for spare parts which could take several days.

Later, Abe learned that this was the off-season for the Port of Ogdensburg. Freight ships arrived periodically to deliver components for a large wind power farm in northern New York, but they operated almost exclusively during the week and used the east berth. They would not be a factor while Ares waited to complete her repairs. Abe cemented the good will by asking the port representative if he could recommend marine mechanics in the area, promising a premium on wages for moving Ares to the head of the line. Everyone at the port was friendly and understanding of their alleged predicament. They also added that, while the port is a 24/7 operation, they would be on minimal staffing on Sunday.

Meanwhile, in his office, Abe began to make plans. He needed to rework the timing to fuel and position the ship. He needed to re-calculate the precise trajectory for the missile. And, he needed to map a new escape route. "The missile will be heading south," he thought. "We shall take advantage of the confusion and head for the Canadian Maritime provinces. We should have no problem gaining passage home, especially with a reconditioned Land Rover to use as a bribe." His confidence was growing.

TWENTY

Saturday, August 3rd

15:15 GMT – 10:15 am EDT

St. Lawrence River, New York, USA

SAVANNAH WAS in the galley stowing groceries. Joseph was on the flybridge with Jerry asking if he could pilot the boat. "Sure, buddy." Jerry stepped aside. Joseph took the wheel and pushed the throttle all the way down. To keep his balance, Jerry grabbed the back of Joseph's seat. He heard a thump below.

Savannah had fallen back and knocked a pan and some groceries off the counter. "I'm fine," she yelled to the empty air.

"Sorry," was the response from above. Joseph pulled back on the throttle. "She's got a kick, doesn't she?"

Jerry started chuckling. "Are you talking about the boat? Or Savannah? Or Lucia?"

"Shut up, baldy."

"Sorry. Do you want to talk? You seemed a little confused when you called the other night."

"You were right. I'm just going to let things play out. Whatever is meant to happen, will happen."

"*Amor fati*, buddy."

"Shut up!"

As they passed the Port of Ogdensburg Jerry pointed to the freighter now docked at the pier. He told Joseph about the strange events he'd seen earlier. Docked behind the freighter was a U.S. Coast Guard boat checking on its condition and completing an incident report.

Ten minutes later the Bayliner was rounding Chimney Island. On Jerry's instructions, Joseph positioned the boat about 20 feet off the middle of the island on the Canadian side. His research indicated this was directly over the portion of the island that had been removed during construction of the Seaway. Jerry dropped anchor and waited a few minutes to make sure it held. Charts indicated the current was only one knot in this part of the river. But, he was still a little concerned about the venturi effect increasing the current as the river rounded Chimney Point and flowed around Chimney Island. Under such conditions the current could double, which was a concern when diving.

While Savannah and Jerry were preparing their diving gear, Jerry had asked Joseph to hang an oversized diving flag from the flybridge, facing the river. Because they were so close to the shipping channel, he thought the traditional buoy flag wasn't enough. "Let's make sure people know what we're doing here," he told everyone. "The flag is under the seat on the flybridge," he told Joseph.

"Better safe than sorry," Savannah agreed.

Looking at the silver metal case holding Savannah's underwater camera housing, Jerry commented, "The camera was a great idea. This is still state property. If we find the marker, we can't bring it up. It belongs to the State of New York."

Savannah was bothered by Jerry's comment. "Nobody would ever know."

Joseph jumped in the conversation. "Jerry would know. Remember, he was a cop and he plays by the rules."

"I was a trooper. Anyway, it's not the marker we're really looking for. It's what's on the marker. If we find it, you can take pictures and that's all we really need."

"You're right. It would just be nice to have it as part of my father's legacy."

"First, let's see if we can find it. You realize it's still a long shot."

Reluctantly, Savannah agreed.

Jerry gave Joseph a short lesson on being a spotter for the divers. Because of the mild current both Jerry and Savannah were tethered to lines clipped to their buoyancy compensators. "We'll swim out 100 feet or so and work our way back upstream. As we make our way back, bring the line in slowly so there's not too much slack."

"Got it." Joseph was glad to help. He worried that he might be sitting around doing nothing on this trip.

Jerry and Savannah slowly made their way upstream. Swimming ten feet apart they carefully examined any anomaly they saw on the river bottom. As they brushed silt away from the rocks, it drifted downstream, behind them.

After 40 minutes, Jerry helped Savannah onto the platform

"Find anything?" Joseph asked.

"Nothing," was Jerry's flat response.

"Nothing *yet*!" Savannah quickly added.

The three had sandwiches and macaroni salad for lunch while they discussed further plans.

"One more dive today," Jerry said, "and we will have covered about half of the 'former' Chimney Island. If we don't find anything, we can come back in the morning."

"Are we going to stay here tonight?" Joseph asked.

Jerry's cell phone rang before he had a chance to answer. Looking at the phone he excused himself. "Business," was his only comment as he walked to the forward cabin and closed the door.

Savannah was puzzled. "I thought he was retired."

"He is. He does do some consulting work for the government."

§

"Hey Lil, thanks for calling back." Jerry was fishing around in his luggage for a notebook and pencil, something he'd carried throughout his career and never broke the habit of having handy.

"I'd never forget you, baby." Lillian was smiling, as she always was, while she looked over the records on Ares. "I looked at the AIS data on your ship. She's flagged in Isle of Man, owned now by a holding company with an address in the Cayman Islands. Nothing unusual there. She sailed from Reykjavik on July 28th, and cleared inspections in Montreal on the first of this month. No problems there. She's carrying no commercial cargo, just a few containers of spare parts, and one motor vehicle. Hmmm . . . a car . . . an old Land Rover. The ship and everything in it are scheduled for delivery to a purchaser in Michigan. I guess they're gonna make her a laker."

"Nothing odd there I guess. Who are the crew? Did they all get through Customs?" Jerry was jotting notes as Lillian was going through the data she'd collected.

"They sure did. No documentation problems. Invoices for everything they were carrying. Basically just Korean engines and parts, and all accounted for. Makes sense they have a lot of parts with them. Lemme look at the crew. Not a lot of them, only a handful. No problems there. No background problems, no warrants, no watch-listed. All of the passports were good, everyone had return passage.

"Nothing? On *any* of them?" was Jerry's question, more rhetorical in nature. Lillian knew what he meant. She'd dealt with sailors for most of her adult life and never knew of a ship whose crew consisted of men whose only offense was singing too loudly in the church choir. This bothered Lillian now that Jerry mentioned it, as did the cobra logo.

"I see what'cha mean. I'm gonna look some more at these boys and let you know what's up with them."

"Anything on the smoke?"

"Not yet, that info isn't in the system yet. It'll take a couple of calls to get the story on that. I'll holler at'cha tonight or tomorrow, baby."

"Sorry about the interruption," Jerry said back on deck. "To answer your earlier question Joey, I don't think we should spend the night here. Too close to the shipping channel. Besides, marinas can be lively places at night. Lots of pleasure boats traveling up and down the river dock there. Usually lots of partying going on. It might be fun."

After talking to Lillian, Jerry had another reason for wanting to return to the marina. His old trooper instincts, along with what he had just heard, had raised his interest enough that he wanted another look at the freighter docked at the Port of Ogdensburg.

§

After the second dive produced nothing, Savannah seemed down. It was late afternoon and they agreed to head to the marina, relax for the rest of the afternoon, and have an enjoyable evening on the boat. Freighter traffic on the river seemed light, but because it was beautiful weather, there were a great many pleasure boats on the water. Jerry took the helm as they headed back, the binoculars hanging from the side of his seat.

Joseph and Savannah were on the main deck enjoying a soda. "Joseph," Jerry called down from the flybridge. "Come up and give me a hand for a second."

"What do ya need?"

"Do me a favor and take the wheel for a minute. I want to get a better look at that freighter I showed you earlier. Pull up close to the pier. Take her real slow, buddy. I want a good look." From the edge of the port side of the Bayliner, Jerry had a good view of the pier through the binoculars. The Coast Guard boat was gone. Getting closer, he could see something on the pier itself that hadn't been there earlier. "Real slow buddy," he cautioned Joseph.

It was one of the two smaller containers he had seen rising out of the smoke sitting on the pier with its doors open. The large crane nearer the front of the ship was rotating its arm over the side of the ship with the second of the small containers swinging below. Jerry and Joseph watched as it was gently lowered to the pier. The Bayliner had now come to a complete stop. The large light blue container remained on the deck of the ship. The painting of the cobra faced the pier, so they couldn't see it.

Jerry looked closer at what appeared to be cargo lined up behind one of the containers. "Joey, slowly pull around to the front of the ship. Let's get a look from the other side."

"The name's Joseph, you bonehead. What are you looking for, anyway?"

"Just do it." Jerry's tone was uncharacteristically curt.

As they were passing the length of the ship, Jerry focused his binoculars on the bridge almost 60 feet above. He could see two people in the wheelhouse. One had binoculars and was looking back at him.

Pulling around the bow of the ship, he didn't need the binoculars to see that what he'd thought was cargo was actually a line of luggage, apparently waiting to be picked up.

Out of the container with the open doors came rolling an old Land Rover with a man behind the wheel. For a split second, Jerry thought it strange there was no sound of a motor coming from the vehicle. As the vehicle cleared the container, he saw two men pushing from the rear. The Land Rover came to a stop just a few feet from the container.

The arm of the crane was again rotating across the side of the ship with a wooden pallet. Jerry could see a load of additional luggage being lowered to the pier.

"Okay, I've seen enough. Let's head back to the marina. Jerry took control of the Bayliner and slowly headed upstream. With a quick glance back, he could see someone on the bridge of the ship, still watching them with binoculars.

Tied up at the marina, the three began to talk about the afternoon dive. Joseph asked a flurry of questions about what they had seen at the bottom of the river. Savannah tried her best to describe the underwater scene.

Jerry, however, was unusually quiet and seemed distracted. Savannah noticed he kept looking at his watch. She finally asked, "Jerry, is there anything wrong?"

"No. Not really. But that call I got earlier means I have to take a quick ride back home to take care of a few things." He chose his words carefully to avoid upsetting his friends. "I guess you guys are going to have to have dinner alone." He looked at his watch again. "I should be back by nine. Plenty of time to party." He looked at Savannah. "Sorry to leave you with the cooking tonight. I was planning on fixing you guys a nice dinner." He thought for a second. "One piece of advice. Don't let Joseph anywhere near the galley."

Jerry got up and went into his cabin to gather the notes he had taken on his call with Lillian.

"Well, that's odd," Savannah said. "Why's he leaving?"

Joseph shrugged his shoulders. "That's Jerry."

As he walked down the dock, Jerry turned and called out, "I'll be back in four hours. Stay out of trouble you two."

Behind his lighthearted tone, Savannah thought she sensed seriousness in Jerry she had never seen before.

TWENTY-ONE

Sunday, August 4th
15:45 GMT – 10:45 am EDT
St. Lawrence River, New York, USA

LILLIAN WENT INTO WORK Sunday morning. The quiet in the office gave her the opportunity to focus on Jerry's problem. She searched for shipping companies, shippers, suppliers, or parts manufacturers that used a cobra as a logo. She found none that would fit the circumstances described by Jerry. More disturbingly, she couldn't get any history on Ares prior to Iceland. She knew the ship wasn't built there, so it had to come from somewhere, but there was no indication that Ares or the ship's owners had existed before Reykjavik. She looked for records on the seller, but found nothing.

Probing sources in Iceland was out of her bailiwick. But the more puzzling this ship seemed, the more suspicious Lillian became. The calls she made to the Seaway Development Corporation and the US Coast Guard about the smoke gave only the basics: small on-board fire started by a burned-out bearing, ordered out of the channel, moored in Ogdensburg. Lillian, never satisfied with the amount of information she possessed, made a call to the Port of Ogdensburg. A talk with personnel there told a story of a very friendly group of officers who'd discharged their international crew and were waiting for parts to be delivered before repairs could be made. Once good-to-go, they planned to hire a US crew to make their delivery.

Lillian felt something was wrong. The discharge of the crew stuck in her head as soon as she heard it. This ship is old enough that no one would have any experience with it or her Korean components, yet they discharged the crew. They'll have to retain an entire crew for a few days' voyage. *Maybe they'll just ship over the crew that'll work on her in Detroit*, she thought. But it still seemed odd. The lack of history was especially troubling. Then another thing began nagging at her. The only cargo they're carrying is spare parts. Why would they need to wait for parts? They were dealing with a failure of drive train components. If they aren't carrying spare bearings and drive shafts, exactly what spare parts are they carrying? One would think they'd have spares simply for the trans-Atlantic crossing.

She decided to collect everything she had and pass it on up the line. Since most of this information was international in nature and dealt with the merchant marine, her access to some data was limited. Knowing they would have the necessary access to fill in the gaps, she addressed her memo to the Pentagon, Office of Naval Intelligence.

§

Abe, Adam and Rosie stood in the cavernous cargo hold of Ares, their voices echoing as they went over the process of fueling and preparing the missile for launch. Frequently they had to clear their throats due to the residue of smoke that still pervaded the space. The singular container that was not mounted on the elevator platform held the requisite load of spare parts, two pallets deep, behind which were secreted two pressurized storage tanks. One held liquid oxygen, *LOX*, and the other held RP-1. *Rocket*

Propellant 1 or *Refined Petroleum 1* is a highly refined version of kerosene, similar to jet fuel. Combined with a suitable oxidizer it produces a tremendous amount of thrust. It is much more stable at room temperature than other liquid fuels such as liquid hydrogen, making it much more practical for use when transported long distances.

The danger of carrying both the fuel and the oxidizer tanks in the same shipping container could not be overstated, but was necessary to maintain their subterfuge. The doors of the intermodal container were opened, and the pallets of parts had been removed, still, no odor of kerosene was detectable. They'd accomplished this by filling the open spaces surrounding the fuel and oxygen tanks with foam blocks impregnated with activated charcoal. The adsorbent property of the carbon traps any fuel vapors, making it undetectable from the outside.

The fueling process they were about to begin was sensitive and dangerous. Despite their desire to launch quickly, it couldn't be rushed. Loading both chemicals simultaneously could result in an explosion that would destroy all the years of effort and millions of dollars invested. Adam had removed the fueling and launch instruction manual from the control room of the Klub-K missile container. While all three men had studied and practiced the process numerous times, they would review it again and use the checklist supplied in the appendix. Adam had brought a box of spark-free tools from the engine room.

They began carefully removing the foam blocks surrounding the two tanks. If there were a leak in one of the containers, they might not know about it until now. If there were leaks in both, they would have known already. The combination would have been disastrous.

"This is delicate," Abe reminded his colleagues. "We do not have the same equipment soldiers would use on the battlefield, so we must be careful. This is not a race." Adam and Rosie nodded their agreement and continued removing the foam until they could access the fueling hoses and valve assemblies.

The Klub-K container, already relieved of the two containers that piggy-backed on it, had been lowered into the hold and rested adjacent to the container holding the missile's fuel. The gauges and labels were all printed in Korean. They had practiced all the steps in the open Atlantic, and they had translations available, but with each step, it would take time to be certain they had everything correct before proceeding to the next. Once the missile was fueled, they had only to move the ship so the port side was facing south. Anchored and pointed in the desired direction, the missile could be launched in a matter of minutes.

Their escape plans had been reworked. The ship's damaged drive shaft would be removed, allowing her to flood slowly, eventually bottoming out on the riverbed thereby blocking one of the primary routes for the transportation and delivery of relief supplies. They would abandon Ares while it was still anchored in the channel.

With a motor old enough to be unaffected by the Electromagnetic Pulse, the inflatable Zodiac boat would be deployed and tied to the port side ladder and used to get back to the Port of Ogdensburg. The Land Rover had been off-loaded and the luggage, documents and cash already had been loaded. The vehicle was fueled, and extra barrels of diesel fuel were loaded. The Land Rover would be used to escape, driving directly into the disaster area. The disabled computers, communications, and infrastructure, combined with their flawless documents, would allow them to pass through rural areas in northern New York and Vermont, easily cross the border into Canada, and eventually to Montreal where they could book a flight out of the country.

If aviation was crippled, they'd drive to the shipping ports in the Maritimes. From there it wouldn't be difficult for men of their experience to gain passage to Europe or Asia. Then, it would be on to Saudi Arabia and the hero's welcome of the adoring throngs.

§

After two days of heavy surveillance on Athena in the Port of Boston, many of the organizations in Mickey Evans' task force had withdrawn their personnel for more weighty matters. Every member of the crew was watched intently. Communication of any kind was recorded and analyzed by cryptologists and experts. Their replacement cargo had been stalled to the point where the ship's officers and their agents were growing frustrated and even angry.

The crew explored Boston, but were anxious to get underway and stayed close to the ship in the event their cargo arrived. The Port of Boston authorities were tiring of a ship occupying a valuable berth and doing nothing. The two Maritime Safety and Security Teams (MSST's) and the Hostage Rescue Team (HRT) were taking 12-hour shifts, fully ready to engage any adversary. Nothing was unusual. They hadn't even seen anything that would suggest a perpetrator scoping out the ship, possibly making plans to recover the source surreptitiously. The federal agents were getting impatient, too.

FBI was still eager to watch the ship and discover the identity of the perpetrators, but this could not go on forever. Plans were being made to pick up and interrogate every member of the crew and their stateside shipping agents. Nevertheless, there was still a radiation source aboard that ship, and it would have to be watched until it was secured by US personnel.

As Mickey sat at the table reviewing updates, his mind drifted to the email he'd received from his superiors the prior Friday afternoon. It acknowledged the radiation source was a significant cause for concern, and that the actions taken to date were prudent. His bosses also advised that inasmuch as the absence of explosives was verified by the OD Teams aboard the Stratton, and the source was in a US port under the watchful eye of the FBI, Department of Homeland Security, and Department of Energy personnel, the task force would be disbanded as of Monday, August 5. The communications links, along with the attendant bank of monitors and live connections, had been removed earlier that morning. His assistant had been given other duties. Mickey's superiors were quick to tell him they were not unhappy, but the tone of the message telegraphed disappointment. Mickey was equally disappointed. He sat puzzling over this case, wondering what could have been missed. He reviewed Athena's operation at every port prior to Boston, but found nothing out of the ordinary. He wondered how long this source had been aboard. Had it been abandoned by the perpetrator? Or was it set to be collected at a future port?

There were so many questions, and now it appeared he'd likely never have the resources to discover the answers. He could hear the second-guessing starting already: shouldn't have boarded the ship, shouldn't have allowed it into US territorial waters, should have raided her in Halifax… He focused on the positives. The cesium would never get into the wrong hands. The crew were all going to be thoroughly debriefed. Nothing bad had happened to anyone. The only casualty was an allergic reaction by a DOE member, who was now doing fine.

Elsewhere in ONI, an analyst received an email loaded with attachments. It came from DHS, Office of Infrastructure Protection, and regarded a break bulk freighter involved in a maritime incident on the St. Lawrence Seaway. She wondered why it had come to her until she read the entire message from Lillian LaForte. In examining the ship's history, she had run into trouble pulling anything prior to its time in Iceland. It had left Reykjavik on July 28. Before that, its history was blank. *Should be simple enough*, the analyst thought, *just some checks with our sources in Iceland*.

Figuring it would take only a few minutes to look into this and enter it into the database, she was surprised to see an intelligence entry regarding the ship while it was berthed in Reykjavik. That entry was made by an intelligence officer who was working on a different case, that of Athena, which was listed as open. She decided to pass it along to someone working on the Athena case as she continued investigating the history of Ares.

That afternoon, it landed on the desk of Mickey Evans's assistant. He initially dismissed it as unrelated to the task force, but since he'd been pulled from exclusive duty to the task force, he looked further. It was the intelligence insert by the officer in Reykjavik that got him to look harder at it, particularly at the photograph of a ship almost identical to Athena, the name "Ares" visible on the stern. His attention was further grasped by the remark about them going to America and never coming back.

He decided to probe a little more into the history of the Ares. He didn't get far initially, except to discover it had been in Iceland for a week, with no prior AIS entries. The real "propeller heads" as he called them, the people who do the most intense data mining, wouldn't be in the office until the next day, so he reviewed what he did know. Sale to a holding company, shipped essentially empty to the US, cleared Montreal a few days ago . . . the same day Athena was boarded. He decided to hold onto the case and look into it further the next day. Right now he had a task force meeting.

The number of participants at the task force table had dwindled. The remaining agencies were all domestic: DHS, Energy, FBI. The analyst knew it wouldn't include Naval Intelligence as of tomorrow. They went around the table, contributing what they knew. FBI was still watching everything and ready to pick up the entire crew when ordered to do so. Energy and DHS weren't taking their eyes off of the cesium. All the tools they needed to recover it were assembled in a plain van, waiting for the green light. Their superiors were growing weary of the travel costs and didn't want to wait much longer. FBI was still committed to solving the case, and made several mentions of taking the lead on the case now that it was domestic in nature. The rest had nothing to report.

Letting out a long sigh, Mickey Evans leaned back in his chair. He was frustrated. "Anything more to add from anyone?" His question was met with blank stares and shaking heads. Then his assistant piped up, "I have another case that may be tangential to this one. There's a connection in Reykjavik." The other representatives, all engaged in domestic operations, were clearly uninterested in sitting through a briefing. Mickey dismissed the group then turned to his assistant.

"Sorry Gary. They don't want to hear it. What do you have?"

His assistant briefed him on what he knew and how the information came to him. After 15 minutes, Mickey looked at the clock and said the rest would have to wait until tomorrow.

His day was over and he had a final dress rehearsal for a Taiko show the following evening. He couldn't recall a time when he felt better to end his workday. He changed out of his uniform and headed to the rehearsal. This was going to be a big show. He was thrilled to have been selected to perform before such an august audience and he wanted it to be perfect.

Moreover, he needed the distraction from the trouble at work.

He arrived as the rest were warming up and fell in with the group without a word having been spoken. His focus on what he was doing pushed the problems and distractions out of his mind. The transcendent nature of the intense physical activity combined with the thunderous rhythm transported his consciousness away from his worries of the day. He was in a different place, just him and those around him. The rhythmic roar of the drums resounded throughout the rehearsal building. The sweat running from his brow and the shouts of his colleagues drove out the last remnants of the day's vexations.

TWENTY-TWO

Sunday, August 4th
12:45 GMT – 7:45 am EDT
St. Lawrence River, New York, USA

SAVANNAH WAS the first to wake. It didn't take long for the smell of coffee and sizzling bacon to wake Joseph and Jerry. There was little movement around the marina docks at this early hour. The breakfast conversation focused on the plan for the day's dives.

"When we find the marker I've got to get good photographs," Savannah declared. "My batteries are charging in the cabin now. It's not too deep, so as long as the sun stays with us, I think we'll be fine with light. The camera has a good flash."

Jerry smiled at her positive attitude.

"And if it doesn't?" Joseph asked looking at the sky.

Savannah looked at Jerry. "I brought fabric and wax to make rubbings. If the light's not good enough to photograph it, can we bring it up and make a good rubbing? Then we'll put it back?"

"I don't see any problem with that. The law just says it's the property of New York State. As long as we put it back, I think you're fine documenting the find."

"Excellent."

In the back of Jerry's mind was the freighter docked just downriver. He wanted to take another good look on their way out to the island. His suspicions had been raised enough after his last call with Lillian that he'd driven back to Cranberry Lake for a few 'tools of the trade.' When he had brought the black duffle bag and large plastic case aboard upon his return, he simply said, "I brought a few things that might be useful tomorrow." Neither Savannah nor Joseph questioned him.

Jerry and Joseph cleaned the galley after breakfast. Before they left the marina, Jerry reached into the duffel bag and pulled out a pair of binoculars he had brought from home the night before. "Now these are real binoculars," he proudly announced. "Joey, grab those fenders when we clear the slip, will ya?"

"Yes sir, Captain."

Jerry pulled the Bayliner right up to the Port of Ogdensburg pier. As they approached the freighter, it appeared no one was on the bridge. He positioned the bow of their boat right under the bow of the freighter. Jerry figured if their approach had gone unnoticed, their position under the bow would keep them concealed . . . at least for a while.

The luggage that had been on the dock yesterday was gone. The two 20-foot containers and the Land Rover were still there. There was no sign of Port personnel in the area which wasn't unusual for a Sunday, Jerry thought. With no dock hands and no crew in evidence, it almost looked as if the ship had been abandoned.

They continued on to Chimney Island, taking their usual route around the south side of the island and heading west on the north side. They dropped anchor about two-thirds of the way along the short length of the island.

Once all the safety checks were complete, Jerry and Savannah headed down, with Joseph monitoring the lines. They swam 100 feet out and started their methodical search back toward the boat.

The bottom of the river was remarkably smooth with silt. Jerry wasn't surprised because they were not in the main channel. They were over what had been part of Chimney Island, or the 'former' Isle Royale. He had expected they might find a few relics from the massive four-day battle that took place here during the French and Indian War. "Then again," he thought, "This area was dug up 50 years ago. The other side of the island is where the relics would be."

Jerry had been enjoying the dive and thinking about the battle that had taken place over 250 years earlier, just 25 feet above him, when he saw Savannah frantically waving her arms. He swam in her direction and saw she was pointing to a rock jutting from the river bottom about 18 inches. Most of it was roughly rounded but one side was unusually flat.

Jerry put his hands on either side of the rock and tried to move it. Slippery with sea slime and covered in tiny plant growth, it didn't budge. Savannah reached to her diving belt and found a soft brush to wipe away the vegetation. Her heart was pumping hard. The brush wasn't accomplishing much other than moving the slime around and making matters worse. She took off her dive glove and ran her hand across the flat side of the rock. Silt clouded the water, though they tried to prevent their feet from disturbing the river bottom. The one knot current wasn't clearing the silt fast enough and it was becoming difficult to see. Jerry tapped Savannah on the shoulder and pointed up, indicating they should surface.

As soon as she broke the water's surface, 30 feet from the boat, Savannah took off her mask and yelled to Joseph, "We found it!"

"What?"

Jerry broke the water's surface and could hear her yelling at Joseph.

"We found it, we found it," she kept yelling.

The two swam to the diving platform and sat on the edge. Savannah was out of breath, but kept talking. "Joseph, we found my father's marker. I felt his spirit as soon as I got in the water today. I knew we were going to find it today."

Jerry looked at her, "Calm down, Savannah. You're gonna hyperventilate. We found a rock. We don't know it's your father's marker."

"I know it's the marker. That flat side was man-made. I took my glove off and I could feel indentations. There's writing under the algae. We just need a metal brush to clean it off."

"You could actually feel indentations?" Jerry was surprised. "Wow! Maybe you did find it. Let's take a break and get fresh tanks. By the time we get back down there the silt will be cleared away. This is one time the current will help us."

"Where can we find a metal brush?" Savannah's excitement was evident in her tone and sense of urgency.

Still sitting on the dive platform, Jerry yelled up to Joseph, "I think there might be one in the tool box, in the middle back bench."

"I'll look." After a momentary pause he yelled, "Got it!"

"Let me see."

Joseph reached over the rail and dropped a five inch wooden brush with metal bristles onto Savannah's hands. "That'll work just fine." She turned to Jerry, "let's go."

"Slow down, sunshine. We haven't even changed our tanks yet. That rock isn't going anywhere."

"Sorry, I'm just excited."

While exchanging the air tanks Jerry instructed Joseph to keep the lines taught once they reached the rock. "We'll let you know we're ready by giving you a tug on the line. If we tug a second time pull us back just a little bit."

"Understood. This is getting interesting, but you guys are having all the fun."

"We couldn't do it without you, buddy. Your job on the boat may not be as much fun, but it's just as important."

"He's right, Joseph. Thank you!" Savannah blew him a kiss and the two divers with their fresh tanks disappeared under the water.

When they reached the rock they gave their lines a tug and could feel Joseph pulling them taught against the current. Savannah carefully positioned herself with her feet on the river bottom, downstream from the face of the rock. Jerry did the same. She reached for the brush and started scraping the rounded side of the rock, making sure she didn't disturb the silt on the riverbed. After cleaning a test area, and satisfied she wouldn't do any damage, she moved to the flat portion of the rock. Jerry was watching in anticipation.

The shape of a pyramid was beginning to appear on the left side. As Savannah continued brushing, it became apparent the pyramid was the top of the letter 'A', clearly carved in the stone. To the right, the letters 'C' and 'K' appeared. As more letters appeared, Savannah brushed faster and harder. Below the letters ACK, the name 'Sara' came into view, followed by the letter 'N'. Once she saw 'Sara,' Savannah knew this was her father's marker.

Savannah grabbed Jerry by the shoulders and shook him. He returned the excitement with an "OK" signal. He offered to take the brush and finish cleaning the rock, but Savannah wouldn't give it up. She thought to herself, *my father made this for me, and I'm going to finish the job.*

Two sets of numbers appeared near the bottom of the flat surface, 9 - 22/23 and below that 3 - 20. At first, Jerry thought they might be dates, but there was no year. *Maybe they mean something completely different*, he mused, *like a combination to a safe*. At the bottom right corner of the flat surface of the rock, the letters, 'JTC', came into view. When she saw the three letters, she stopped brushing and stared.

Jerry watched her take off her gloves and slowly run her fingers over the indentation of each letter. He knew Savannah had been very close to her father and he didn't want to interrupt this moment. He thought he saw her lips moving. Touched, he felt privileged to be there, though he felt he was intruding on Savannah's private moment with her father. Jerry thought of a similar moment, just a few months ago, when he saw his friend, Joseph, look into the cave and see the treasure left behind by his ancestor, King Joseph Bonaparte.

Savannah turned to Jerry and held her hands in front of her face, as though she were holding a camera. She pointed up. Jerry understood, and they both headed toward the Bayliner.

On the dive platform, Joseph started with a barrage of questions. "Did it say anything? What did it say? Where's the treasure buried?"

Savannah gently looked at Joseph. "Yes, it said something. I don't know what it means. But father's initials were carved in the corner. And Sara's name was there."

"There were numbers too," Jerry added.

"Joseph, it was incredible. I could feel my father's spirit. He was right there next to me. I've never experienced anything like that before." Savannah took off her tank and went on deck to grab the camera case. She had put the charged batteries in earlier and checked the underwater housing to make sure it was sealed properly.

"Jerry, after I get several photos of the marker, would you take a few with me next to it?"

"It would be a pleasure." Savannah showed him the shutter button.

"Let's go." She looked to Joseph. "This won't take too long. We'll be back before you know it."

"I'm not going anywhere."

Again, the two disappeared under the water. The bright sun, combined with the flash, provided the necessary light. Savannah took several pictures of the marker, and Jerry snapped a few of the marker with Savannah next to it.

Back on board, they stowed their diving gear and headed for the galley table where the sun wouldn't obscure the computer screen. Savannah pulled the memory chip from the camera and inserted it into the side of her laptop. A few clicks later, the photos began to appear. A click on the first photo enlarged it to fill the screen and the three looked in amazement.

ACK

Sara N.

9 - 22/23

3-20

JTC

Joseph was the first to speak. "What does it mean?"

Nobody answered. Joseph asked again. "So where's the gold? Hello, are you guys there?"

Savannah looked at Joseph. "Sweetheart, I have absolutely no idea what it means. The only thing I know for sure is those are father's initials in the corner."

"Look guys, here are the two big questions we have to figure out. Who was this Sara, and what do the numbers mean?" Jerry looked at Savannah. "Did you bring the pages of the Journal? I'd like to read that entry again."

Savannah went to her cabin and returned with the manila file folder with the photo copied pages. She turned to the page with the yellow sticky. Silently, the three read the entry together.

> ***August 13, 1955*** *– Sara was buried today, leaving behind the* ***grand old lady dog****. The marker can be found on the former Isle Royale. Visit the marker and it will provide you great comfort.*

"I'm not feeling great comfort," Joseph quipped.

"Maybe the date of the entry is important," Savannah added. "But it doesn't match any of the numbers on the marker. Maybe these numbers are the combination to a safe."

Jerry had already decided what to do. "I thought of that, but most combinations are only three numbers. There are five numbers on the marker. Look guys, I don't think we are going to figure this out here. Why don't we pack up and head back to Cranberry Lake. We can talk about it in the car and put a plan together. It can't be that difficult."

Everyone agreed.

He added, "Tomorrow, we'll take a drive to Canton and check old newspapers to find out who this Sara was. It should be easy. After all, we know the exact date she was buried. There has to be an obituary some where, and a burial permit. Once we know that, it should be easy to figure the rest."

"Great idea." Savannah decided to give Jerry a hard time. "By the way, Jerry, you owe Joseph and me a dinner. You were supposed to cook last night, and you ran out on us."

"Fair enough. We'll stop on the way home and pick up some steaks and veggies and throw them on the grill. Will should be home too. You'll finally get a chance to meet him."

Savannah was closing her computer and packing her camera equipment in its case. "I'm looking forward to that."

"Joe Boy, why don't you get the anchor?"

"The name's Joseph, you moron."

Savannah just shook her head and mumbled, "Boys will be boys."

Jerry started the engines when he heard her yell.

"Stop! Latitude and longitude!

Thinking she was talking about the numbers on the marker, Jerry yelled down to her, "Not enough numbers."

Savannah was climbing the steps to the fly bridge. "That's not what I meant. Let's write down the latitude and longitude of where we found the marker. Maybe it's connected somehow. Remember, father was with the Army Corps of Engineers. He knew that kind of stuff."

"Good thinking." Jerry pressed a button on the GPS and read the coordinates to Savannah as she was writing. "It may be nothing, but at least we'll have them."

As he slowly increased his speed, Jerry thought to himself, how smart this woman was, and what a fun project this was turning into. He was looking forward to looking in old newspapers and government records to find out who Sara could be. Surely her identity would lead them to Savannah's gold.

His thoughts were interrupted at the sight of the break bulk freighter in the channel. "*I guess they got their mechanical problems fixed*," he thought. He then realized the Bayliner was gaining on the freighter too fast. Suddenly it hit him, "*They're not moving!*" Reaching for his binoculars, he could see the light blue container on her deck, the doors on the port side open. He quickly looked to his right and saw the two smaller containers and the Land Rover still sitting on the pier at the Port of Ogdensburg. Looking back at the ship, the large letters, ARES, filled the stern. "The god of war," he thought to himself again. "Strange for a merchant ship." It was then he noticed there was an inflatable Zodiac tied to a ladder near the stern.

Jerry slowed the Bayliner and made a wide turn to port, close to the Port Authority pier. As he circled around to head back downriver he was surprised to see that the Ares was anchored in the middle of the shipping channel.

"Hold on down there," he yelled to his friends.

He pushed the throttle down and the boat jerked forward heading back toward the stern of the freighter. As they passed the stern, he noticed there was no churning of the water by the Ares' propellers. "She's at a dead stop and anchored in the channel. Something is seriously wrong here," he said aloud.

He continued a ways past her stern and circled again, bringing the Bayliner to a full stop about 500 feet behind the Ares. As he looked through the binoculars, a dozen different scenarios were racing through his head.

His heart stopped as he watched what happened next. The front six feet of the blue intermodal container on her deck remained still, while immediately behind that section, the much larger portion of the container pointing south started to rise on an axis point near its rear. Instantly, he knew exactly what was happening.

TWENTY-THREE

Sunday, August 4th
20:45 GMT – 3:45 pm EDT
St. Lawrence River, New York, USA

MICKEY EVANS HAD worked up a sweat. The intense physical activity, the concentration on the music, and the thunderous rhythms settled his mind. He was living in the moment, thinking only of the enormous drum before him and the music he would call forth. His fellow drummers were equally exquisite, flawlessly producing an awe-striking collection of sound that no one could help but find impressive. He was in a place where his mind flowed freely, where time stood still and history met with the present and the future.

When the ringing in his head stopped, he found himself standing still, with the remainder of his Taiko group staring at him. His mind had wandered so far that a connection was made. It dawned on him so suddenly that he accidentally struck himself in the head with one of the huge drumsticks in his hands.

His university degree was in classical studies, the world of the ancient Greeks. Athens, Sparta, Troy . . . and the Olympian gods. The gods. Athena: the goddess of wisdom, intelligence, philosophy, reason, literature. He'd thought of her often while engaged in the Athena Joint Task Force. She was a daughter of Zeus. She had a brother: Ares, the god of order, courage . . . *and war*. The instigator of violence. Ares, the trouble-maker.

Just before leaving work, he'd been briefed on another case, sent up the line from some DHS contractor in the northeast. Another break bulk freighter. Left Iceland about the same time. Something about a cobra painted on an intermodal container. The serpent. The sacred animal of Ares. Ares cleared inspections in Montreal at the moment all eyes were on Athena.

Could it be? Has Athena been an elaborate ruse? It would explain a lot. Mickey hastily made his apologies, saying to his colleagues he had to leave to return to work. He said he hoped to be back in time for the performance the following evening, but could not be sure.

He dashed to his car and headed to his office. On the way, he called to the duty desk, asking to be connected with his commanding officer. It took some work to convince the young petty officer to put the call through. The old man didn't like being disturbed on a Sunday afternoon, especially during baseball season. Mickey trotted out the old, "life and death, the nation's fate depends on it," story, but got nowhere. Then he said he'd take all of the blame for whatever repercussions followed. The call was connected in less than 30 seconds.

Waiting for the phone to be answered, he narrowly avoided a collision while passing a red traffic signal. He was telling himself to settle down when his boss picked up. Mickey knew he had one shot at convincing him to recommend immediate action. As he relayed the information he'd received that afternoon, he realized it was sounding flimsy. It didn't take long for the captain to get irritated.

"Where are you going with all of this, Evans?"

"Sir, Athena is the mythical sister of Ares, the god of war. I believe they're connected, and Athena was used as a diversion to allow Ares to more easily gain access to the US interior. She passed through Montreal at the same time we were boarding Athena."

"Mythology? That's what you're basing this on? Where's your evidence?"

"No, sir. Not just mythology. They were both in Iceland at the same time. No one knows where Ares came from before Iceland. Now she's in the St. Lawrence River and . . ."

"Evans, you want me to hit the alarm buttons to raid and inspect some cargo ship that's already been inspected? What am I supposed to show them, a copy of *The Iliad*? We've already raided one ship like that, and we saw where that got us. I'm not about to do any such thing again based only on your conjecture."

"It's more than conjecture, sir. There's a good deal of data here that is very compelling."

"Fine, get it together and brief us in the morning. If the ship is in the Seaway, it's a domestic case. It's not ours."

"I'm asking that you get this to the TTIC and ask them to get assets out there as soon as possible. Get the State Police or the local police department if they have SWAT assets. I think we're in a time-sensitive situation here. Today is the Islamic holy day . . ."

"Enough, Lieutenant Evans. Enough. I'm not about to recommend committing those kinds of resources on some circumstantial vagaries, and the suspicion of some contractor to DHS. We saw what happened last time. I'm not risking that kind of embarrassment again. If the domestic side of the house wants to tackle it, they can be my guest, but this office is keeping its hands off. We're finished here, Lieutenant. I'll see you tomorrow morning."

The line went silent.

A second later, the petty officer who'd connected the call came on the line and asked if he could do anything else. Mickey thanked him and said no.

Evans reached the parking lot in Langley. Bailing out still bare-chested, he dashed for the door, trying to dig out his ID so he could get inside. Out of breath and half dressed, he ran to the door, showing his identification to a shocked guard. He smashed headlong into the inner door, having missed the handle because he was looking through the contacts on his cell phone. He was sure it was saved. At least he hoped it was. "Damn, it isn't. *It's OK, there will be a rep in the Task Force*," he was now talking to himself.

He took the stairs. When he got to the Task Force's room, he discovered it empty and dark. "*They shut it down as soon as I left*." He spun around and went for his office. Pouring through paperwork he finally located the phone number he needed. During the run-up to the boarding of Athena, Lieutenant Snow of the Coast Guard had given Mickey his personal cell phone number, asking that he be called if circumstances changed. He didn't want to miss the boarding.

Mickey stared at it a moment. He knew that what he was doing was frowned upon. He was not following his chain of command, circumventing the enormous and complicated national security apparatus and going directly to a different agency with data. He'd experienced this frustration before, where anyone, anywhere in the chain can stop or stall something. Everyone has to say "yes" to passing information along in order for it to be shared. It takes only one person, anywhere along the chain of communication, to stop something. He felt strongly about this. Perhaps he was fooling himself, wrapped up in confirmation bias, but he thought the stakes were high enough to act.

If Athena were a diversion, it took substantial preparation, transportation, and finances to make such a large acquisition of Cs137 and get it on a freight ship. A diversion that elaborate and costly wouldn't be used to cover the smuggling of a firecracker. This might be big. Very big. Knowing every communication going through that building was recorded, Mickey picked up his cell phone and dialed. The phone just rang. When the ringing stopped, Mickey expected to hear a voice mail message. Instead, it was Lt. Shawn Snow.

"Mickey? What's going on? Sorry to hear they pulled the Task Force."

Evans's voice was flat. "Shawn, I'm going to tell you something. I have information that I think is significant. I think it's very significant and I think it requires immediate action. My command isn't listening. So I'm coming to you. If you hear what I have to say and want nothing to do with it, just say the word and this conversation never happened. I'll respect your decision."

Snow's experience with Evans had never given him a hint that Mickey was driven by emotion or prone to wild conclusions. If anything, he was more the opposite. Snow sat silent for a beat, then answered. "Shoot."

Mickey relayed to him all of the information he had in the most concise and well-organized manner he could muster, pausing only briefly for Shawn to get to another room and start taking notes.

By now he had calmed, but his anxiety about Ares hadn't waned. As he told the story, he realized some of it sounded outlandish, particularly the connection to Greek mythology.

Nevertheless, when Mickey was finished, Snow asked only one question: "Mickey, do you really think we need to jump on this?"

Mickey could hear the sound of the infant in Shawn's lap as he answered, "I do."

"Hang on, let me get my command on the other phone." Mickey listened as Snow dialed and waited. "Hey, Smitty, this is Shawn Snow. No, I'm not in until tomorrow, but I came across something that needs attention ASAP. Can you connect me with the District Nine command center? Whoever the duty officer is. Thanks." He switched phones. "Mickey, I'm going to give it right to the district response division, enforcement branch, whoever can launch somebody right away." Evans held his breath as the conversation continued with a Coast Guard officer in Cleveland, the headquarters for District Nine, the "Guardians of the Great Lakes." As the conversation progressed, Shawn knew Mickey was right.

"Mickey, the district advised that Sector Buffalo launched a Search and Rescue/Law Enforcement (SAR/LE) boat out of Alexandria Bay to investigate a possible ship in distress in the shipping channel down river from them, near Ogdensburg, N.Y. They're leaving the station now. They just got a call from St. Lawrence County 911 center of an incident in the channel near the Ogdensburg – Prescott Bridge. No details yet."

§

Jerry Doolin continued to look through the binoculars he held in his right hand as he squatted down, his left hand probing around the floor for the duffel bag he'd brought aboard. When he found it, his left hand slid inside and withdrew a long flat piece of black leather. Joseph and Savannah, swapping their gaze between the ship and their friend, didn't realize what Jerry was holding until it fully exited the black bag. It was a belt with a holster and ammunition carrier. They looked up in shock and bewilderment as Jerry gently placed the binoculars on the deck and fastened his old duty belt around his waist. He confronted them with a look Joseph had seen only once before. He knew that Jerry meant business, and communicated it to Savannah by tightening his grip on her forearm.

Jerry spoke quietly and without emotion. “Get down on the deck, up against the bulkhead. Protect your heads. Do it now.”

Before they could ask what was going on, or why, the twin engines of the Bayliner roared to life. Jerry had thrust the throttles as far forward as he could. A field of white foam spewed from the boat’s transom as the vessel accelerated to an alarming velocity, its bow climbing out of the water to such an extent that loose items were sliding aft.

Joseph was sitting on the deck, his back to the bulkhead. He reached for Savannah’s arm to pull her close, but she held back. He saw the look of surprise in her eyes but had no idea what produced it. She was looking through the windshield and over the bow of their boat and saw quite clearly that they were on a collision course with the cargo ship resting quietly in the water in front of them. She let out a gasp, then threw herself down beside Joseph, shouting, “We’re gonna hit!”

Joseph’s eyes widened, “Hit what?”

“That ship!”

Not believing what he heard, he started to get up but Savannah pulled him down, knowing the collision was imminent. “Hold on!”

Jerry aimed the Bayliner directly toward the port stern of Ares. As he got closer he saw that one of the crew aboard Ares was watching their approach. He set the wheel straight and at the last second dove to the deck of the fly bridge, hoping it would stay attached after the crash. The container on Ares’ deck was pointing south. Jerry didn’t think he could hit the huge ship hard enough to knock the container over or to disable it, but maybe he could at least change the missile’s trajectory. And with luck, he could distract the crew enough to prevent a launch, or at least delay it until more help arrived.

The pulpit of the Bayliner crumpled like a cardboard box against the steel hull of the freighter, followed by the fiberglass and wood bow. The impact threw everything forward and pressed the three passengers up against the bulkheads. Dive tanks, which had been secured with bungee cords, flew at Joseph and Savannah, narrowly missing them. One tank went through the windshield, another shot into the cabin. Savannah scrambled to her feet to see the destroyed front end of the boat heaving out of the water as it pushed against the Ares. Jerry reached up to make sure the throttles were still wide open. He adjusted the rudder to try to force the giant ship to swing on its anchor line.

Rosie had seen the boat coming only seconds before it smashed into theirs. No one heard his warning shouts, but the heaving deck brought Abe running out of the missile container's control room. The Captain initially thought they'd struck bottom. It was a logical conclusion since Adam hours earlier had removed the non-functional drive shaft and made other alterations intended to begin slowly flooding the ship. Abe ran up to the port side gunnel to see a smaller boat pushing on the stern forcing the Ares to move, much as a tug boat would.

Abe and Rosie looked at each other, both realizing in the same instant that they hadn't secured the ship's wheel. The pressure from the smaller boat would cause Ares' rudder to turn, making the job of the makeshift tug easier. It would be easier still because it was pushing with the current. They also knew their point-and-shoot missile was being moved off course. Rosie thought about making a run for the bridge, but he was stopped by Abe who was calling to him, now in Arabic, to follow him to the missile container's control room. Rosie saw why. Abe emerged holding an AK-47 rifle, one of two secreted in the control room. Abe ran along the port side gunnel, toward the low point near the aft crane. He looked over the side of the ship to see if the collision was an accident. He knew immediately it was not.

Jerry had no cover and barely any concealment. What he did have was a moment to kneel down, brace his arms against the rail of the fly bridge and look down the sights of the Glock 37 which he'd drawn from his holster. He could feel his heart pounding in his chest and in his ears. The metallic taste in his mouth was accompanied by a sense of tunnel vision. He thought to himself, *this is normal.* He heard himself shout, "Police, don't move!" as he'd done so many times during his 23 years as a State Trooper. He doubted it could be heard over the deafening noise of the engines which were bearing down with all they had. He saw a man look down at him, and a second later saw the unmistakable barrel of a rifle come over the rail.

He squeezed the trigger, over and over, trying to keep his sights on his target despite the lurching platform on which he found himself. He saw a muzzle flash. Then another. Jerry wasn't sure if the man was aiming at him or at the boat's engine compartment, attempting to disable the thrust of the boat. Jerry fired until the Glock was empty. Rapidly reloading from one of the spare magazines on his belt, he looked through his sights to find no target visible. Only a limp arm hanging over the gunnel of the ship.

Jerry relaxed for an instant, just long enough to take a breath before he heard another shot and felt a burning sensation in his left calf muscle. The impact caused him to spin and roll onto his back. At first he couldn't tell where the shots were coming from, but as more rounds ripped through the fiberglass around him, he realized they were coming almost from overhead.

The canopy of the fly bridge provided enough concealment that the shooter was firing blind into the area where he'd last seen Jerry.

Everything seemed to be moving in slow motion. Jerry rolled over toward the instrument cluster and tried to look up at the source of the shots. He could see nothing through the windshield. He lay back, aiming upward and through the shredded canopy. It was then that he saw the muzzle flashes again. The shooter had to lean over the side of the ship to get a shot. His entire torso was visible from the waist up. Jerry sat as still as he could and took careful aim. Hearing nothing but his own breathing, he began firing. Ten rounds were fired as quickly as he could keep the handgun under control and on his target.

He replaced his empty magazine with the last one on his duty belt. Rounds kept coming toward him, splintering fiberglass everywhere. Squinting to keep the shards out of his eyes, Jerry slid forward to use the seat as a brace. He peeled off the final ten rounds, not knowing if he'd hit the shooter until the wounded body landed on the Bayliner's twisted foredeck.

Rosie had known the mission would almost certainly fail when he saw the Bayliner headed on a collision course with Ares. He no longer cared about the missile, the mission or harming American innocents. All he wanted was to get off the ship with his friends and escape North America. Merely discovering the unused missile would scare the Americans enough. He was on his way to urge Abe and Adam to abandon ship and get out of there in the Land Rover. Suddenly Abe was shooting, and the people who'd crashed into them were shooting back.

Rosie grabbed a rifle, not to harm anyone, but to protect himself and his friends. When he saw Abe go down he got angry and began firing. Then he felt the burning sensation of the rounds penetrating his chest and neck. He barely felt anything as he landed on the smashed deck of the Bayliner. Taking his final breaths, he hoped the missile would not function. He hoped it would fail. He closed his eyes and asked the Heavens for forgiveness as he exhaled and waited for Paradise.

Jerry poked his head out from under the canopy. He knew from his conversation with Lillian that there had been more than two people left on the Ares. Maybe three, maybe more.

The pain and blood loss from the gunshot wound was beginning to affect him. He reached into his duffel bag and pulled out a t-shirt, twisted it into a narrow rope and tied it tightly around the wound. The entrance wound was clean, but the exit was worse. He broke out in a cold sweat and tried to shake off the mild shock that accompanies a significant injury.

Joseph had been on his cell phone from the moment the Bayliner connected with Ares. He called it in as a crash, trying to explain something about a friend losing control of the boat and hitting a freighter. The 911 dispatcher was trying to collect the necessary information but was having trouble hearing over the noise of the boat's engines, which were running at full throttle beneath Joseph's feet. The information was being simultaneously transmitted to US Coast Guard sector headquarters in Buffalo, N.Y. As the dispatcher was asking additional questions about injuries and fire, Joseph interrupted with, "They're shooting at us. We need help right now!" Surprised, the dispatcher paused for a second, then lost her caller as Joseph and Savannah dove for the deck to dodge bullets coming from Abe.

When the firing momentarily ceased, Joseph picked up his phone and was surprised to hear the dispatcher still connected. Shouting over the noise of the boat, which was still pushing with ferocious effort, he attempted to give as much information as possible about the armed conflict in progress. Then he suddenly stopped. The last thing the dispatcher heard him say was, "Oh, mother of God."

Jerry had limped his way down the ladder to the main deck to find his other gear and see if he had any more ammunition on board. Everything was in a heap in what was left of the cabin. Savannah was out of sight. Jerry was looking for his gear when he saw what Joseph saw. He went pale. He felt his blood drain.

A Rocket-Propelled Grenade (RPG) is the size of a hunting rifle. From a distance, a person could mistake it for one. At this close range, no such mistake could be made. Adam, the last remaining crew member, had been attempting to launch the missile when the electronic compass in the container control room gave a heading error alarm. The missile was so far off its intended course it would be foolish to launch. He had to try to stop the ship from moving and get the missile pointing roughly to the south. He had already initiated the launch sequence and activated the delay timer before he grabbed the RPG-7 out of the control room. Expecting to be delayed only a minute, he left the control key in the active position. He ran to the edge of the deck leveling the RPG on his shoulder.

Jerry knew this was the end. The thin fiberglass of the boat would produce more shrapnel once the rocket-propelled grenade exploded, far too close to them than is survivable. There was nothing Jerry could do except jump into the water. He tried to shout to Joseph to jump, but his mouth was too dry and Joseph wasn't listening. He was looking for Savannah, intending to cover her with his body in hopes that at least she would survive. She was nowhere to be seen. There was no more time to look for her.

Then Jerry heard the familiar bark of an M-4 rifle. He recognized the sound, but for a moment couldn't make sense of why he was hearing it. It hadn't occurred to him that Savannah would recognize the plastic case he had brought with him the night before. As an ex-Marine, she had the skill and muscle memory to employ it with deadly accuracy, aiming from the remnants of Jerry's stateroom. The RPG dropped to the deck, its owner crumpled over it like a wet rag. Rifle shouldered, Savannah made her way to the rear deck to join her companions, still looking, as Jerry was, for additional adversaries.

Jerry hauled himself back aboard and located one more magazine. As he was reloading, he saw Joseph dive overboard, and understood he was swimming toward the Zodiac tied to the ladder of Ares. They'd need it to make their way back to shore. Joseph got it started and brought it to the remains of the Bayliner just as her engines flooded and stalled. They grabbed Savanna's laptop and camera, the weapons, and their records and piled onto the inflatable boat. Jerry and Savannah, falling back on their training, covered the ship as they moved. It wasn't until then that Savannah noticed Jerry's blood-soaked leg and shoe.

"You're wounded."

"Yeah. I have a medical kit somewhere in the cabin."

Joseph looked at the remains of their pleasure craft. "It's under water now. All that whiz-bang medical gear you're always toting around and you use a t-shirt. Brilliant."

"Joseph, get us over to the Port. I have to get to get to a phone and call this in, and I need this leg looked at."

Joseph nodded and twisted the throttle of the little boat, navigating quickly across the river and to the pier at the Port. He was tying the Zodiac when they heard a siren blaring from the west.

"That will be the Coast Guard," Jerry remarked. He recognized the approaching vessel as the stealth boat prototype discussed at his last Operation Stone Garden meeting. Joseph and Savannah helped Jerry out of the boat and the three headed toward the administration building to find a telephone so they could explain what had happened, where they were, and to get some medical attention for Jerry's leg. Jerry was having trouble walking. They paused. Joseph held him up as Savannah kneeled to tighten the remnants of the tee shirt around his damaged calf.

The Coast Guard circled Ares, looking for movement on the deck. They'd received a report of shots fired, and had a gunner on the bow of the stealth boat behind a mounted M-240 machine gun. Detecting no sign of motion on the freighter, they tied off to her ladder on the port side and boarded her, rifles ready. Once on board, they saw the two bodies on the deck.

One petty officer was gesturing to the gunner aboard the stealth boat when it happened.

TWENTY-FOUR

Sunday, August 4th

21:15 GMT – 4:15 pm EDT

St. Lawrence River, New York, USA

SUDDENLY, THE QUIET BLUE CONTAINER aboard the Ares roared to life. A deafening blast emanated from the steel box, followed immediately by a trail of smoke as the missile launched upward into the ether.

Savannah, Joseph and Jerry were still 20 yards from the port administration building. Everyone, including the crew of the stealth boat, and the occupants of a handful of pleasure boats who had been alerted by the Coast Guard siren, jumped and turned toward the freighter. Jerry looked up. "Shit." Savannah pulled a compass from her pocket and measured the azimuth of the launching missile: "065, to the northeast."

The glow seemed brighter and lasted longer than they thought it would. "Shit, I thought it would only be chemical," was the only remark heard. It came from Savannah, who pulled Joseph and Jerry to the ground as the Coast Guard crew instinctively turned away and waited for the shock wave and fire ball that follows a thermonuclear blast. Nothing happened. After a few seconds Jerry and Savannah looked back for the signs of a mushroom cloud. The sky was clear.

Jerry noticed the Coast Guard boat and all of the other boats on the river stalled. The administrative building went dark. Jerry and Savannah looked at their watches and saw they were dead. They looked at each other and simultaneously said, "Electromagnetic Pulse."

The Coast Guard boat was hardened against an EMP weapon and a technician got their engines restarted. Communications were disabled so they couldn't report what they were facing. Every other vessel within sight appeared dead in the water.

Joseph was bewildered. "What just happened? What's an electro-whatever pulse?"

Savannah responded, "It's a special type of weapon sweetheart."

Jerry tried to explain. "It put out strong gamma rays that disable any electrical device in its line of sight. We didn't see an explosion so it had to have been pretty high . . . 100, maybe even 150 miles high. A large area must have been affected."

Joseph was still confused. "I didn't feel any gamma rays. How come all the boats are stalled? They're not electric."

Jerry had other priorities and didn't want to answer the question. "Their engines all have little microchips that were affected. I'll explain it later."

Other than the Coast Guard boat, there were no sounds. No boat engines, no automobiles, no other clutter noise in the background. The scene was eerily quiet as the three stood on the pier.

In the river, the Coast Guardsmen were trying to decide how to handle all the competing priorities they faced. The missile must have detonated some kind of warhead and they knew there was damage experienced over a large area. They had a major incident on their hands, with an apparent gunfight and deaths. The freighter appeared to be low in the water, and it didn't take long to determine that she was flooding in the middle of what was going to be one of the most important routes for relief supplies in the northeast. If it were to sink where it was, the shipping lane could be blocked for weeks, if not months. They needed operational tugs to get the freighter moved. They also needed operational communications and additional manpower.

The boat that smashed into Ares was destroyed and barely visible in the water. The Coast Guard wondered if there were any bodies in the water, or if those on the pleasure boat had escaped. Perhaps one or more of them were among the dead aboard the freighter.

The petty officer in charge spoke to his crew. "That electromagnetic pulse, and that's what it was, was produced by a nuclear detonation in the atmosphere. Draw a line from here to…probably Newport, Rhode Island. Everything from that line north is likely wiped out. Everything with a microprocessor. Every car, computer, telephone, the electrical grid, radio towers. Everything. Do we have hardened communication at the Alex Bay station? I don't think so. We're going to do everything we can to clear the shipping channel and open up a supply route for the recovery that's going to last months, probably years. Let's head back to Alex Bay and see if they have communications. We have to get someplace where we can notify command and get more resources here. We'll leave three guys aboard the freighter to secure her and begin collecting evidence."

It would not be until the stealth boat had gotten far enough south to reach some intact telephone lines that they would realize the full gravity of the incident they had witnessed.

§

Mickey Evans sat glued to his phone as Shawn Snow relayed information coming to the District Nine Headquarters by radio from a Coast Guardsman attached to Alexandria Bay, New York. The radio operator was reporting his observations as they were happening, including a freighter anchored in the channel and sinking, the evidence of a collision, a missile launching, and bodies and weapons discovered aboard the ship. Then everything went dead. They stopped answering their radio.

Shawn apologized, but said there was no more information he could provide. It was then Mickey realized it was his turn to provide information.

"NORAD detected the missile launch," Mickey said. "They placed it somewhere in the northern New York or eastern Ontario region." He grabbed another phone and called in the exact location of the ship-launched missile. "NORAD detected the EMP as well, and early indications are that the effects are massive," he told Sean.

As Mickey was collecting information he left the line open so Shawn could continue to feed information through his command allowing the Coast Guard to mobilize resources instantly. "Make sure they pass the information to the DHS framework," he yelled.

"They are," was the quick response.

It wasn't long before Lillian LaForte heard the news. Instantly, she knew who was involved. A call to Jerry's phone only returned a recording. Lillian's perpetual smile disappeared. She worried about her friend, feared their suspicions were correct, and dreaded the thought that serious harm had come to Jerry.

Domestic resources were immediately marshaled for recovery. National security apparatus were engaged to determine who was responsible. Mickey Evans was waiting with the answers, at least to the extent they could be known. He and the Coast Guard knew exactly where the evidence was.

In Washington, the President, Vice-President and members of Congress were being rounded up and moved to secure bunkers. Nobody knew if this was a single attack or if more missiles would be launched. What was known was disturbing enough. The impact area was large and electronics were heavily damaged. The electrical grid had experienced a cascade of failures all the way to the west coast.

Mickey's next action was his last as the leader of the Athena Task Force. He sent word through the hardened communications network to their assets in Boston: secure the cesium, seize the ship Athena, detain and interrogate the crew. He knew this would be difficult. Not every military vehicle or facility was sufficiently hardened against the effects of an EMP. But he knew some were.

§

"Let's go." Jerry was motioning Joseph and Savannah back toward the end of the pier.

Joseph objected. "That way? Our cars are nowhere near here. What're you planning, you bald-headed lunatic, a swim? You have a hole in your leg."

"Relax, Joey. Relax."

Joseph opened up again. "Terrific. What're we gonna do? We have to get back to the car at the marina."

Savannah was quick to reply. "Cars are wiped out. They won't start."

"Savannah's right buddy. Our car is dead, that's why we're not going back to the marina. Anything new enough to have a microprocessor is toast."

"So what the hell do we do now? Commandeer horses from the Amish?" Joseph was red-faced and frazzled.

"No, we drive home. Give me a hand, Joey?" Jerry had been limping around the side of a small intermodal container near the edge of the pier. When they rounded its corner they were standing in front of a fully restored 1962 Land Rover, complete with spare fuel. "I think once we get the fuel in the back we're ready to go." The truck started without difficulty. They tossed the terrorists' luggage into the intermodal container and closed the doors. Jerry retrieved a soggy business card from his wallet and left it on the locking handle of the container. It would have to suffice as communication under the circumstances. Taking all the diesel fuel they could hold, they piled in. Jerry stretched out on the back seat, elevating his throbbing leg. Joseph jumped behind the driver seat and sat for a moment. "Right-hand drive is bad enough, but I haven't driven a stick shift in decades."

Sitting in the passenger seat, Savannah immediately got out. "I'll drive."

Weaving through the streets of Ogdensburg, now littered with dead cars Jerry spoke up, "We should take back roads to be safe. I just hope Will got home safely. At least he had the truck."

Joseph chuckled, still shaking. "That old oxcart is finally good for something. You realize this buggy doesn't belong to us, right? It doesn't even have plates on it."

"Who's going to pull us over? There's not a single police car that works. Still, we're not going to go through any large towns. We don't want to chance a road block."

Joseph turned in the seat to face Jerry. "What if someone tries to car-jack us?"

"I don't think that'll be a problem. If it is, it won't be a problem." Jerry slid down onto the floor of the vehicle. "This seat is uncomfortable."

"Yeah, I don't think that's enough of a deterrent, Baldy."

"The reason for the discomfort is . . ." Jerry lifted the bench seat. Beneath were mounted two AK-47 rifles. "Counting my M-4, that's one each. I don't think we'll need them. But they're here if we do."

At that moment, Jerry would have eagerly traded both rifles for a couple of aspirin.

TWENTY-FIVE

Sunday, August 4th
23:45 GMT – 6:45 pm EDT
Cranberry Lake, New York, USA

JERRY'S LEG WOUND was throbbing as they drove into Cranberry Lake. He had been giving directions to Savannah that had kept them on back roads. During their trip they encountered abandoned vehicles as well as scores of people walking in every direction obviously confused about what had happened and why almost every vehicle had suddenly ceased to function. Many people tried to flag them down, but Jerry instructed Savannah to keep moving. Other than a few Amish buggies, they saw only one other operating vehicle, an old pick-up truck. Jerry suspected the Amish weren't the only ones who didn't yet understand that something catastrophic had happened.

Jerry asked Savannah to stop at the Cranberry Lake fire hall.

"You need to take care of that leg," Savannah insisted.

"I will. There will be an EMT there."

They had a few hours of daylight left and Jerry really wanted to assess the situation in town and make sure emergency responders understood what actually happened and what to expect over the next few days, weeks and months. It had been less than four hours since the EMP had hit. Jerry suspected there were a lot of confused people with more questions than answers.

Normally, with a major event like an ice storm or a fire, there would be at least dozen cars in the parking lot. There were none as they turned in. A few people were milling around. Inside the fire house, there were a half dozen volunteers around the equipment bays, all speculating on what was happening. As soon as Jerry limped in, the questions were directed at him. "Jerry, do you know anything?" "Have you talked to the State Police?" "Why aren't our communications working?" "We've been trying to get our generator going for over two hours." "We can't even reach St. Lawrence County dispatch." "Why aren't the trucks working?" "How come you have a working vehicle?" "None of our vehicles are working." "Why are you limping?"

Jerry ignored the barrage of questions and looked for an EMT. He found Debbie Grenier. "Debbie, could you please get the first-in bag out of the ambulance and take it to the other room? I need a wound attended to." He then looked around and asked a few people to set up tables and chairs in the hall. "I'll explain everything in a few minutes. First, let me have a few private minutes with the Chief." He asked Joseph and Savannah to help with the set-up as he followed Fire Chief Walter Dial into the Chief's office and closed the door.

Dial had almost 20 years behind him as a firefighter, and three as chief. He was used to dealing with emergency situations. His reputation during emergencies was that of a calm leader.

"Walt, we have a major incident on our hands."

"Don't I know it. None of our equipment is working."

Jerry was adamant. "Walt, listen to me. It's gonna get worse. In fact, it's going last probably for months. Maybe longer."

"Jerry, you're overreacting. Calm down. We'll be fine. They'll have the power back on in a few hours."

"Really, Walt? You think this is just a power outage? And I guess with no electricity, that's why not one vehicle in town is working, including your emergency vehicles? That's why your generator didn't kick in. That's why nobody's generator kicked in? That's why your radios don't work?"

Chief Dial had a feeling Jerry knew what he was talking about. Growing more concerned he looked at Jerry, "So what do you think is happening?"

"What you see happening in Cranberry Lake, Walt, is happening over a huge geographic area. The United States was attacked. An EMP weapon was detonated somewhere off of the east coast. I don't know if others were detonated over other parts of the country or not. Certainly, most of New England and eastern Canada is involved. I'm not sure how far west it goes."

Dial's mind was beginning to plan ahead. "How long do you think the effects will last?"

Pointing out the window Jerry answered. "A long time. Months, maybe more. Haven't you been listening? By morning there will be hundreds of people in that parking lot looking for help. They're going to want an explanation of what happened. They're going to want answers. They have no transportation and no running water. In a few days they're going to start to run out of food and you're going to have thousands of people out there looking for help."

"The State or Feds will send help," Dial insisted.

"Walt, listen to me, you can't expect any help from the outside. No supplies of food, fuel, electricity, anything. They're dealing with their own problems."

Walter Dial sat silently for a moment taking in everything Jerry had said. "What is that weapon you said went off? An EMT? How do you know all this? Why's your vehicle working?"

"It was an EMP, an electromagnetic pulse. It probably destroyed the electrical grid for 1000 miles in every direction. It also probably destroyed every microchip for 500 miles in every direction. That's why the electronic ignition in your car doesn't work. Even if the ignition did work, all the other electronics wouldn't. There probably aren't a half dozen working vehicles in town. Only those made before 1978, and they'll run out of gas soon. We have to be careful. That's also why not one radio in town is working, including the fire departments'.

Dial interrupted, "People are going to want answers."

"You're damn right." Jerry could see that the Chief was beginning to understand. "Nobody has running water because their pumps aren't working and they're going to start running out of food in a few days. We need to get ready."

As the enormity of the situation began to sink in, Walter Dial's mind started racing. "Let's go out and brief the others. Then we'll need to put together an Incident Action Plan. It looks like we'll be busy for a while. Jerry, will you write the IAP?"

"I'll help, Walt, but I've been shot. I have to get this leg fixed then I have to handle a few things at home. I'll be back first thing in the morning."

"Sure, Jerry. Thanks."

The two started to get up to head into the hall. "Walt, one more thing. I'll need a good assistant who can take over when I leave."

Walt was surprised, "Leave? Where are you going?"

"I'm guessing as soon as they get their act together the FBI will find a way to get up here and pick me up. It might take them a few days though."

"You've been shot and the FBI is looking for you. Are you in trouble?"

Jerry smiled through the increasing pain in his leg. "No, let's just say I was a witness. I need to brief the FBI on what I know. Right now they don't even know where I am and I have no way of contacting them. But, I'm sure they'll figure it out and come find me so I want to work with somebody who can replace me when that happens." Jerry's leg was beginning to bleed again.

In the hall, Walt Dial and Jerry sat at in the front of the room. Dial started the briefing while Debbie Grenier worked on Jerry's calf. She removed the blood soaked t-shirt not knowing what to expect. As soon as she cleaned wound, she knew exactly what caused it. She looked at Jerry with concern and a question in her eye. He simply looked at her and shook his head no. Debbie nodded, and continued to work without saying a word.

Chief Dial tried to explain what was happening but quickly turned the meeting over to Jerry who gave more details and outlined what they could expect over the next few days.

By the time Jerry had finished, Dial had finalized his plan and was ready to hand out assignments. "Jack, you're Operations Chief. Frank is Logistics. Doolin is in charge of planning. Mike, Jerry has asked that you work with him as his deputy. Debbie, you're going to be our Safety Officer. Tim, you handle Public Information. There won't be media to deal with, but you have an entire community to keep informed. Keeping the community in the loop is going to be the key to making sure things stay calm.

"Prepare yourselves everybody, we're in for a long hard ride. I need everybody rested and focused. We're losing light, so make your way home. Chiefs, start your planning, and we'll meet here at 0600. I need two people to spend the night here at the firehouse. Any volunteers, other than Tim?"

Tim Moore, a barrel chested man in his mid-40s wasn't surprised Dial 'volunteered' him. He was single and didn't have to worry about anyone at home.

Debbie Grenier, who lived close by, volunteered to stay. "I'll run home and make us some sandwiches and be right back."

Tim announced that he'd start by making message boards to put up outside and notices that could be posted around town to keep folks informed.

As the meeting broke up, Debbie pulled Jerry aside and whispered, "That's a GSW. What the hell happened to you Jerry?"

"I got shot."

"I know that, but how? What happened?"

"It's a long story. Let's just say I got tangled up with the wrong people. I'll give you the details when we have more time. Right now we have a big job to do and I need to get home to see if Will made it home okay."

Debbie was concerned. "You need to get off that leg. I'll get you some crutches."

Debbie left to retrieve the crutches. Joseph and Savannah were standing close by. Jerry was anxious about getting home to see Will. He was worried about him. When Debbie returned with the crutches, Jerry asked her to issue him some ketorolac to help with the pain.

"You need morphine," she insisted.

"I don't want morphine. I need to focus. Anyway, we may need it down the road." Jerry was unusually curt. "Just get me the ketorolac."

It was a relief to get back in the Land Rover and be heading home. But for Jerry, between the pain in his leg and his concern over Will, the five minute ride up Columbian Road seemed to take forever.

As they turned into the driveway, they saw the old pick-up. Jerry knew that Will was fine.

Chester ran up to greet them and as they got out of the Land Rover and almost knocked Jerry off his crutches with his 110 pounds of excitement.

"Hey, buddy," Joseph called, trying to get the dog's attention away from Jerry. "Savannah, meet Chester, The Wonder Dog."

Savannah knelt down and let Chester greet her with sloppy puppy kisses.

"Chet, where's Will?" Jerry asked. The dog barked and immediately headed for the house. The three treasure hunters followed.

Hearing the commotion, Will met them at the door. "So, did you find the treasure?"

He didn't wait for an answer. "You must be Savannah?"

"Will? It's nice to finally meet you."

Realizing he was on crutches, Will turned his attention to Jerry. "I missed you honey," he said, as he gave Jerry a kiss. "Why the crutches? Did you slip on the boat?"

"I'm fine. I'll explain later. Are you all right?"

"Of course I'm all right. But, some really strange things are happening around here."

"I know."

"There's no electricity and my cell phone is dead. A dozen people have stopped by the house looking for you."

"Okay, sit down everybody and let's talk," Jerry said.

Jerry explained everything that had happened in Ogdensburg. As he started to describe what he expected the next several months to be like, he did his best to strike a balance between frightening everybody and trying to be realistic.

"I think our biggest issue is going to be communications—keeping the public informed and keeping them calm. If people start to panic there's going to be violence. And just about every house in town has firearms."

"Once folks start running out of food," Savannah added, "that's when the real problems will start."

"You're right," Jerry said. "So we have to let the town know we have a plan. If we don't, people will be breaking into the Lodge, the Diner or the General Store, or even into their neighbor's homes, looking for food. It could get ugly.

"That's why it's so important we get the word out that we have everything under control and arrangements are being made to make sure everyone gets fed." Jerry looked at his partner, "Will, I'm going to need you to work with Tim Moore on communications."

Though Will worked primarily as a stained glass artisan, he was a divinity school graduate, an ordained minister and chaplain at the fire department. Jerry knew that Will's remarkable ability to convey calm would be a critical asset. His biggest worry was panic setting into the community. The other concerns regarding food, water, transportation, safety and preparation for winter, were simply a matter of good planning and coordination by the fire department. The community would pull together to make sure basic needs were met.

Will put together a light dinner for the group but was still shaken by the fact his partner had been shot. "Twenty-three years as a state trooper and you never even fired your gun in the line of duty until a month before you retired. Every morning you left for work, I worried. When you retired, I thought I could finally relax. And you get shot again. What am I going to do with you?"

"As your mother would say, sell me to the gypsies for ice cream."

"I might just do that. I love ice cream." There was a pause. "But, I love you more, so I guess I'll keep you around." Will thought for a moment then looked at Joseph, "Actually, it's your fault."

"What are you talking about?"

"Whenever Jerry helps you on a treasure hunt, he gets shot. I never realized treasure hunting was such a dangerous activity. I may have to separate you two boys for a while."

After dinner, Jerry suggested that Joseph and Savannah move into the spare bedroom. "Safety in numbers," he said. He also suggested Joseph and Savannah drive to Joseph's house on the other side of Cranberry Lake to collect all the frozen and refrigerated food Joseph had. Jerry had a large freezer in the garage and he expected it would keep the food cool for a few days if they were careful.

Lying in bed, Jerry had a hard time getting to sleep. His leg was burning and the Incident Action Plan was on his mind. His thoughts turned to what was happening in the big cities like Boston and Montreal. Feeding the residents of Cranberry Lake would be comparatively easy. There was plenty of wildlife, fowl and fish available. Most residents were experienced hunters. Wood for cooking was plentiful; after all, they lived in the middle of the largest forest east of the Mississippi. Most residents lived on the lake, so fresh water was just a few steps away.

In Boston, it would be a completely different story. Jerry remembered reading de-classified reports while he was a state trooper that estimated two-thirds of the population—200 million people—would die from starvation, disease or societal collapse within a year of a nationwide EMP attack. The casualty rate in the big cities would approach 90 percent. In the cities there would be millions of people with no immediate access to food or water. Panic would prevail. There would be a complete societal collapse. Vigilante groups would form, roaming the streets for food and water. People would be willing to do anything to feed their families. Even kill their neighbors.

He rolled over and held Will close, thankful they lived in Cranberry Lake.

TWENTY-SIX

Tuesday, August 6th
13:45 GMT – 8:45 am EDT
Langley, Virginia, USA

THE TONE IN THE small task force room was much different than it had been just a few days earlier. The people were the same but he responsibilities had changed. Mickey Evans was no longer in charge.

In cases of domestic terrorism, the FBI is the lead agency. Rather than being engaged in intelligence-gathering and analysis for possible threats, everyone in the room was devoted to gathering information and evidence in response to an attack on the United States.

Special Agent Frank O'Neal assumed the role of FBI liaison to the agencies represented in the task force. Evans was briefing O'Neal on the substantial information gathered by the task force during their investigation of Athena prior to the attack. He also brought O'Neal up to speed on what little he knew about Ares.

As they were finishing their briefing, Lt. Shawn Snow, the Coast Guard liaison, knocked on the door of the small office just off the task force meeting room. He stuck his head in, "The President is getting ready to address us from the Situation Room. Two minutes."

Mickey Evans looked up, "Okay Shawn, we're on our way."

In addition to CIA Headquarters at Langley, the secure feed was being watched at FBI, DHS Headquarters and the Pentagon Situation Room.

The Situation Room in the White House was tense. The President entered and sat at the head of the mahogany table and didn't mince his words. "The slightest hint of stove-piping and people will be replaced. I will have no tolerance for petty differences between agencies. We need to find out who did this, and we need to find out quickly. Preliminary suspicion is that the attackers were part of a terrorist organization. Looking at the cost of this operation, a small cell of independent operators is not likely; they needed substantial financial support to pull off such an expensive enterprise. Given the sophistication of the weapon, a government cannot be ruled out. North Korea and Iran are at the top of the list. Others are being explored as well."

The President looked at his notes then regained eye contact with the camera. "I want to commend Lt. Preston Evans on the information his team gathered and the connections he made regarding the ships before this attack. Thank you Lieutenant." Mickey's face went red. The President also made clear that there was no time to waste: additional attacks could be imminent. The more quickly intelligence could be gathered, the more likely the US would be capable of thwarting them.

"The FBI is in charge now," the President went on, "but I'm expecting the task force at Langley to continue your good work. Everybody watching this feed needs to think outside the box the way Evans did. The American people are counting on you and I'm counting on you." The screen went black.

O'Neal stood in front of his group. "We have our orders. Let's get to work."

Mickey and several other new people from The Office of Naval Intelligence focused on the history and ownership of Ares. The CIA and FBI were looking into financial support of both freighters.

Lt. Snow reported that the Coast Guard had summoned operational tugs and moved Ares out of the shipping channel. Crews enlisted from the Port of Ogdensburg were assisting with repairs and making the Ares capable of being towed to the Port of Oswego to be processed for evidence. The FBI was not thrilled the ship was headed to Oswego.

"Oswego is really our only choice," Snow pointed out. "It'll have to do; apart from two near Toronto, there are no major shipyards or dry dock facilities on Lake Ontario. And it's equidistant from the FBI field offices in Buffalo and Albany."

O'Neal dropped his objection. "Okay then, we'll get a team of forensics experts headed to Oswego."

Lt. Snow continued his report. "A small Coast Guard crew deployed divers to look for more evidence or bodies. Nothing more has been located. After the FBI is finished processing, the Coast Guard has requested that the ship be forfeited to the possession of the United States and its damaged electronic components replaced. We need it for relief shipments to the disaster zone. Fortunately, much of the ship's upgrades were made with hardened equipment, undamaged by the EMP. Prior to removal from the St. Lawrence River, the ship's crane was used to hoist the remains of the Bayliner onto the deck of Ares. The bodies have been brought below deck."

Autopsies and identification will take place in Oswego. The weapons and other evidence aboard will be collected and trucked to Washington. The Oswego County Coroner has been notified the bodies are on their way. After the initial identification and death certificates are complete in Oswego, the bodies will be released to the FBI and sent to their lab in Virginia."

Agent O'Neal updated the group on the FBI side of the investigation. "Communications with Montreal were interrupted," he said. "All electronic records maintained by the inspection services were likely destroyed, along with any recordings of radio traffic on the Seaway or 911 calls. Coast Guard tells us paperwork aboard Ares was intact. We have copies of inspection forms, certificates, and passport data. The AIS was completely wiped out by the EMP. While awaiting preliminary repairs in Ogdensburg, the small shipping container left on the pier was pulled back aboard Ares to get it to Oswego. The Zodiac discovered at the Port of Ogdensburg was also loaded onto Ares in case it had anything to do with the incident. An inventory of the property aboard compared to the paperwork left one glaring anomaly: a 1962 Land Rover was unable to be located."

This gave rise to speculation about accomplices who may have used it to escape. O'Neal continued, "According to the Coast Guard, all crew members were accounted for; departure records matched the crew manifest, with the exception of the three bodies on the ship."

"Who, then, would have taken the vehicle? Who would have known it was there?" one of the new ONI reps asked.

"Good question," the Special Agent responded. DHS has been notified to watch the borders and we're trying to alert local police authorities to look for and detain the vehicle. Of course, word will get to everyone outside the impacted region. Everyone inside is, quite literally, in the dark."

Mickey Evans jumped in. "What exactly is the impact area?" he asked. Mickey and his group had been working on background information on Ares and had not heard any news.

"The grid was knocked out as far east as the Mississippi," O'Neal said. "But the worst effects are in northern New York and New England. In that area, if it has a microprocessor, it probably doesn't work. Thankfully, New York City appears to have missed the major effects."

Evans shook his head. Re-focusing, he knew that Ares and Athena were related, but it took a tremendous amount of probing, beginning with CIA sources in Reykjavik where shipyard workers recalled sand blasting off the name "Nova" and later painting "Ares" in its place. This gave the ONI and FBI a trail to follow, which led to a series of shell corporations. A similar run up the family tree of Athena revealed one corporation in common. The FBI, with the assistance of the NSA, were able to follow the sophisticated and convoluted financial transactions surrounding the two ships.

The capabilities to conduct an investigation in Boston were so degraded, FBI forensic resources from New York City were sent by bus to the Port of Boston. The crew of Athena was returned to New York City for interrogation. While the crew members were cooperating, as they were ordered to do by Captain Jibril, neither the interviews nor the documentation seized produced any usable intelligence. Agents were beginning to think they knew nothing about the operation.

The National Nuclear Security Administration use hardened vehicles. They were able to cut the steel plate on Athena's hull and secure the sphere of cesium. It was placed in a containment vessel and trucked to the DOE facility in Oak Ridge, Tennessee for analysis. Often, the specific preparation of the metal will identify where and by whom it was manufactured.

The Coast Guard assisted to the extent it could, but they were extraordinarily busy with the fleet of disabled ships inland and in the North Atlantic. Hundreds of Coast Guard and Navy assets were being shifted to the impact area, but conditions aboard these disabled merchant, pleasure and passenger vessels were deteriorating rapidly. Lives took precedence over all else. But this was a challenging task. Without communication or operational AIS units from these ships, there was no way to locate the vessels in the most need. Satellite imagery and ship-based RADAR were used to locate ships one at a time. Ships, unable to be towed to an operational port, were anchored in place and left behind along with their cargo. Idle cruise ships were redirected to the area of operation to assist with the removal of sailors and passengers. Periodically, Coast Guard ships would come across the remnants of aircraft which crashed into the ocean after being disabled by the EMP.

Beyond rescue, a massive clamp-down was placed on all commercial shipping throughout North America. All ships and intermodal containers were to be searched, by hand if necessary. The Coast Guard and its auxiliary were going to be operating at full throttle into the foreseeable future. As massive as the rescue efforts were on the seas, it paled in comparison to the monumental task awaiting responders on land.

The FBI was trying to put together information from the Langley task force when their best lead came from a completely unexpected source. A senior analyst from the Department of Homeland Security's Office of Infrastructure Protection, Lillian LaForte, contacted them regarding a contractor who had been asking questions about Ares prior to the attack. That contractor, a former state trooper, was in the affected area and now out of contact, she told them.

Coast Guard had located the owner of the Bayliner. The registration number came back to a marina in Ogdensburg. FBI speculated the party or parties on the Bayliner were responsible for the deaths of the crew of Ares and the missing Land Rover. Coast Guard was able to dispatch a small working boat to Ogdensburg and discovered the Bayliner had been rented to a Jerry Doolin, from Cranberry Lake. The name was passed on to Washington.

New York State Police were mobilizing to shift operational assets to the impacted areas of the state. They committed only four troopers to the FBI investigation until the public emergency was mitigated. Time and manpower were two commodities in very short supply.

Two FBI Agents were waiting in Oswego when Ares arrived. The forensics team was on their way. Initial fingerprint results from both the Bayliner and the Zodiac revealed a number of prints, but one stood out; a former New York State Trooper. The same individual who'd rented the Bayliner. It wasn't until the information reached Washington that the name was connected to the DHS contractor who had inquired about the Ares.

The FBI moved quickly. "Okay people, we have a person of interest. Actually several people, but we only have two names. A Jerry Doolin rented the Bayliner. The marina owner in Ogdensburg tells us there were two other people with him. A female, we assume Savannah Christian. Her fingerprints were also found on the Zodiac. The only thing we know about her is she is a former Marine. Honorable discharge more than a decade ago. There was another set of prints that were unidentified. All other prints belonged to the dead suspects.

"This is top priority. I want everything you can get on these people. We need to find these people. Now," was the emphatic order from the FBI. "The Pentagon is giving us four Black Hawks and Special Forces Teams. Two are heading to Cranberry Lake and the other two are heading to Saranac, New York."

TWENTY-SEVEN

Thursday, August 8th

15:45 GMT – 10:00 am EDT

Cranberry Lake, New York, USA

By 10 AM, more than 70 people had gathered at the fire hall. Many were helping to prepare and distribute food. Others were waiting for the latest set of bulletins to deliver to the stations that had been established around town where notices concerning community meals and special needs were posted twice a day.

Debbie Grenier was holding a small medical clinic in the back of the hall

Chief Dial was bringing an elderly woman to Debbie Grenier when he heard the commotion. People were running out of the fire hall to see what was happening. There was an unusual noise in the distance and Dial had heard the same sound two days earlier when a convoy of Army vehicles had passed through the village heading east toward Saranac Lake and Lake Placid. After a brief lull, the commotion suddenly intensified. Dial heard a shotgun blast. People began running back into the fire hall angrily yelling, "they're not stopping, they're not stopping."

Just outside, Dial found Tim Moore. "Who fired the shotgun?"

"Old Mrs. Knapp."

"You've got to be kidding, why?"

"I don't know. She showed up a few minutes ago, crying. They say she's looking for Will."

"He's inside. Find him and let him deal with her. And tell him to take that shotgun away from her."

Tim Moore found Will and together they went looking for Mrs. Knapp.

"Will?" Tim tapped Will on the shoulder and pointed to the frail elderly woman sitting on a bench facing the lake. The shotgun was at her side and her long flowing grey hair was gently moving in the light breeze.

"Thanks, Tim. I'll talk to her."

"Millie?" Will waited. There was no response. "Millie, I heard you were looking for me. Are you okay?"

Mildred Knapp gently patted her wrinkled hand on the empty space next to her, motioning Will to sit.

Will sat and put his arm around the woman he had known for years. "What's wrong, sweetheart?"

There was a long silence. Then, in a whisper, the words came out. "He's gone."

"Who's gone, Millie?"

"Amos. God took him home day before yesterday."

Will held the woman close. "Oh, Millie, I'm so sorry."

In the distance, someone called out. "Briefing in five minutes!"

The two just sat looking at the lake for several minutes. Will finally spoke softly, "He was a good man, Millie."

"Yes he was, but I'm worried he may be in trouble."

"Why do you say that, Millie?"

"I'm not sure God will be as patient with his little pranks as I was."

"I think God can handle Amos." They both laughed. "Millie, why did you wait so long before coming here to find me?"

"I was sitting with him."

Will understood. The two had been married for 52 years.

"We'll have a service here at the hall tomorrow. I'll arrange to have him picked up. We need to get him buried. I'll find someone to stay with you for a few days."

"I'm not an invalid, Will. I can take care of myself."

"When was the last time you ate something?"

Millie shrugged.

"Let's go inside and get you something to eat." Will took the shotgun in one hand and Millie's arm in the other as they walked toward the hall. "So why did you fire the gun, Millie?"

"Nobody was paying attention to me. They all were concerned about those blasted Army trucks driving by."

Will smiled. "I understand. I'll hold on to the gun for now. I'll see that you get it back."

"I wasn't trying to hurt anyone."

"Of course you weren't." Will gently squeezed Millie's arm.

The crowds were getting larger each day at both the fire hall and the community center. Clearly, people were beginning to run out of food and becoming more dependent on community resources. Anger was building. Inside the fire hall, Dial was trying to calm the crowd. People wanted answers and Dial had none. As he was speaking, multiple helicopters could be heard overhead. From his time in Desert Storm, Dial recognized the unmistakable sound of Sikorsky Black Hawks. They seemed to be circling looking for a safe location to land. "It sounds like we'll have some answers soon."

Dial looked around and saw Bill Gleason in the back of the hall and motioned him forward. "Bill," he whispered, "they'll probably land behind the Community Center. Take the Land Rover and go down and see who they are."

Will found Jerry helping at the medical clinic and told him about Amos Knapp.

Jerry briefly closed his eyes. "I'm not surprised. He had a pacemaker. Is Millie alright?"

"I think so. She hasn't been eating. They're getting her something right now."

"Jerry," he asked, "is that going to happen to everybody who has a pacemaker? Walt has one . . ."

"I know. It depends on why they have a pacemaker. I'm guessing you'll see more of this."

"You mean 'we'll see more of this?"

Jerry shook his head and thought of Lucia. Joseph had told him about her pacemaker. His thoughts quickly turned to the helicopters.

"Will. Remember I told you the other day the FBI would be looking for Savannah, Joseph and me. I don't think those helicopters are here to provide help. I think they're here for us. Could you go find Savannah and Joseph? I need to finish up here."

Bill Gleason was waiting behind the Community Center when the Black Hawks landed in a large grassy area. A crowd was gathering to see what kind of supplies they were bringing. Gleason was shocked when the sliding doors opened on both choppers and a dozen Special Forces troops emerged in full combat gear with their M4's at the ready, looking like they were prepared to engage in battle with the residents of Cranberry Lake. As the troops took up position around the choppers, two men in civilian clothing emerged with the Special Forces Team Leader and approached the crowd. Gleason realized the civilians were FBI agents wearing FBI ball caps and protective armor. He put his hand out, "I'm Bill Gleason, I think I know why you're here. You're looking for Jerry, right?"

Surprised, Special Agent Morley shook Gleason's hand. "That's right. Is he here?"

"He's up at the fire hall. He's been waiting for you. So are Joseph and Savannah."

"Savannah Christian? Really? Why didn't they call us and let us know they're here?"

Gleason was surprised at the question. "You're kidding, right?"

"They're the most wanted people in America right now. "

"Do you have any idea what's going on here? Look around. These people don't have any food. We have less than a half-dozen working vehicles in town and they're low on gas. People are getting sick and people are dying. There's not a phone in town that works. Tell me, how in the hell was Jerry supposed to contact you?"

Buried in an office in Washington, D.C., Morley hadn't really thought about the specific effects of the EMP. "Really?"

"He knew you would find him."

"Is he going to give us any trouble?"

Again, Gleason was shocked at the question. "What are you talking about? Why would he give you trouble?"

"He was there when the missile was launched. He may have been part of the plot."

"Are you crazy? If it wasn't for him you'd be dealing with these problems in Washington. He almost killed himself and his friends by ramming the ship with his boat and changing the trajectory of that missile. He's a national hero. All three are national heroes."

Agent Morley raised his eyebrows. "We want to talk to him."

Gleason motioned to the Land Rover. "Hop in."

"Whose vehicle?"

"Don't know. Jerry used it to get back to town after the EMP hit."

Jerry had just finished talking with the parents of a young boy with diabetes. They were concerned that they only had a two week supply of insulin left and no refrigeration. Jerry assured them they were doing everything possible to get more insulin.

Outside, Jerry joined a conversation with Tim Moore, Kathy Morris, the Town Clerk, and Sam Pickering, the sexton of the town cemetery.

"I can't bury him without a burial permit from Kathy, and she can't give me that without a Death Certificate."

Jerry was tired and frustrated. "Amos is just the first. Are you going to tell Millie Knapp we can't do anything with Amos? There are going to be more. A lot more. What do you suggest we do? Stack the bodies behind the fire hall? We're in the hottest part of the summer. These bodies will start to decompose. That's untenable. Kathy, you're the only government there is right now. You two need to come up with a solution. Figure out how you're going to get Amos buried. And quick!"

Jerry began to storm away but was interrupted by John Dragun, the owner of the Windfall Bar and Grill.

"What's up, John?"

"We have refrigeration now."

"What? How?"

"You know I have the neon sign shop. I remembered the old refrigerators that used ammonia and had no moving parts. I have one here and one back at the restaurant. I used glass tubing and some other stuff to rig one up. We can keep the fish the guys catch cold for a couple of days at a time now."

"And insulin," Jerry added. "Finally, some good news. You're brilliant. If I had a medal, I'd pin it on you. Right now though, I have some people waiting for me."

Will had located Savannah and Joseph and they met Jerry in the parking lot as the Land Rover was pulling in.

"Remember you guys, the FBI probably has no idea what happened up on the river. Just stay calm and we'll get all this worked out. Don't say anything about what happened until we get to wherever they're taking us. Then just tell the truth." Out of the corner of his eye he could see Bill Gleason and the two FBI Agents walking toward them. He looked at Will. "Honey, don't worry. We'll be back before you know it. Take good care of Chester. Give him a scratch for me." He gave Will a hug.

Agent Morley approached the four. "Jerry Doolin?"

"I'm Jerry Doolin."

"Mr. Doolin, please turn around and put your hands behind your back. I'm taking you into custody as a person of interest in an attack on the United States of America."

Jerry turned around and Morley secured the handcuffs.

Bill Gleason started to walk toward the FBI agent. "What the hell are you doing?"

The second FBI agent positioned himself between Jerry and Bill. "Stand back Mr. Gleason or you'll be arrested for interfering."

Jerry looked at Bill. "It's okay. They don't know what happened. They're just doing their jobs. Everything will be fine. Bill turned and headed toward the fire hall to find Walter Dial.

Agent Morley looked at Savannah. "Savannah Christian?"

Savannah shook her head yes.

"Ma'am, please turn . . ."

Before he finished, Savannah had her hands behind her back. Joseph had also turned around and had his hands behind his back.

"And you are . . . ?"

"I'm Joseph B. Benton. I was with Jerry and Savannah when it happened."

"Okay Mr. Benton. I'm taking you into custody as well."

The group headed toward the Land Rover. Chief Dial was waiting at the Land Rover with two AK-47's. He introduced himself and handed the rifles to the FBI agents. "You'll want these as evidence. Jerry asked me to hold them until you arrived." He looked at Jerry, "You need anything?"

"Just take care of things here. I know you will."

Chief Dial looked at the agents. "You don't have enough room for a driver so you have to drive yourselves back to the Community Center. We'll get the Land Rover later. It'll be waiting when you guys can get someone up here to pick it up. It's evidence too."

A crowd had formed around the Land Rover and Walt Dial asked everybody to move aside. The whispers in the crowd were getting louder and several people were beginning to shout at the FBI Agents. They didn't understand why Jerry, Savannah and Joseph were in handcuffs. "Best get going now," Dial whispered. "People are on edge and who knows what they'll do."

The Land Rover slowly backed up and headed through the crowd toward the waiting choppers. A few minutes later, Will looked up and watched as the two Black Hawks headed west. His thoughts were with his partner as he waved goodby and wiped a tear from his cheek.

TWENTY-EIGHT

Thursday, August 8th
17:45 GMT – 12:45 pm EDT
Washington, DC, USA

THE VISTA OF CRANBERRY LAKE, his home, and his partner shrank away from Jerry as the helicopter ascended to the west and turned south. It had been almost a day since he had taken anything for the pain, which hadn't abated in the days following his wound. He would have gladly accepted more ketorolac, or even morphine, but they were running low at the fire hall and he knew it had to be saved for more pressing needs.

Trying to make himself more comfortable in the cramped helicopter, Jerry squirmed in his seat in an attempt to elevate his leg. The sharp sting of his wound now gave way to a dull ache and a hot burning sensation. Jerry knew he needed surgery and suspected he was beginning to cook an infection. Before the arrival of '*the boys in the white socks*,' he'd begun to consider the possibility of losing his leg to gangrene. Now in the custody of the United States government, he would have access to medical care. Not so for any of those left behind.

Joseph sat silently, scowling. Being treated like criminals disgusted him, even though Jerry had tried to prepare him. He wanted to give these people a huge chunk of his mind, but he was determined to follow Jerry's instructions and keep his mouth shut. He looked over to see Jerry mildly smiling at Agent Morley, calmly telling him that they'd be happy to speak with them when they reached their destination. Joseph was already running the names of attorneys through his mind, waiting for a chance to retain one.

Savannah, was all name-rank-and-serial-number. She sat upright, silently ignoring anything said to her. She replied only with her name. No one could help but be impressed with her discipline.

The helicopters landed at Hancock International Airport in Syracuse, NY, a hardened facility because of a sensitive military installation based there. On the tarmac was a plain white Falcon 50 EX jet waiting for them. On seeing it, Jerry was taken aback. This airframe was sufficient for traveling overseas; he wondered where they were taking him and his colleagues. For a moment, Guantanamo Bay came to mind. With air travel being so dramatically curtailed in the northeast, the airplane was immediately in motion and aloft, turning south. It was a brief flight to Washington, DC where, other than electrical power, the EMP effects had not reached and back-up generators provided power to most government buildings.

The steel of the handcuffs were competing with Jerry's leg for his attention by the time they landed. Joseph's shoulders ached and Savannah's fingers were becoming numb, although she showed absolutely no outward sign of discomfort, nor would she admit to it. She would not even admit to the time of day.

They were hustled quickly to separate black SUV's with windows so dark they were almost opaque. Nevertheless, the three erstwhile treasure hunters saw their progress into the city, down Pennsylvania Avenue, turning onto 10th street and eventually driving into an underground parking garage at FBI Headquarters. Jerry had told his friends to just tell the truth. That's all that was necessary. The evidence was all with them.

Jerry's leg felt as though it was on fire. The three were taken to separate rooms and searched. The bandage on Jerry's leg was removed. The wound was ugly. It would get attention. Jerry was counting on it.

With his years as a state trooper, Jerry wasn't worried about himself, but he was concerned with his friends, especially Joseph. They would never be charged with an offense, but Joseph could be a hothead and things could get difficult if he expressed his true feelings. Jerry, unlike his cohorts, knew the drill and was relaxed, albeit uncomfortable. Into the room walked a tall, lean man with a shirt entirely too starched and pressed for the summer temperatures and humidity of Washington, DC. Flanked by two unidentified agents, he sat for several minutes, reading over the file in front of him. *Trying to build tension*, Jerry thought to himself. He'd employed the same tactic more than once during his career. He tried to stifle a smile.

"Mister Doolin," was the first thing said by the starched shirt. "You're in a lot of trouble, my friend."

"You're mistaken."

"You're not in trouble?"

"I'm not your friend."

The agent, who identified himself only as Morales, was trying not to look flustered. "A wise guy, huh? I have enough on you to put you away for a long time, mister. Just the conspiracy charges alone are enough to send you to Fremont for the rest of your life. You don't know half of what I know."

"Nonsense. I know *more* than you know. And you know better. We both know the evidence here, and we both know that none of it points to us as a perpetrators, but rather the opposite. We both know that my actions, and those of my colleagues only attempted to thwart the goal of the perpetrators, whoever they are. I understand you're under the gun here, so to speak, but trying to pin something on us just to satiate the appetite of a bunch of . . . "

"I'm not so sure Mr. Doolin. Not by a longshot."

"I've cooperated at every step. I'm here. If I didn't want to be found, believe me, your people never would have located me."

"Now you want me to believe that you *wanted* to be located? Is that what you're saying? How the hell do you expect any of us to believe that?"

"I communicated to you who I was and that I was on the scene."

"Really. Phone call? Email? Telegram? Carrier pigeon? If you communicated to us, we'd know about it."

"You do know about it."

"Is that so? Perhaps you'd like to enlighten us as to who you spoke to."

"I left my card for you."

"You did no such thing."

"Look on your evidence log. On the small sea can on the pier, pierced right through the locking mechanism was a business card with my name and the DHS offices I'm consulting for."

"Sea can…"

"Pardon me. 'Intermodal container.'"

Morales looked over the extensive evidence list more closely. Jerry could tell by the look on his face when his interrogator found the item he had described.

"And you want me to believe you left it there with the intent to communicate who you were and how to find you? I don't think so."

"It didn't fall there on its own. You knew who to look for, didn't you?"

"Why didn't you make a phone call if that was your intent?"

"There was an EMP weapon detonated that day. Phone calls were impossible. You know that."

Morales just glared. "All you had to do was wait."

Jerry locked eyes with him. He was about through with this. Rather than reply, he hoisted his now un-bandaged and oozing leg onto the table. It was disgusting. The two agents observing were repulsed. Morales left the room. Jerry knew he was going to compare notes with the interrogators of the other two.

§

"We're going to talk about it now. Right now." The perpetual smile on Lillian LaForte's face was gone. The stern visage of a mother short on patience telegraphed business to her supervisor as they approached the office of the Secretary of Homeland Security.

After a tangled series of calls to an army of assistants and deputies announcing a situation that demanded the Secretary's immediate attention, Lillian had insisted on a personal visit. Just as an executive assistant was preparing to intercede, the Secretary's voice came over the intercom.

"Mark, some people from OIP are on their way. Show them right in when they arrive, please."

With an expression suggesting the detection of a foul odor, the assistant heaved himself out of the chair and opened the door to the Secretary's suite. "Mr. Campbell and Ms. LaForte." After they'd passed into the office, the door was closed, not quite slammed, but closed hard enough to be noticed by everyone in the room. Secretary Roberta Antonucci greeted them with a broad smile and quiet grace that concealed the frenzy in which the government and her department in particular, found itself. She was flanked by the FEMA Director and the liaison to the Terrorist Threat Information Center.

It was clear to Lillian she didn't have much time. She had come prepared with documentation, phone logs, a time line, and anything she could glean from the FBI's investigation. Fortunately, the President's warning about stove-piping information was heeded. By the time she was finished with the briefing, all were aghast that they didn't know the FBI had taken one of their people into custody. No one had even requested any records from DHS. Lillian's documentation not only exonerated Jerry and his friends, but also showed that it was his initial suspicions and inquiries that led to the eventual, albeit late, discovery of the Ares's intentions.

Secretary Antonucci sat quietly a moment, then picked up the phone. "Mark, get me the Attorney General, please. It's urgent."

§

Joseph sat scowling in a small room, for what seemed like an eternity, before two agents came in to speak with him. Knowing Jerry as well as he did, he'd picked up enough about interview techniques to recognize a "good-cop, bad-cop" routine. Nevertheless, his best friend told him to tell the truth, and that's what he would do.

Savannah was a tough customer. Her one-word answers quickly became frustrating to the agents. She saw the entire process as an enormous injustice and would make them work for every scrap of information they'd get. She could tell she was wearing them out. Eventually they needed a break and left the room.

Comparing notes, the interviewers found that all their stories were spot on, right down to what they ate, how long the dives were, even the colors of their equipment. On the evidence logs the agents saw that dive logs had been recovered from the Bayliner along with empty air tanks. It appeared the three were either extraordinarily well rehearsed, or they were being truthful.

The investigators were aware of Joseph's previous discovery of historic treasure. The fact that he'd been described by the media as a "master treasure hunter," made his explanation for their presence on the river even more plausible.

All eyes turned to Jerry. How did he know what that ship was up to? What did he do about what he knew? Why didn't he warn anyone? Why did he feel he needed to get weapons?

Returning to his interrogation room, Morales found Jerry trying to attend to his wound. He stood at the opposite end of the blood-stained table and stared for a few moments.

"Save the theatrics, Agent Morales. What's on your mind?"

"No one knows anything about you. I checked on you, you're a stranger to DHS."

"In that case, someone needs to notify the Treasury Department. They've been cutting me checks for almost a year."

"You're in no position to be cute, Doolin."

"You're in no position to lie to me."

"You're calling me a liar, is that what you're saying?"

Jerry took his leg off the table, slid his chair to the wall, and replied flatly. "I'm saying either you did a lousy job checking on me with DHS, or you never checked at all. So I suppose I'm saying you're either lying, or you're incompetent."

Morales' two colleagues had to stifle chortles, which elicited a sidelong glare to each of them from their boss. They continued to sit quietly.

Morales, growing more red-in-the-face, looked at Jerry.

"You need to calm down, agent Morales. The veins on your head are starting . . ." Morales shoved the table across the floor at Jerry, who caught it with his hands and shoved it back.

Jerry understood that Morales was unaccustomed to interviewing people who were unafraid of him. Jerry just sat back, relaxed. Unimpressed.

Morales was visibly startled by a knock on the door. Without taking his eyes off of Jerry he shouted, "WHAT?" The door popped open and a head poked in. Morales and his colleagues huddled at the partially opened door. Jerry couldn't hear much of the hurried whispers, but the words "AG" and "Director" came through. All three left the room. This was the first of the days' events Jerry couldn't explain and the first time he felt uncomfortable. It was also the last time he saw ASAC Morales.

§

Stripped of his wrist watch, Jerry could only estimate how long he waited. It seemed like hours when, at last, a young man walked in. Jerry could tell by his blue shirt and striped tie that he was not from the FBI. The man introduced himself as an Assistant US Attorney (AUSA), and told him that he'd received quite a bit of documentation from DHS, which made it clear that he was not a co-conspirator. Jerry breathed a sigh of relief. Although he'd been confident this would be the result, he was glad it had come. The AUSA noticed the wound on Jerry's leg and stepped back with alarm. "Hang on. We're going to get that wound taken care of." He stepped out, leaving the door open. Moments later, an FBI employee showed up and drove Jerry to Walter Reed Army Medical Center.

The staff had a good deal of work to do, but assured him the leg would be saved. He was started on IV antibiotics and prepared for surgery. Jerry insisted on local anesthesia, partially because he never liked the idea of general anesthesia, but more because he wanted to get the ordeal over with and he wanted to be debriefed as quickly as possible at the hospital. These agents were surprised by the candor and cooperation of their subject.

Joseph and Savannah were visited by the same young man from the AG's office and told about their conclusions and asked to give depositions about their experience on the river. A couple of hours later, they were reunited. After an apology for their trouble, the AUSA told them he'd arrange for their transportation back home. Joseph inquired about Jerry. He was told Jerry had been taken from the building and would not be able to join them. What followed from Joseph was a threat to descend on the FBI, the Justice Department, or the city as a whole, with "a battalion of the most aggressive and vocal attorneys your nightmares couldn't imagine." He wanted his friend, and he wanted him now. The surprised AUSA explained that he'd been brought to a hospital for treatment. "That's where we're going. Call us a cab, please." They were taken by a department car to Walter Reed.

By the time they were able to locate Jerry he was nearly ready to leave, with a pocket full of antibiotics and three hand trucks for the piles of boxes in his treatment room.

"Hey baldy, what'd they give you here, spare legs? You're not *that* sick, are you Jerry?" Savannah looked worried.

"I managed to liberate some supplies that will be helpful at home." Jerry had a cane hooked over his forearm as he was closing the last of the boxes which resembled a cooler.

"What's that? Ice cream won't make it all the way home, you dope."

"It's dry ice. It doesn't have to make it all the way. It just has to keep this stuff cool."

"What is it?"

"Insulin. And some other drugs we need."

"Insulin?"

"There's a ten-year-old at home with his name on a few of these vials. One of these boxes is full of syringes."

"Doolin, you're way more trouble than you're worth, but you're a good man."

"Yeah, whatever. Quit flapping your gums and get us a car. Then start hauling this stuff out."

"Boys," Savannah interjected. "Play nice. We'll need a lot of gas cans to make the trip all the way home."

"Drive?" Joseph scoffed. "They used a plane and a couple of helicopters to bring us down here. Get that guy on the phone. Tell him to get a car over here and to warm up a plane."

Jerry just looked at his friend. "Joey, I don't think they can devote a plane . . ."

"Gimme that guy's card. Where's a phone?" He dashed into the corridor.

Looking at Savannah, Jerry commented, "By now you realize he's a little nuts."

"He's not the only one." Savannah rolled her eyes.

Joseph returned. "Okay. They're sending a van over to get this stuff to the air base. We'll meet them there later."

Savannah and Jerry both looked back at him, a little shocked. Jerry offered up a question, "Later?"

"We're getting something to eat first. I'm starved."

Savannah demanded, "How… how did you get them to do that?"

"Something about a battalion of lawyers and an army of media."

The Cessna Citation that picked them up at Joint Base Andrews landed at Fort Drum, New York, not far from the northern city of Watertown. The three passengers and cargo were transferred to a 2.5-ton truck for the drive to Cranberry Lake. The medical supplies occupied a tiny portion of the space available for cargo, so after some coaxing and a couple of telephone calls, the remainder of the space in the truck was filled with MRE's. "Meals Ready to Eat" can be stored indefinitely, and would supplement the nutritional needs of Cranberry Lake for some time to come.

§

When Mickey Evans walked into the resurrected Task Force room, everyone rose to their feet. The video screens and communications links had been replaced, and the cadre of representatives from the various corners of government were back. Although he'd tried to keep it quiet, word had gotten around quickly about his actions and the President's praise.

Mickey was at once humbled, amused, and touched. "Please, everyone, sit."

The renewed vigor in the room was palpable. Those who had worked hard on the Athena Task Force felt vindicated. Now, the pressure was on to keep producing actionable intelligence about the would-be attack and any possible follow-up.

Mickey began by going around the room to get updates. The Coast Guard had shifted all assets they could to the northeast to assist with rescue and recovery while maintaining assets around the remainder of the country's coastline. All of the National Security Cutters were underway and would remain so for the foreseeable future, as were all regular and auxiliary assets. The US Navy also cancelled all leave and got every available ship, aircraft and surface vehicle operational.

The entire country was scrambling to harden critical infrastructure against another attack. Although the consequences of an EMP, whether caused by a weapon or a natural event such as a solar coronal mass ejection, had long been well known, critical preparation for such an event had always been put off until some other time. That time was now.

While many of the necessary steps toward recovery were simple, the sheer volume of tasks and the difficulty of obtaining replacement components made the job close to impossible. Few had realized that large transformers and other critical elements of the electrical grid are made to order, in most cases overseas, taking weeks or even months to build, and more time to ship.

The rep from the Department of Energy gave a run-down on the analysis of the cesium, now secure and removed from Athena. It was a ceramic sphere of Cs137 pellets. The metallurgy, mass and dimensions were similar to samples secured from radiography cameras and soil density gauges, 100s, if not 1,000s of which had gone missing from Iraq and Afghanistan. Cesium was a common product in industry, available in relatively large quantities and low prices. After businesses fell apart, many employees looted the equipment they once used, and offered it for sale to the highest bidder. Nevertheless, the perpetrators had spent substantial sums collecting two kilograms worth. As a Radioactive Dispersal Device, it could have been catastrophic.

The rep's description of the condition of the electrical grid was much less precise, and her prognosis was not encouraging.

The liaison from FBI gave what he had on the investigation, mentioning that in response to the Presidents orders, he'd shared all of the background information the Task Force had collected on the two ships, with other government agencies. FBI was looking for help in establishing any Naval or commercial shipping connections on the three primary persons of interest. Because the AIS had been wiped out on the Ares, the rest of the crew members would have to be identified by paper records in Montreal. Most had already left the country. International partners were being contacted for their help in apprehending them. He added that three people had been located and transported for questioning as possible accomplices.

When he said the names of the three suspects in custody, Mickey Evans sat bolt upright. Something sounded familiar with one of the names. He began rifling through stacks of papers. "Where have we heard that name before? Eventually he divided up the mountain of documents amongst his colleagues to fish for the name in question. After about ten minutes, Evans stopped short. "Here he is. It's an inquiry on…holy crap, it's an inquiry on Ares. He made it to OIP. No, he made two, the day before the attack. Who is this guy? Why OIP?" Evans instantly remembered. "He's a DHS consultant. He asked about Ares because she reported an on-board fire in the St. Lawrence Seaway. Then I guess he didn't like what he heard and they moved the data on to ONI. That's how we got it and why we started to pull information on the ship, including observations made by CIA in Reykjavik. There's no way he can be a perpetrator."

"Ed," he turned to the FBI liaison, "do your people know what we know about him?"

"I'm not sure. I'll bet not. Let me see what you have and I'll make a couple of calls." He excused himself to phone the ASAC who was overseeing the case. By the time he got through, the conversation was rather one-sided and loud. ASAC Morales assured him that he had been informed of the details regarding the Doolin subject some hours earlier and if this call was a joke, he didn't see it as funny. The conversation ended abruptly.

The members of the Task Force wanted to know who this contractor from "way up North" was. They were more interested in knowing what he'd seen and how his suspicions developed. No one in the Task Force knew where he was. Embarrassed, the FBI weren't talking.

As others in the Task Force attempted to contact Jerry Doolin, Lt. Mickey Evans was summoned to the office of his commanding officer. Mickey dreaded this visit. Several days earlier he'd willfully circumvented his chain of command. He didn't know what would befall him, but a court martial was not out of the question. He went up the stairs, straightened his uniform, and stepped into his captain's office suite.

The meeting was short. Fortunately for Lt. Evans, his boss was made aware of the comments of the Commander-in-Chief. In the end, Mickey wasn't sure if he was being rewarded or being shipped off to a gulag. He was told about how impressed his superiors were with his intelligence gathering, how he would be recommended for promotion, and how they were going to reassign him to a team developing targeting packages in preparation for a reprisal attack on North Korea. While he was glad he wasn't being brought up on charges, he was being assigned to an unfamiliar job, and one to which he was not suited. Was this really a promotion or a set-up for failure? He decided to keep his powder dry for the moment and not discuss the matter further.

TWENTY-NINE

Friday, September 20th
15:00 GMT – 10:00 am EDT
Washington, DC, USA

"I COULD GET USED TO THIS," Joseph commented to Jerry, who was seated with Will, across from him and Savannah in the luxurious cabin of a Sikorsky VH-60N.

Jerry laughed. "Planning to run for President of the United States . . . or maybe Vice-President?"

"You're kidding? This is the President's ride?"

"Yes, Joey. It's one of them."

The four had landed at Joint Base Andrews just outside Washington, DC. The government jet that had brought them from Wheeler Sack Army Airfield in Watertown taxied right up to the waiting helicopter.

"A bit more pleasant than our trip here last month," Savannah said. "I'll bet they don't have many passengers in handcuffs on this helicopter."

The views out the windows were stunning. Because airspace over Washington, DC was restricted, Jerry urged his friends to "Enjoy, not many people get to see Washington this way."

"Where are they taking us?" Joseph asked for the third time.

All the arrangements had been made through Jerry and he hadn't told the others the details.

"Be patient my friend. You'll see."

To the left, out the window, was the Pentagon. To the right was the Washington Monument. Almost directly below them were the Lincoln Memorial and the Reflecting Pool. At the end of the National Mall, the Capitol Building stood majestically. Savannah felt as though she could almost reach out and touch the Washington Monument. "Why are we flying so low, Jerry?"

Will had never been in a helicopter before and he was completely silent, squeezing Jerry's hand so hard it was beginning to hurt.

Out of nowhere a voice announced, "We'll be landing in 30 seconds,"

Will jumped at the sound.

"OH . . . MY . . . GOD," was all Savannah could get out when she realized where they were.

"What?" Joseph asked.

"Just get out and you'll see." At the bottom of the steps, two Marines were standing at attention. The four stood on the lawn in awe.

"Welcome to the White House." A young man greeted them with a smile and warm handshake. "The President is anxious to meet you."

Will just looked at Jerry. "Did you know about this?" he demanded. "Why didn't you tell us?"

"I wasn't sure it was really going to happen and I didn't want you all to get your hopes up."

"Follow me, please." The young man headed toward the White House and was motioning the others to follow. "We'll cut through the Rose Garden and go directly into the Oval Office. Please understand, he doesn't have much time right now, but he did want to meet privately with you before the reception this evening. The meeting itself is classified, so you can't tell anyone you were here. Your luggage is being taken directly to Blair House."

"Blair House?" Savannah asked.

"Reception?" Joseph and Will asked in unison.

The President was waiting just outside the Oval office as the group walked up the several steps from the Rose Garden. "I wish I had the Marine Band playing to give you all a hero's welcome to the White House. But, for reasons that will become clear, this meeting must remain confidential."

"We aren't heroes by a long shot, Mr. President," Jerry insisted. He introduced himself and the others. "We're just simple folks who saw a problem and tried to do something about it."

"That's what they all say, Jerry. By the way, how's your leg?"

"It's fine, Sir. Thank you for asking."

"If Ares had made it to Detroit and launched the missile as planned, the device would have detonated over Kansas. The entire nation would have been sent back to the 1800's. If the missile had launched from the St. Lawrence and you hadn't changed the trajectory, it would have shut down Washington, DC and New York City. Either way, tens of millions more people would have died. So yes, you three *are* heroes. The nation owes you a great debt of gratitude."

The President then looked at Will. "Will, I have something very private to say to Savannah, Joseph & Jerry. Could you step outside just for a moment, please?"

The President turned to Savannah, "Miss Christian, as a thank you I want you to know if you ever find your father's treasure you have nothing to worry about regarding the IRS." Glancing at Jerry and Joseph, "and, with the help you have, I'm confident you *will* find it. When you do, it's all yours. Tax free."

With a big smile she gave the President a hug and a kiss. "Thank you

Mr. President. But, how did you even know about that?"

"Miss Christian, I know so much more than you could ever imagine." The President turned, "Mr. Benton and Mr. Doolin, that goes for you two as well."

Joseph was confused, "Mr. President, the treasure belongs to Savannah, if we find it, it's hers. It was left to her by her father."

With a wink the President responded, "That's not what I'm talking about."

Joseph looked at Jerry, and back to the president. The President just smiled and opened the door to the left of his desk and invited Will back into the Oval Office. "Will, I hope you can keep these three out of trouble in the future."

"Mr. President, I'll do my very best."

"I'm looking forward to seeing you all at the reception this afternoon."

"Thank you, Mr. President," they said in unison.

As they left the Oval Office, the aide who had escorted them inside handed each an envelope labeled, CLASSIFIED. "Please don't open them until you get to Blair House. It's just across the street. It's a beautiful day, why don't we walk?"

"Blair House?" asked Savannah.

Surprised, the aide looked at her, "That's where you're staying. Your luggage is already there."

Jerry jumped in, "I didn't give them the details. I just told them we were going to Washington."

"I see," smiled the aid.

"I guess I'm the only one here who doesn't know what the Blair House is," Joseph mumbled, feeling foolish.

The Presidential aide spoke like a tour guide. "Blair House is the

President's guest house for visiting foreign dignitaries and honored Americans. There are just under a hundred people expected at the reception. The President has arranged a few surprises for you as well."

Joseph pulled Jerry aside as they were making the short walk across Pennsylvania Avenue. "What did the President mean when he said . . ."

"I have no idea Joey. Maybe this envelope will explain."

"The name is still Joseph, you dope."

After signing the guest book and being shown their rooms the four got together in an elegantly appointed sitting room to open their envelopes.

Savannah's envelope contained a waiver of any IRS taxes that would be due in the event she finds her father's treasure.

Joseph and Jerry had individually signed copies of a slightly different document:

THE WHITE HOUSE

Proclamation 6438

September 20, 2013

By the President of the United States of America

A Proclamation

Whereas, Joseph Benton and Jerry Doolin found the Benton family treasure, known as the Bonaparte Treasure, on private property in Tupper Lake, New York and,

Whereas, the exact value of that treasure is unknown and,

Whereas, it is further known a portion of that treasure was donated to the country of France and,

Whereas, it is further known the remaining portion of the treasure was divided between Joseph Benton and Jerry Doolin and,

Whereas, it is highly probable there is a significant unpaid tax liability by Joseph Benton and Jerry Doolin associated with the remaining portion of that find, and

Because, of the unique and significant contribution by Joseph Benton and Jerry Doolin to the security of the United States of America during a terrorist attack on the Homeland,

Now, Therefore, as President of the United States, pursuant to the pardon power conferred upon me by Article II, Section 2, of the Constitution, I have granted and by these presents do grant a full, free, and absolute pardon unto Jerry Doolin and Joseph Benton for all offenses against the United States of America and any states therein, which they have committed or may have committed or taken part in during the period from August 2, 2013 through August 5, 2013.

Be It Further Known, any and all tax liability of Joseph Benton and Jerry Doolin due the United States of America associated with the Bonaparte Treasure is now and will forever be forgiven.

In Witness Whereof, I have hereunto set my hand this twentieth day of September, in the year of our Lord two thousand and thirteen, and of the Independence of the United States of America the two hundred and thirty-seventh.

"Joseph, I can't believe what I'm holding in my hands. This is incredible. I've been waiting for the tax man to knock on my front door since that day in Tupper Lake. Now, we've got to find Savannah's treasure to make her pardon good."

It had been a long several weeks and the beds in Blair House looked so inviting, each could lie down and not get up for a week. All they could manage was a short nap before the stewards' gentle knocks on their doors announced that the reception would start in an hour.

Will was excited. Jerry dreaded official parties. Joseph and Savannah saw it as another chapter in their blossoming romance.

Will was tying Jerry's bowtie when a steward knocked again. "Gentlemen, you have guests waiting downstairs. I've taken the liberty of seating them in the Eisenhower sitting room." The two looked at each other, then at the steward.

"Guests?" Will asked, "Would you mean Savannah and Joseph?"

"No sir," was his reply, "these are guests who arrived early for the reception."

Jerry and Will shrugged and stepped out into the hall where they met Joseph and Savannah. The steward escorted them to the Eisenhower room.

"Mrs. Lillian LaForte, and Lieutenant Preston Evans, United States Navy," the steward announced. Then he introduced the four from New York. Only two of the six recognized one another, although they had never met in person.

"Lillian!" Jerry dropped his cane and leapt forward to embrace his friend. Lillian, dressed in a blue evening gown, wrapped her arms around him, and through her joyful sobs she managed to say, "Oh, baby, oh. I'm so glad you're all right. I thought I lost' cha, baby." The warmth and love of that dear, sweet woman brought tears to his eyes as well. "Not on your life, darlin'." The tears were contagious. When they finally released each other, Lillian looked at the tall, long-haired man in the tuxedo and said, "Oh, Will, I never thought I'd ever meet you. Come on…" She held her arms out and Will stepped forward, a bit cautiously. As soon as he was in range, Lillian had him in her grasp, mashing him up against her.

Three somewhat stunned people remained. Savannah, recognizing the Navy officer's dinner dress uniform, extended a hand from her evening gown. "How do you do, Lieutenant, I'm Savannah Christian."

"Call me Mickey, it's a pleasure, ma'am."

Joseph, beside her, extended his hand next. "I'm sorry, did you say 'Mickey?'"

Shaking his hand, Lt. Evans replied, "Delighted to meet you, Mr. Benton. Yes, I said 'Mickey. It's a nickname, for an old Japanese name, 'Mikoto.' My mom gave it to me."

"Mikoto," replied Savannah. "The noble person. Your mom knows her son."

"You two haven't met Mickey. Lillian was ushering Jerry and Will over for introductions. He's the one who sent the Coast Guard after you that day. When I sent your stuff up, baby, he's the one who got it."

"Well, look at you … my goodness, ain't you just the prettiest thing." Before Savannah could react, Lillian had her arms around her. I'm so glad y'all made it through everything all right. I was worried sick. And you *gotta* be Joey."

"Yes, Mrs. LaForte, it's actually Jos . . ." It was too late. Lillian had him smothered in her enormous bosom. She looked over at Savannah. "You know hon, if this one don't get his hooks on you, I have a son who's a doctor."

The steward reappeared, "Ladies, gentlemen, may I announce you to the reception?" Taking Mickey's arm, Lillian replied for the group, "Please do."

They were escorted through the house to the Jackson Place Conference Room, which had been converted to a lavish buffet, and on to the large interior garden where the guests were mingling. As they approached, the sound of a New Orleans jazz band filled the air, causing Lillian's smile to broaden even more. The steward asked them to pause at the doorway and the band gracefully concluded their tune.

Then the group heard another sound. Powerful. Thunderous. Startling to those not ready or familiar, Lieutenant Preston Evans was stunned. It was *Hiryu San DanGaeshi*, a Taiko composition by Daihachi Oguchi, Master of the Osuwa Grand Shrine. The drummers were calling upon the dragon god three times to honor Lt. Evans.

He could not have imagined anything more moving than this salute from his Taiko group. The other guests were equally awe stricken. Savannah just said, "Oh, my, Taiko." When the piece was finished, the guests erupted in a roar of applause as the performers bowed toward the youthful Navy officer standing before them. Mickey wiped the tears from his eyes. After months away from his practice, he'd worried that his group had forgotten about him, or even dismissed him from their ranks. Yet, here they were, paying him an indescribable honor.

Even the President was in awe. He came over and was saluted by Lt. Evans. The salute was returned and the two shook hands. After congratulations and a short conversation, he asked Mickey if he would introduce him to the members of the Taiko group.

As the evening progressed, the mingling and socializing did as well. The initial surprise at the number of people of such power and import eagerly introducing themselves and wanting to speak with them eventually gave way to pleasant exchanges and news of the conditions on the ground in the rural parts of the northeast. Mickey and Jerry finally found a moment to sit alone and talk, getting each other's full story of how the events of the past month had unfolded. Eventually, the conversation turned to Mickey's career move. Jerry was rather interested and Mickey shared the details with Jerry, who provided a sympathetic and understanding ear.

As the crowds thinned, Will, who had walked an older woman to the door, went in search of her husband. He found the White House Chief of Staff in the rear drawing room with Jerry. They appeared to be engaged deep in conversation. Will stood out of the doorway but was able to hear Jerry's comments.

"I'm telling you now, if I get one hint of any sort of retaliation on any of these people: Lillian LaForte or that young Coast Guard Officer, I'm going to get vocal. Very vocal. And loud."

The chief made a cursory attempt to allay his concerns, saying they were unfounded.

"Really? Tell that to the FBI agents who reported issues with student pilots before 9/11. What happened to them? You know what happens as well as I do. It's great to be right, unless your boss was wrong. Then they get rid of you. No one wants a subordinate who is an example of their mistake. I'm serious Sam, I'll tell it all, and you know who'll be left holding the bag. These people need to be protected from ladder climbers who'll get rid of good people to make themselves look slightly less bad. If this Navy kid gets reassigned to something he can't do, there's going to be a lot of red faces and uncomfortable explanations to make."

"Don't do anything foolish, Jerry. It wouldn't be good for you."

"What're you going to do, Sam, fire me?"

"Point taken. I'll be sure they're not messed with. I will, Jerry."

"I trust you, Sam. And I'll be watching. You have a good night. I think your wife's waiting with Will."

When the guests had all gone, the four honorees invited the staff and musicians to sit with them and share some of the beautiful food. Rather than packing up, the band played some quiet jazz from the 40s.

Joseph and Savannah, Jerry and Will, danced.

THIRTY

Saturday, September 21st

05:30 GMT – 10:30 am EDT

Somewhere Over the East Coast, USA

THE CLOUDS WERE THICK as they took off from Joint Base Andrews. The trip had been a twenty-four hour whirlwind none of them would ever forget. As the jet leveled off above the clouds, Will was reading a history of Blair House they all had been given. Savannah was staring out the window. Her thoughts had turned to her father and his mysterious legacy.

Jerry and Joseph were musing over a piece of paper with the handwritten notes about the marker in the St. Lawrence River.

ACK

Sara N.

9 - 22/23

3-20

JTC

"The only thing we know for sure is that the 'JTC' stands for John T. Christian." Joseph pointed out. He was frustrated. "Maybe Sara was the 'Grand Old Lady Dog.' I give up. It makes no sense."

"I don't think Sara was a dog. Maybe we're trying too hard." Jerry knew how easily Joseph could become agitated. "Relax, Joey, it'll come to us."

Will was half listening to the conversation. He glanced over at the paper Jerry was holding. "So, who was Sara?"

"We don't know, sweetie. That's what we're trying to figure out."

Joseph told Will maybe they're asking the wrong question. Maybe the question is not, *who* is Sara? Maybe the question is *what* or *where* is Sarah?

"Okay, I'll bite. *Where* is Sara N. Ack?"

There was no response. Everybody was puzzled. Several moments went by until Savannah, who had been absolutely silent up to this point, started to laugh. It started as a chuckle but developed into a full belly laugh she couldn't control.

The laugh was contagious. Everyone was smiling, not really knowing why. Joseph's smile was turning into a laugh. "What are we laughing at?"

Savannah couldn't get her answer out.

Finally, Will got it. "I know what she's laughing at."

"What?" Jerry asked.

"Figure it out yourself. You're the treasure hunter." Will was now laughing as hard as Savannah. He stifled the laugh just long enough to tell Jerry he was right. "You guys are trying too hard. Your analytical mind isn't going to help you with this."

The laughing stopped with a strong jolt of the jet. The pilot came over the intercom, "Sorry folks. Just a little rough air. We'll be out of it in a few minutes."

"Okay, you guys, Jerry and I are in the dark. Are you going to tell us?"

Will and Savannah looked at each other. "No," they said in unison.

Savannah continued, "Just ask yourself the question. Will figured it out."

Joseph thought about it for a second. Then, out loud he asked, "Where is Sara N. Ack?" There was a pause. He asked again, "Where is Sara N. Ack?"

"Oh, no. It was that simple. I can't believe it." Jerry finally figured it out.

A moment later Joseph figured it out. "That's stupid."

Savannah had a smug look on her face. "I thought for a moment that Will and I were going to have to finish this treasure hunt by ourselves. At least we're a lot closer than we were before. Father must have buried it on the farm. That only leaves us 140 acres to search. The numbers must somehow tell us where it's buried."

The jet was preparing to land at the Wheeler Sack Army Airfield at Fort Drum. A military vehicle was waiting to drive them home. When their luggage was transferred, the SUV made its way out of the locked-down base and headed for State Route 37.

"We're going the wrong way. Cranberry Lake is the opposite way," Joseph remarked, looking out the window.

Jerry told the group, "We're on a supply run. A ship is berthed in Ogdensburg with supplies for us."

"I wish I'd known. I'd have dressed differently." Savannah looked at her very sharp, very white, and very clean outfit.

"You'll be fine."

When they arrived at the Port of Ogdensburg, they saw her. The bow of the break-bulk freighter rose above the pier, as it had the day before the tragic events weeks earlier. All but Jerry shuddered.

"Is that the same one? I never wanted to see that thing again." Savannah nevertheless was staring.

Jerry, in his soothing tone replied, "She used to be, but the United States seized her, rehabbed her, and now she's a relief ship." They climbed out of the truck next to one of the ship's heavy mooring lines. Will had never seen the ship. He whistled softly and said, "Talk about swords to plowshares."

Jerry ushered them toward the stern of the ship where they could see an enormous US flag flying. As they walked, Jerry relayed some more information. "While I was in the hospital in DC, I had a visit from one of the deputy secretaries at DHS. They told me they were taking possession of the ship and said they wanted to name her after me. I told them I was flattered, but no. There was someone else who was responsible for my being in the right place at the right time. He deserves the honor." By that time they'd walked past the ship sufficiently to see the white letters painted on the massive steel stern of the ship. It bore the name *USS John T. Christian*. Savannah was dumbstruck. Tears welled up in her eyes and she began to tremble. Joseph wrapped an arm around her, pulled her close, and gave a wink to his old friend.

Will held Jerry's arm, "You never cease to amaze me."

"He helped build the seaway. Now his namesake sails rescue missions on it." Jerry was elated that Savannah liked what she saw. The driver from Fort Drum actually had a working phone and snapped several pictures of the group, with the *John T. Christian* in the background. The Captain and First Officer of the ship greeted them on the pier, thanking them profusely for all they'd done for their country, and for providing him with such a marvelous ship to command. They were given a guided tour of the entire vessel, including the empty, cavernous cargo hold. The supplies had already left for home. It was time for them to head back as well.

Electricity was still out throughout northern New York. Gasoline was unavailable, except for a few military tankers positioned at key points along the highway and available only for emergency and military vehicles. Any private vehicles had to carry extra gas cans for their round trip into and out of the affected area.

Other than a few people walking toward the fire hall, Columbian Road was quiet as they drove the last mile. Everything changed as they came around the final curve before Jerry's house. Seven media trucks ranging from panel vans to large box trucks, all with their satellite dishes pointing toward the sky were parked along the road. Each truck had five or more large fuel cans on a platform mounted to the back of their vehicles. There was one truck parked in Jerry's driveway.

Savannah was amazed. "I thought we did our thing with the press during the reception. Why are they here?"

"They all want exclusive stories." Jerry told her. "They want the details. Don't say a word to them."

Once inside the house, Jerry asked Will how much gas was in the pick-up.

"It's full. I filled up in Tupper Lake on the way home from my show in Burlington."

Everyone agreed they should pile into the pick-up and head to Savannah's house. "The media won't know where we're going. They won't be able to follow because none of them will know for sure if they have enough fuel." Jerry was satisfied with the plan. He was confident everything was fine at the fire hall. Otherwise there would have been notes posted to his door. Anyway, nobody knew he was back, so they wouldn't miss him.

"What about Chester and Bailey?" Will asked. "I'm sure Chester is sick and tired of Bailey irritating him."

Joseph jumped into the conversation. "Bailey doesn't irritate him, she just wants to play with him. Don't blame me if your 110 pound dog can't handle my ten pound cat. Chester can take care of himself. Anyway, Jimmy has been taking care of those two creatures for years whenever we're all away. Although, we probably should stop on our way out of town and check. I'm sure he won't mind keeping them a few more days."

As they drove past the trucks on the now one-lane road, Savannah and Joseph were in the cab and Jerry and Will were in the back of the pick-up. After checking on the animals, they headed toward Saranac. Two of the media trucks were following. “They’ll drop off before Tupper Lake . . . if they make it that far,” Jerry yelled through the back window.

Half way to Tupper Lake Joseph looked at Savannah. His tone had changed considerably. “Savannah?”

“What honey?”

“Would you mind terribly if we stopped in Saranac Lake to check on my ex-wife? I want to make sure she’s okay.”

“Of course I wouldn’t mind. I think that’s a great idea.”

“Thanks, that means a lot to me. Can I tell you something, Savannah?”

“Of course you can. What is it?

“I think you have handled yourself remarkably this past month.”

“Thank you, Joseph.”

“One more thing. I think I’m falling in love with you.”

Savannah didn’t say a word. Joseph saw tears rolling down her cheeks.

“Did I say something wrong?”

Still no response.

“Savannah?”

She finally composed herself enough to speak. “You didn’t say anything wrong Joseph. It was absolutely perfect.” Her hand patted his leg and she grabbed his hand and squeezed. “I’ve been hoping to hear those words, because I fell in love with you a long time ago.”

Savannah kept driving. The two were silent, simply enjoying the moment.

Jerry was right. The two media trucks had dropped off in Tupper Lake. The only vehicles they saw on the road were military. In Saranac Lake,

Joseph gave directions to Lucia's house. As they turned off State Route Three, Jerry knocked on the window. "Where are we going?"

"We're making a quick stop to check on Lu."

After what had happened to Amos Knapp, Jerry had a sinking feeling in his stomach.

The black Lexus was in the driveway and it gave Joseph hope she was fine.

"Come with me Savannah, I want you to meet Lucia. I know she would love to meet you. I told her all about you."

"No, sweetheart. You need to do this alone."

"You sure?"

"It's better this way."

Joseph got out, went to the front door and started knocking. There was no answer and he knocked again. After waiting a minute he decided to walk around the house to see if Lucia was in the back. As the minutes passed, Jerry's concern grew. He got out of the truck and walked up to the driver's side window where Savannah was sitting. "He may need you, right now."

Savannah didn't understand. As he was talking to Savannah, a neighbor called over from her front porch, "Can I help you?"

"We're looking for Lucia. Do you know if she's here?"

"Hold on," the lady said. She went back into her house and in a moment returned with a white envelope. As she walked down the front steps, Jerry headed to her front lawn to meet her half way. He could hear Joseph in the distance knocking on the back door and calling Lucia's name.

"I'm sorry to be the one to tell you, but Lucia passed away three weeks ago. It was shortly after everything happened. Are you Joseph?"

Jerry's heart was broken, not only for Lucia, but for his friend. Jerry shook his head. “That’s Joseph knocking on the back door.”

“I was with her when she passed. Her final request was to see that Joseph got this envelope.” She handed it to Jerry. “Would you see that he gets it?”

“I will. Thank you so much. I’ll talk to Joseph.” Jerry headed to the back of the house. He could hear Joseph calling for Lucia.

“Joseph? I just talked to the neighbor. Lu’s not here.”

“I’ve figured that out, where is she?” There was a new concern in Joseph’s voice.

“Let’s sit down.” There was a settee on the back patio.

“I don’t want to sit down. Where is she?”

“Joseph, Lu passed away three weeks ago.” There was a long silence. “I’m so sorry, buddy. It was probably her pacemaker. It must have failed after the EMP.” Jerry put his arms around his friend. “Let’s sit for a minute.” The two sat down. Joseph put his head on Jerry’s shoulder.

“She was a special person, Jerry.”

“I know she was, buddy. You know how much I cared about her.”

“I know. She loved you too.”

“Lu left this envelope for you.” Jerry handed the envelope to Joseph.

Without opening it, Joseph knew what was inside. He could feel the outline of King Joseph Bonaparte’s coronation coin. Holding the unopened envelope, he looked at Jerry, “You know what this is?”

“I know, buddy. You told me you left it here.”

“Ya know, Jerry, I had just finally made peace with the divorce. Lu and I had a wonderful time together a month ago. Nothing happened sexually. We just enjoyed catching up. We had agreed to be friends. I was looking forward to that. Now that will never happen.”

Jerry didn’t respond. He held his friend.

Several minutes passed before Jerry spoke. “We should go.”

“*Amor fati* sucks, Jerry.”

Jerry remained silent.

Joseph lifted his head with a newfound strength. “Then it’s time for me to find my own destiny. Let’s go, there’s nothing more we can do here.”

Joseph put the envelope in his pocket and the two headed for the truck.

“Everything okay?” Savannah asked as Joseph climbed into the cab of the pick-up.

“It will be,” Joseph responded. “We’ll talk about it later.”

Savannah didn’t pursue the subject. She suspected what had happened. She and Joseph didn’t say a word during the 30 minute ride to the farm in Saranac. Savannah simply found Joseph’s hand and held it.

In the back of the truck, Jerry told Will what had happened. “Is Joseph going to be all right?”

“He’ll be just fine.” Jerry was confident in his words.

Groceries were being shipped into a few of the larger stores from outside the affected area. The group had stopped for supplies but selection was limited. Savannah was pleased bacon and eggs were available as were pasta, bread, flour, powdered milk and a very limited supply of beef. With what was available in her vegetable garden and what she picked up at the store, she knew she could feed four people for several days. Savannah planned an Adirondack breakfast for the morning.

It was dark by the time they reached Saranac. Without lights the four went to bed early. They all were exhausted from the past 24 hours.

“We’ll start early and figure out where this treasure is buried,” Savannah announced.

“Not too early,” Joseph said.

Savannah kissed Joseph on the cheek. “You sleep as long as you want sweetheart. We'll be able to find the treasure without you."

§

Savannah, in her usual fashion, had gotten up early. By six, the aroma of coffee had filled the farmhouse and woke Jerry and Will. The three were in the kitchen drinking their first cup. Grateful she had a gas stove, Savannah was just putting the bacon on low.

Jerry smiled. "I don't think even the smell of bacon will wake Joey."

"You may be right," Savannah agreed. "Why don't you two enjoy your coffee in the garden. It looks like it's going to be a beautiful sunrise. Due to unforeseen circumstances, I haven't had much of a chance to work on it this summer. I'm afraid it needs some attention."

"I'm looking forward to seeing it. Joseph told me all about it." Silently, Jerry thought Joseph had been exaggerating and wanted to see for himself. As they exited the back door, Jerry and Will were stunned by the breath-taking view. It was as fine a sight as could be seen in any botanical garden in America.

"Joseph wasn't exaggerating at all. This is impressive."

Will, who was not easily impressed, simply said, "Wow!"

Along the back of the farmhouse were beds of colorful flowers. Beyond the house were three tunnels created by flowering trees and vines. The main tunnel seemed to head straight out about 60 feet from the house. Two others, the same length, angled off either side. There were several benches strategically placed near the confluence of the three tunnels. At the beginning of each tunnel were large concrete bird feeders. The three bird feeders were lined up 20 feet apart between the house and the start of each tunnel. At the end of each tunnel were steps leading to a large grassy area and more flower beds. Mostly roses.

It was a crisp fall morning. The two sat down to enjoy the magnificent flowers and sounds of the morning birds. Will held Jerry's hand. "What a beautiful place to just sit and contemplate life."

"It sure is."

Several minutes passed, each just thinking and listening. Will finally broke the silence. "I just figured it out."

Jerry looked at him. "You figured out where the treasure is?"

"No, silly. I figured out what kind of garden this is. It's an astronomical garden. It kinda connects you to the universe and reminds you of your place in it."

Jerry didn't understand what Will was talking about. "You're not making any sense, Will"

"Most astronomical gardens use stones. The best and oldest example is Stonehenge, in England. This is remarkable, it's all plants. It's alive!"

"What are you talking about, Will?"

"Look, Jerry, there are three tunnels. The middle one faces due east." Will then pointed to the tunnel on the left, "That one points northeast." He then pointed to the right tunnel, "And that points to the southeast."

Jerry was still confused. Will was excited at such a clever design. "Here's the best part, sweetie, at exactly sunrise on the summer solstice, the sun will shine directly down that tunnel." Will was pointing to the left tunnel. "It will only last a few minutes, but I bet it's very cool." Will shifted his arm to point to the tunnel on the right. "During the winter solstice the sun will shine down that tunnel at sunrise. Finally, on each equinox, the sun will shine right down the middle. Depending on the date, the sunshine will illuminate the corresponding birdfeeder here at the end of each tunnel."

Jerry had completely lost interest. "That's great Will."

The aroma of cooking bacon was beginning to replace the sweet smell of the flowers. Savannah had just come out to refill Will and Jerry's coffee. As she was pouring the coffee she looked up and saw the very top of the center birdfeeder begin to shine.

"I completely forgot. You boys are in for a treat. Today is the autumnal equinox.

Joseph walked out the kitchen door, rubbing his eyes. "What's going on?"

"Father created a natural light show with this garden and it only happens four times a year. Today is one of those days."

The four watched in amazement as the center tunnel flooded with light as the rising sun crested over the horizon. The center birdfeeder was awash in light. It was a magnificent sight. Two cardinals landed on the birdfeeder right on cue.

Suddenly, the look on Jerry's face changed completely. "Savannah? What's the date today?"

"It's September 22nd. Why?"

"What's the date of the vernal equinox?"

"It's March 20th. What's going on Jerry?"

Jerry reached into his pocket and pulled out a piece of paper. He unfolded it and looked at the numbers.

"Savannah, does the date of the autumnal equinox change?"

"Yes, but it's always either the 22nd or 23rd of September."

"Does the date of the vernal equinox change?"

"Never, it's always the 20th of March."

Jerry passed the paper around. It was the inscription on the marker from the St. Lawrence River.

ACK

Sara N.

9 - 22/23

3-20

JTC

Jerry repeated the dates. "September 22nd/23rd or 9 - 22/23. March 20th or 3-20."

All four just looked at the center birdfeeder.

"Underneath?" Joseph asked in a whisper.

"I'd be willing to bet on it." Jerry responded. "Ladies and gentlemen, I think our work is done here."

Savannah continued to stare at the center birdfeeder. Tears were running down both cheeks. "Father shone a light on the treasure twice a year for me. I never knew it."

Savannah composed herself. "Now then, the mystery is solved. Let's go in and have a celebratory breakfast."

Will spoke up, "Wait, before we go in, I'd like to say this is one of the most beautiful gardens I've ever seen . . . and experienced."

Jerry took Will's hand in his and with a gentle squeeze looked him in the eyes. "It occurs to me this would be a beautiful place for a wedding."

Joseph smiled and looked at Savannah, "I think it would be a beautiful place for a double wedding."

AUTHOR'S NOTE

THE LEGEND OF GOLD buried on Isle Royale at the site of Fort Lévis, has been circulating in northern New York since the conclusion of the French and Indian War more than 250 years ago.

The Prologue and overview of the French and Indian War is historically accurate, including the Native American names used for various locales.

During our research, we picked up several pieces of classified information relating to our National Security infrastructure and its response to a terrorist event. We deliberately chose not to knowingly reveal any classified information. All information in this book is available through public sources. Additionally, throughout the book, dozens of acronyms are used. Many refer to agencies of the United States government. All government agencies mentioned are real. We have provided a Glossary of Acronyms used throughout the book.

References to radiation sensors in the story are accurate. As noted in Chapter Five, bananas can actually touch off gamma radiation sensors. Bananas contain Potassium-40, a naturally occurring radioactive isotope. Law enforcement expect positive readings whenever bananas appear on a manifest. Gamma radiation sensors used by domestic law enforcement and American intelligence agencies are remarkably sensitive and some have the capability to reject such natural sources and reduce false alarms.

Versions of the stealth Coast Guard boat described in Chapter Six are currently in use by a number of local and federal agencies. The boat is designed to deflect radar signals, thus its stealthy, low-radar profile. The task of making a boat less visible to radar is the same as for an airplane—the objective is to make radar waves bounce off, but not back toward the sender. According to engineers, a ship must be designed to deflect radar coming from the side or above, whereas an airplane has to deal with radar from below.

All of the geographic locations in the book are accurate, including the sites mentioned during Rosie's walk around Reykjavik, Iceland, in Chapter Seven. Additionally, with 20 percent of the world's coral reefs and over 6,000 species of fish, Indonesia does boast some of the best diving in the world.

During construction of the St. Lawrence Seaway, one-half of Chimney Island (formerly Isle Royale) was dug up to widen the shipping channel, and was moved by barges to the mainland on the American side of the St. Lawrence River. If you drive east from Ogdensburg, toward Lisbon, NY, on State Route 37, you can see grass-covered mounds between the highway and the river. These mounds are the former Chimney Island. Today Chimney Island is owned by the New York State Power Authority.

All vessels entering the Great Lakes from abroad are required to exchange (pump out) their ballast water and flush their empty tanks with ocean water. This practice helps to remove foreign organisms, including invasive species, from ballast tanks. The high salinity of seawater will kill most freshwater organisms. To ensure compliance, the U.S. and Canadian governments inspect and test every ocean-going ship entering the Great Lakes in Montreal, the gateway to the St. Lawrence Seaway. Typically, this exchange takes place in the open sea but, under special circumstances, as in our story, a ship may make the exchange in the calmer waters of the Laurentian Channel, east of 63° west longitude.

While we did our best to describe a plausible inspection process in Montreal, specifics of such inspections are classified. We know they generally include border control, sea worthiness, customs and ballast exchange. We strongly suspect a real inspection would be much more robust than ours.

The AIS described in Chapter One is used on all commercial ships today. In 2004, the St. Lawrence Seaway was the first waterway in the world to introduce an Automated Identification System.

The description of the trip through the St. Lawrence Seaway and its locks is accurate. Known as Highway H_2O, the Seaway is one of the most important inland waterways in the world. More than 3,600 ships pass through each year. Between the Atlantic Ocean and Lake Superior, a ship is raised almost 600 feet by the locks. That's the equivalent of a 60 story building! The larger ships are 78 feet wide and the locks they pass through are only 80 feet wide.

In Chapter Seventeen, we used several French phrases. We understand the French Canadian dialect can, at times, be different than traditional French. We chose to use standard French to make it easier to translate for readers unfamiliar with French Canadian colloquialisms and usage. Apologies to our French Canadian friends and neighbors.

Break bulk freighters were the mainstay of international shipping through the 1950's. There are few remaining in use in the west. Break Bulk freighters have since been replaced by larger freighters and intermodal container ships. You can still see break bulk freighters in use along the coast of Africa and throughout Indonesia. As far as we know, there are no freighters operating anywhere in the world under the names Athena or Ares. Athena and Ares are, however, the children of Zeus, in Greek mythology.

Ares is the god of war, bloodlust and violence. He's the son of Zeus and Hera and among his sacred animals are venomous snakes. We took a little liberty by being specific and making his sacred animal the striking cobra.

Athena is the goddess of wisdom, warfare, battle strategy and heroic endeavor. According to most traditions, she was born from Zeus's head fully formed and armored. Her symbols include the olive tree. She is commonly shown accompanied by her sacred animal, the owl.

Our character, Mickey Evans, is an avid Taiko drummer. Taiko is the modern expression of an ancient Japanese drumming tradition. The drums themselves were originally developed in India where they were used in religious ceremonies to represent the voice of Buddha. Taiko arrived in Japan around 500 AD and quickly became an integral part of Japanese culture. Priests played Taiko to dispel evil spirits and drive insects from rice fields. Samurai employed Taiko to instill fear in the enemy and courage in themselves. There are active Taiko groups in most major cities in America. If you ever have an opportunity to attend a Taiko concert, it will be an experience you will never forget.

In Chapter Twenty-Nine, the Taiko group preformed *Hiryu San DanGaeshi*, a composition by Daihachi Oguchi, Master of the Osuwa Grand Shrine. We took a little liberty when we said the drummers were calling upon the dragon god three times to honor Lt. Mickey Evans. In reality, the drummers call upon the dragon god three times to help humanity. Legend says if the dragon circles over the village thrice a good crop is foretold.

Blair House mentioned in Chapter Twenty-Nine, is the President's guest house for visiting foreign dignitaries and honored Americans. It is located in Washington, DC, on Pennsylvania Avenue, directly across from the White House. The description of the interior is accurate.

In addition to other effects, a nuclear weapon detonated in or above the earth's atmosphere will create an electromagnetic pulse (EMP) or high-density electrical field. An EMP acts like a stroke of lightning but is much stronger and briefer. All of the EMP effects described in this book are real. It will seriously damage any electronic device connected to power sources or antennae. This includes communication systems, computers, generators, electrical appliances, and automobile or aircraft ignition systems. Depending on its proximity to the detonation, the damage could range from a minor interruption to actual burnout of components. Most electronic equipment within 1,000 miles of a high-altitude nuclear detonation would be affected. Blackouts due to a cascade of the electrical grid could extend nationwide, even if the detonation is over New England.

The existence of the electromagnetic pulse has been known since the 1940's when nuclear weapons were being developed and tested. However, because of a lack of data, the effects of an EMP were not fully known until 1962 when the United States was conducting a series of high-altitude atmospheric tests, code named "Fishbowl." The nuclear explosion, "Starfish Prime," which was detonated in the Pacific Ocean 800 miles from Hawaii, caused an EMP that disrupted radio stations and electrical equipment throughout Hawaii. Consequently, in 1963, the United States and the Soviet Union signed the Atmospheric Test Ban Treaty to counter the considerable threat posed by EMPs.

Unfortunately, the destructive potential of an EMP increases every day as society becomes ever more dependent on electronics. Military experts consider EMP weapons the single most serious threat to the United States. Many of the details surrounding EMP weapons remain classified, but those we discuss in this book are real.

In 2004, Russia admitted to the *Commission to Assess the Threat to the United States from Electromagnetic Pulse (EMP) Attack*, that they had designed a 'Super-EMP' weapon with a low nuclear yield and a very high gamma output. According to physicists, *'Super-EMP' theory is complex; the technology is not.*' They testified this weapon was within the capability of rogue nations or terrorist organizations to build. Moreover, they admitted the technology '*may*' have been leaked to North Korea.

Within two years of this disclosure, North Korean nuclear tests were widely panned by the American government and western media as failures because of their low yield. Yet, according to staff of the *Report of the Commission to Assess the Threat to the United States from Electromagnetic Pulse (EMP) Attack*, the North Korean massive radiation signature appeared alarmingly similar to a low yield 'Super-EMP' weapon. Finally, in April of 2013, a Washington lawmaker announced that an unclassified Pentagon report, not yet released to the public, suggests that North Korea has the capability to arm missiles with nuclear warheads.

Recently, legislation was introduced in the United Stated House of Representatives titled, the *Secure High-voltage Infrastructure for Electricity from Lethal Damage Act*. The intent of the legislation is to protect transformers in the nation's electrical grid from a catastrophic cascade, throwing more than 300 million Americans into darkness after an EMP event.

The Klub-K container missile launching system described in the book is real and is advertised on the internet. Manufactured by Concern Morinformsysten-Agat JSC, Moscow, Russia, it is actually advertised as Club-K. As authors, we exercised a bit of literary license and changed it to Klub-K. Their universal launching module is configured within a standard marine intermodal container and includes from one to four universal launching modes. Their website (http://www.concern-agat.com/products/defense-products/81-concern-agat/189-club-k) includes a chilling video of a Club-K container configured for four cruise missiles.

Throughout the process of researching and writing this book, we learned a great deal about the rich history of northern New York, the St. Lawrence Seaway, the structure of the federal intelligence and national security communities, and the disturbing vulnerability of the United States in the event of an Electromagnetic Pulse, natural or manmade. It was a remarkable experience and we truly hope you enjoyed sharing it with us.

MJG & MJD

GLOSSARY OF ACRONYMS

ADD – Attention Deficit Disorder
AIS – Automated Identification System or Automated Information System
AG – Attorney General
ASAC – Assistant Special Agent in Charge (FBI, DOJ)
AUSA – Assistant United States Attorney (DOJ)

CIA – Central Intelligence Agency
CPA – Closest Point of Approach
COMM – Communications Link
CHRS – Criminal History Record Search
C.O.B.R.A. – Chemical, Ordnance, Biological, Radiological
Cs137 – Cesium 137, a radioactive isotope

DNDO – Domestic Nuclear Detection Office (DHS)
DHS – Department of Homeland Security
DNA – Deoxyribonucleic Acid
DOD – Department of Defense
DOE – Department of Energy
DOJ – Department of Justice
DPRK – Democratic People's Republic of Korea (North Korea)

EDT – Eastern Daylight Time
EMP – Electromagnetic Pulse

FBI – Federal Bureau of Investigation (DOJ)

FEMA – Federal Emergency Management Agency (DHS)

GPS – Global Positioning System
GMT – Greenwich Mean Time
GSW – Gun Shot Wound

HRT – Hostage Rescue Team (FBI, DOJ)
HST – Health Service Technician (US Coast Guard)

IAP – Incident Action Plan
IRS – Internal Revenue Service
IT – Information Technology
ITA – Infrastructure Threat Assessment

LED – Light-emitting Diode
LOX – Liquid Oxygen

MRE – Meal Ready to Eat
MSRT – Maritime Security Response Team (US Coast Guard)
MSST – Maritime Safety and Security Team (US Coast Guard)

NATO – North American Treaty Organization
NBR – Natural Background Rejection
NNSA – National Nuclear Security Administration
NORAD – North American Aerospace Defense Command
NSA – National Security Agency (or National Security Advisor)

OCA – Office of Court Administration

OD – Ordnance Disposal
ODNI – Office of the Director of National Intelligence
OIP – Office of Infrastructure Protection (DHS)
ONI – Office of Naval Intelligence (US Navy, DOD)

POTUS – President of the United States

RAD – Radioactive Disposal
RADAR – Radio Detection and Ranging
RDD – Radiation Dispersal Device
RED – Radiation Exposure Device
RIID – Radioactive Isotope Identification Device
RP1 – Rocket Propellant 1 (or Refined Petroleum 1)
RPG – Rocket-propelled Grenade

SAR/LE – Search and Rescue / Law Enforcement
SEAL – Sea, Air Land Teams
Source – Shorthand for "source of radiation," (or "radioactive material")
SWAT – Special Weapons and Tactics

TCPA – Time to CPA
TTIC – Terrorist Threat Information Center

USCG – United States Coast Guard

WMD – Weapons of Mass Destruction

Other books by

Matthew J. Glavin

ADIRONDACK TREASURE

The Bonaparte Legacy

"*. . . The North Country's own DaVinci Code.*"

A Regional Best Selling Novel by Matthew J. Glavin

Coming Soon

ADIRONDACK TREASURE

The Noble Hermit

A Novel by

Matthew J. Glavin & Michael J. Dolan

"*. . . An extraordinary tale of suspense.*"

Follow the progress of *Adirondack Treasure – The Noble Hermit* on Facebook

Like 'Adirondack Treasure Books' on Facebook